Custode

Lavanderia

Necroscopia

Cappella

Contagiosi

Contagiose

Agitate

Agitati

Semiagitate

Semiagitati

Infermeria

Infermeria

Panificio

Sudice

Bagni

Bagni

Sudici

Servizi Generali

Tranquille

Tranquilli

Tranquille

Tranquilli

Uffici

Osservazione

Osservazione

Alloggio del Direttore

Alloggi dei medici

Custode

Rampe di accesso

VERLAG *für* MODERNE KUNST

Libera Viva

Elisabeth Hölzl

17 **Libera Viva**
Emanuela De Cecco

33 **Fardellario – Registro degli effetti ed oggetti**

53 **Ospedale Leonardo Bianchi**
Silvie Aigner

113 **Fardellario – Register of Inmates' Belongings**

130 **La casa dei matti**
The Madhouse
Anna Sicolo

I. Abteilung Männer, Garten, Winter
I. Sezione uomini, giardino, inverno
I. Men's wing, garden, winter

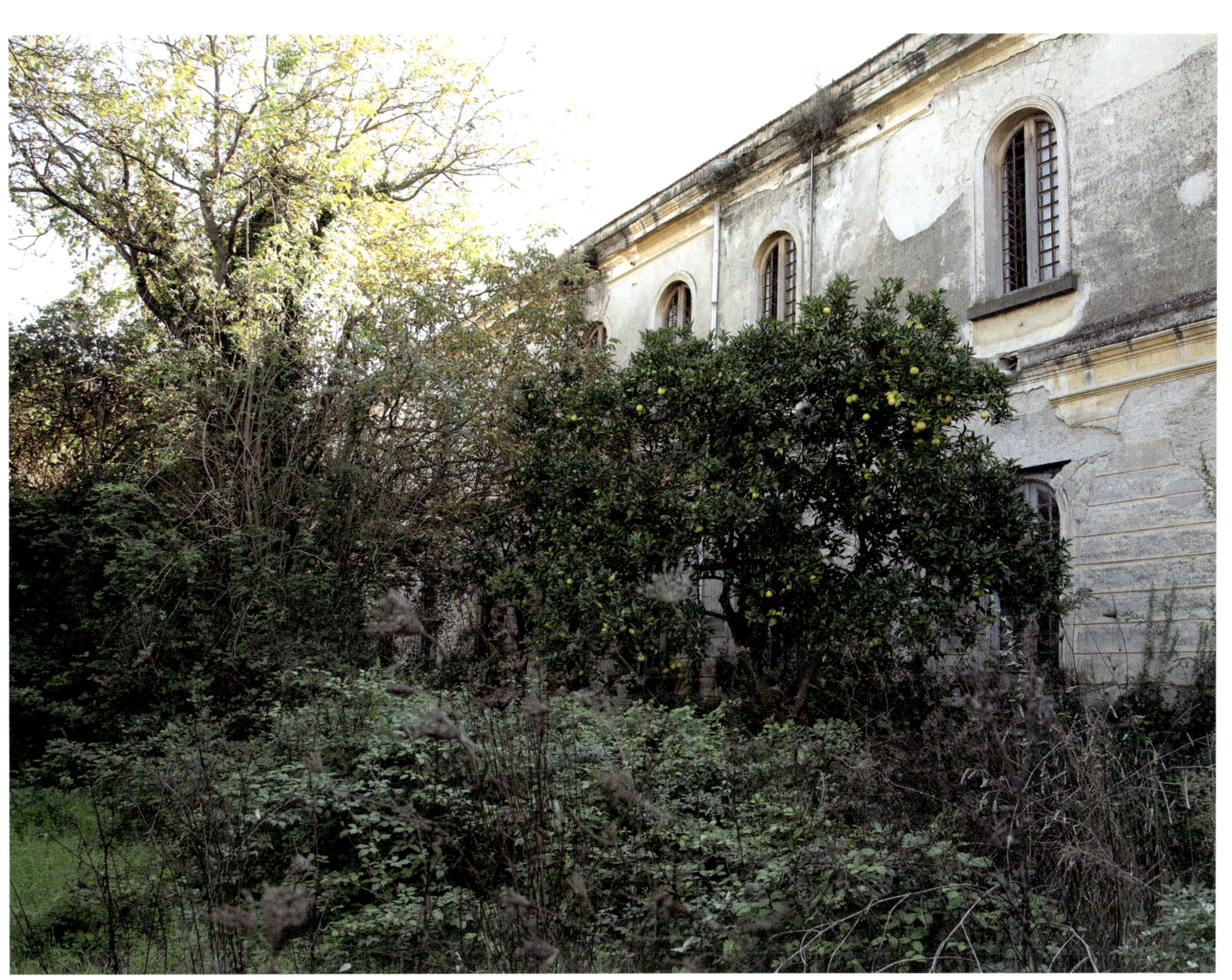

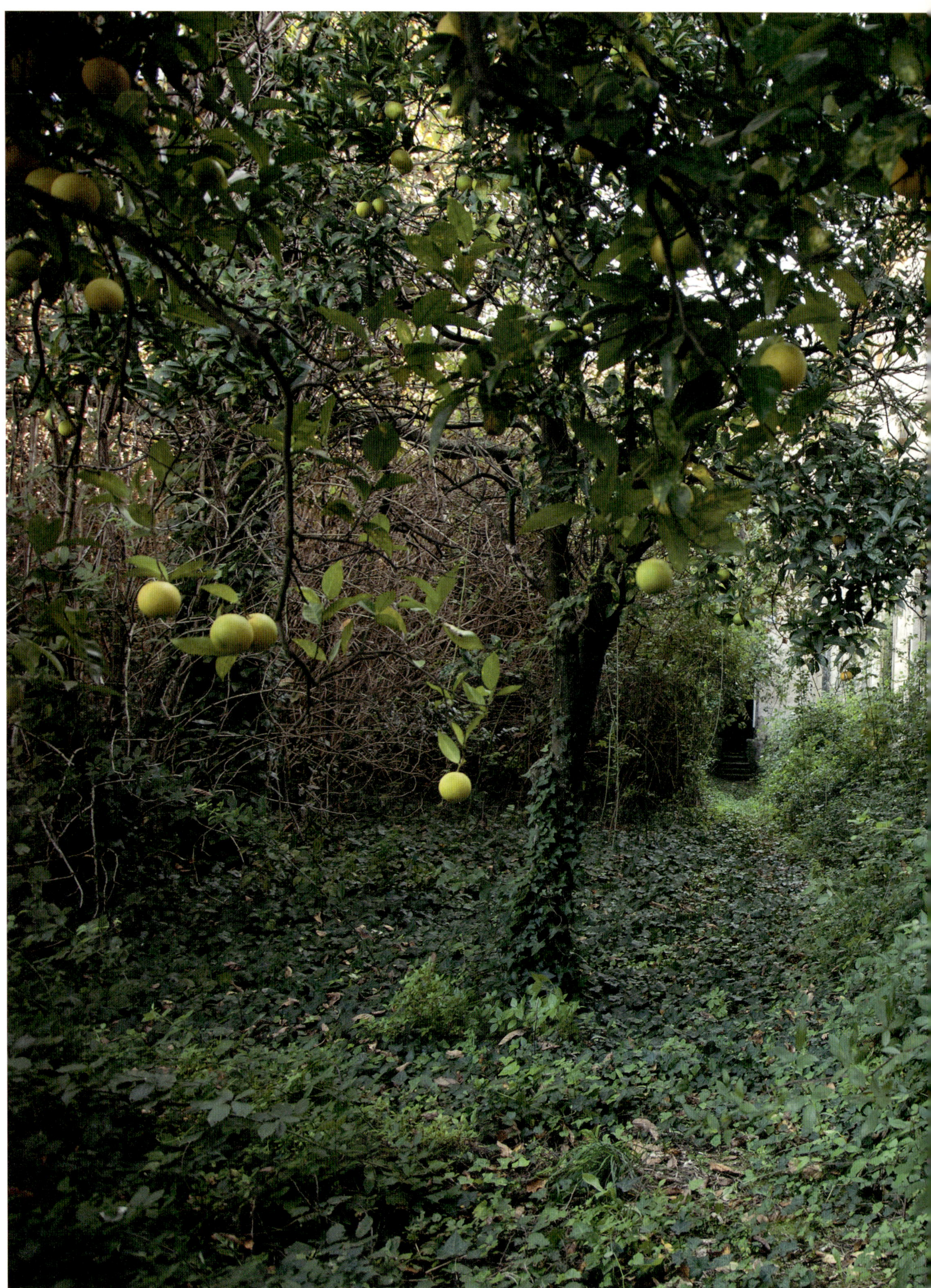

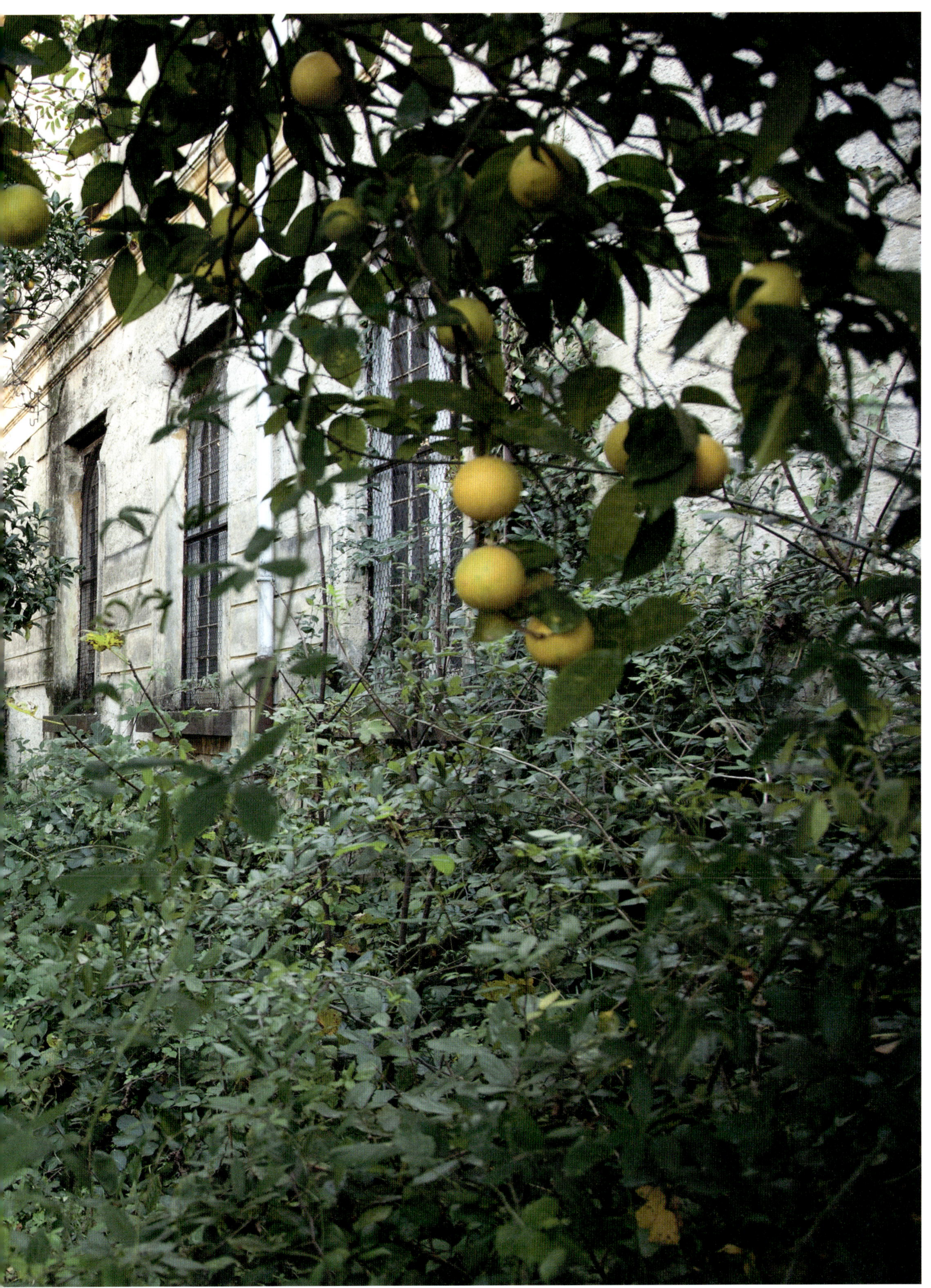

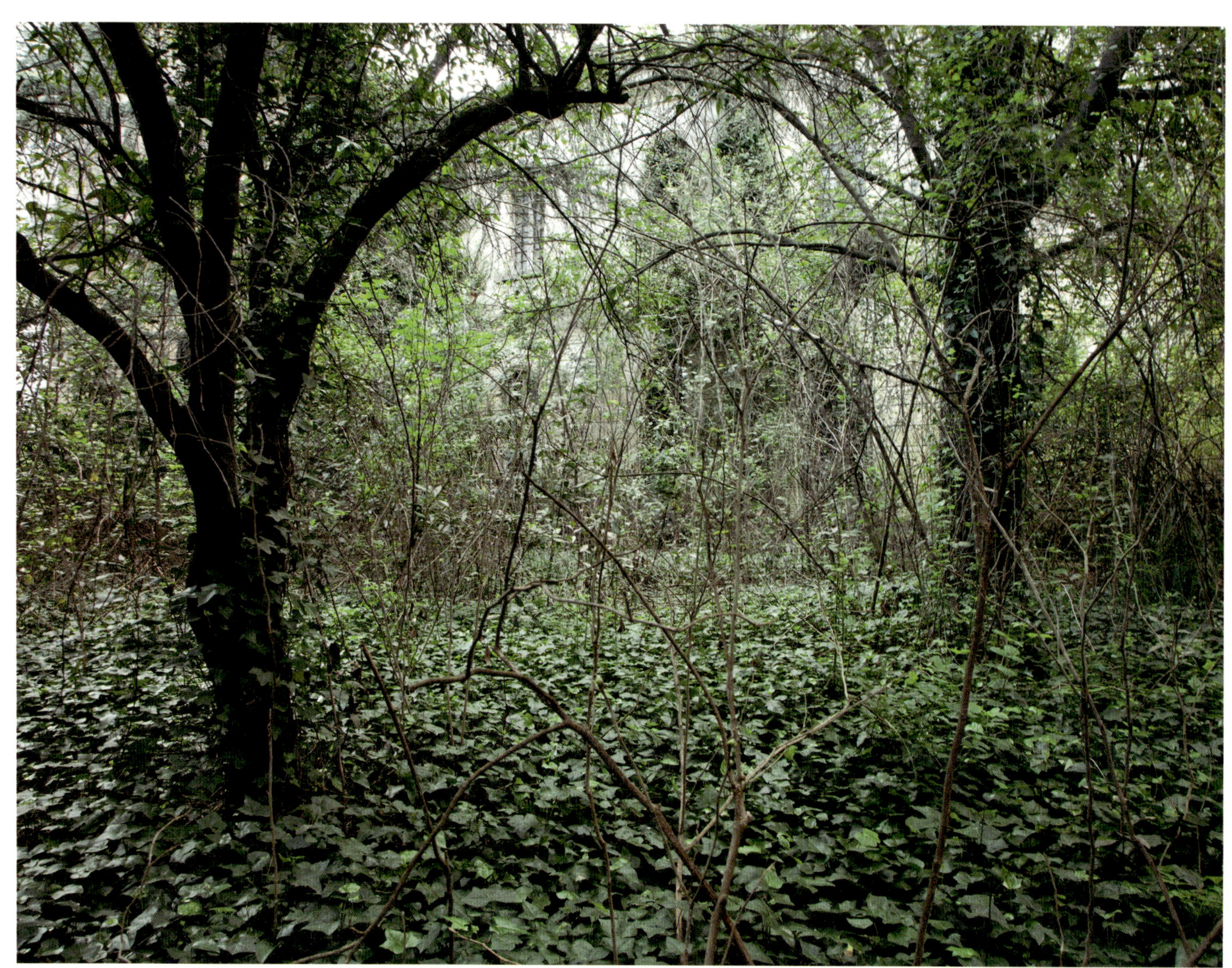

II. Abteilung Frauen, Garten, Winter
II. Sezione donne, giardino, inverno
II. Women's wing, garden, winter

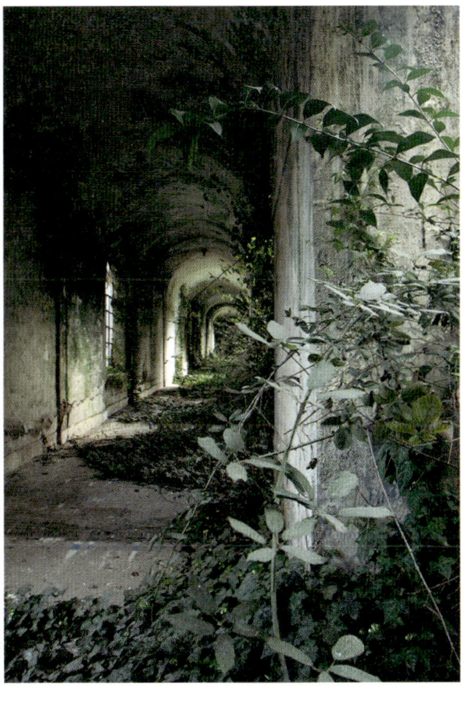

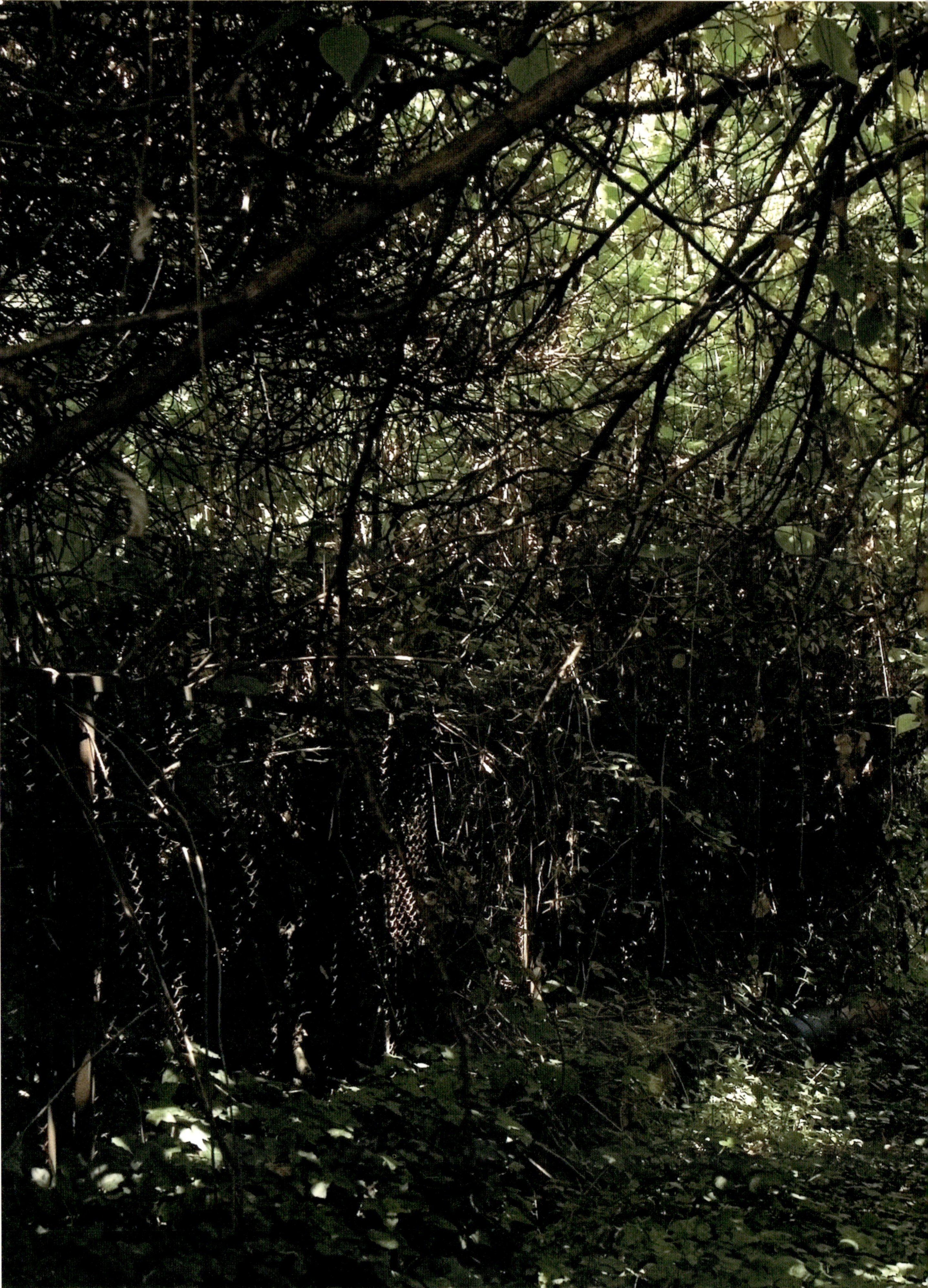

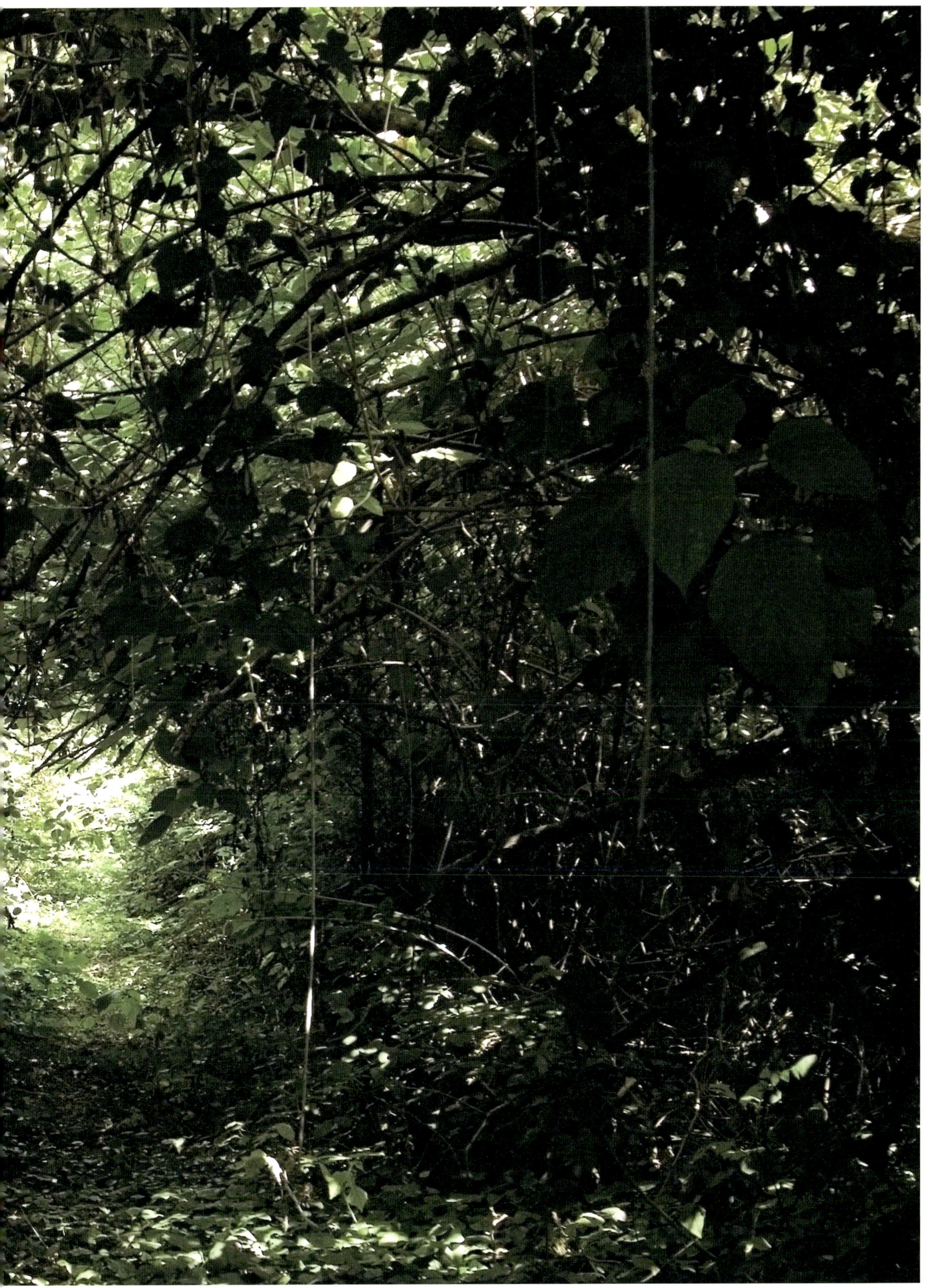

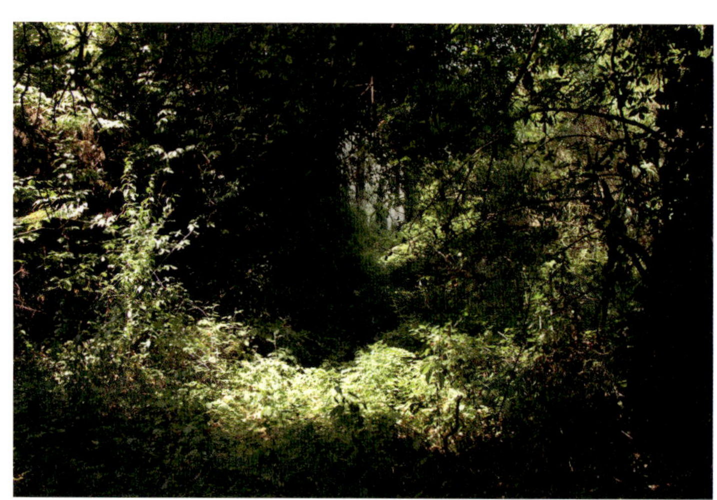

Garten, Sommer
Giardino, estate
Garden, summer

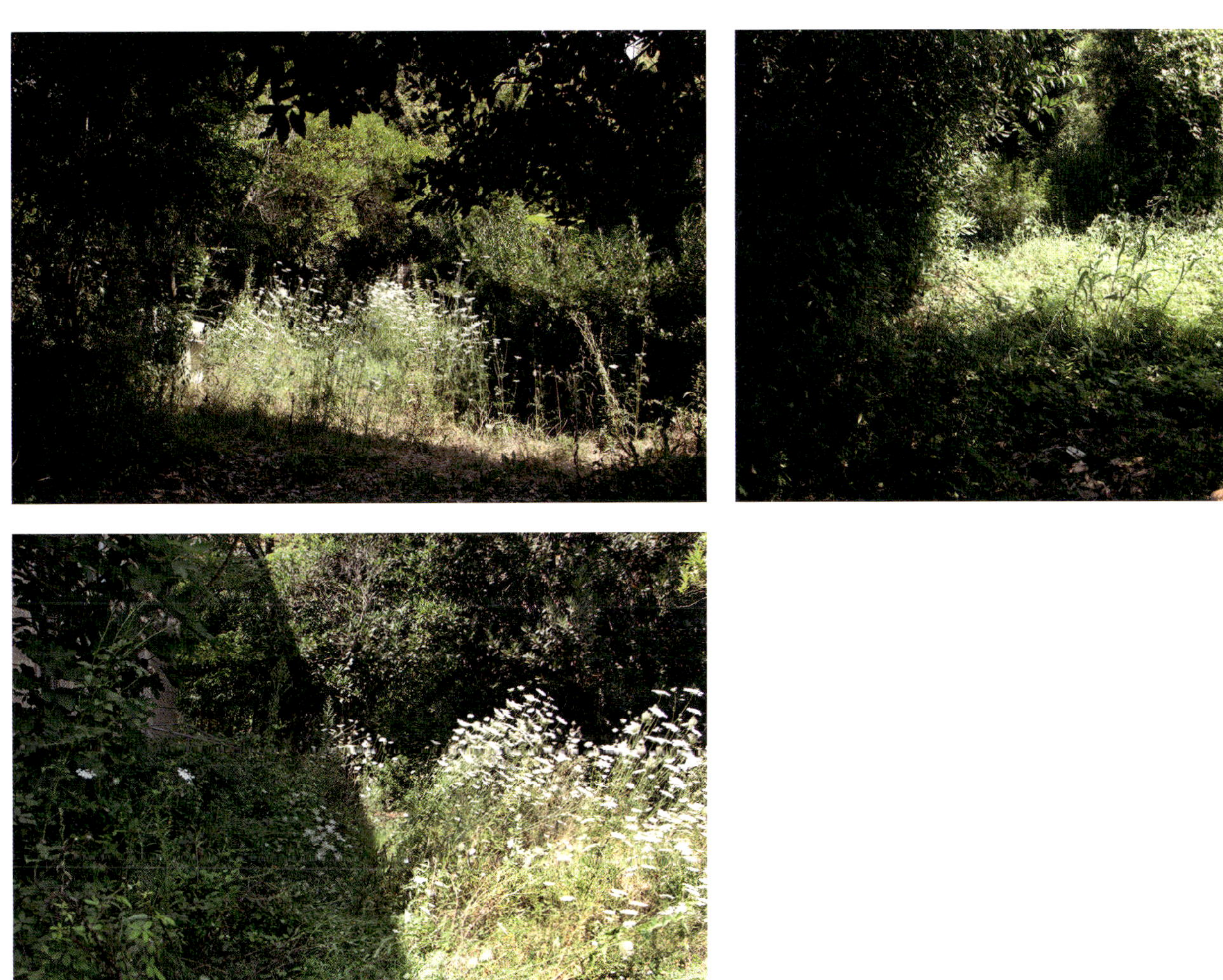

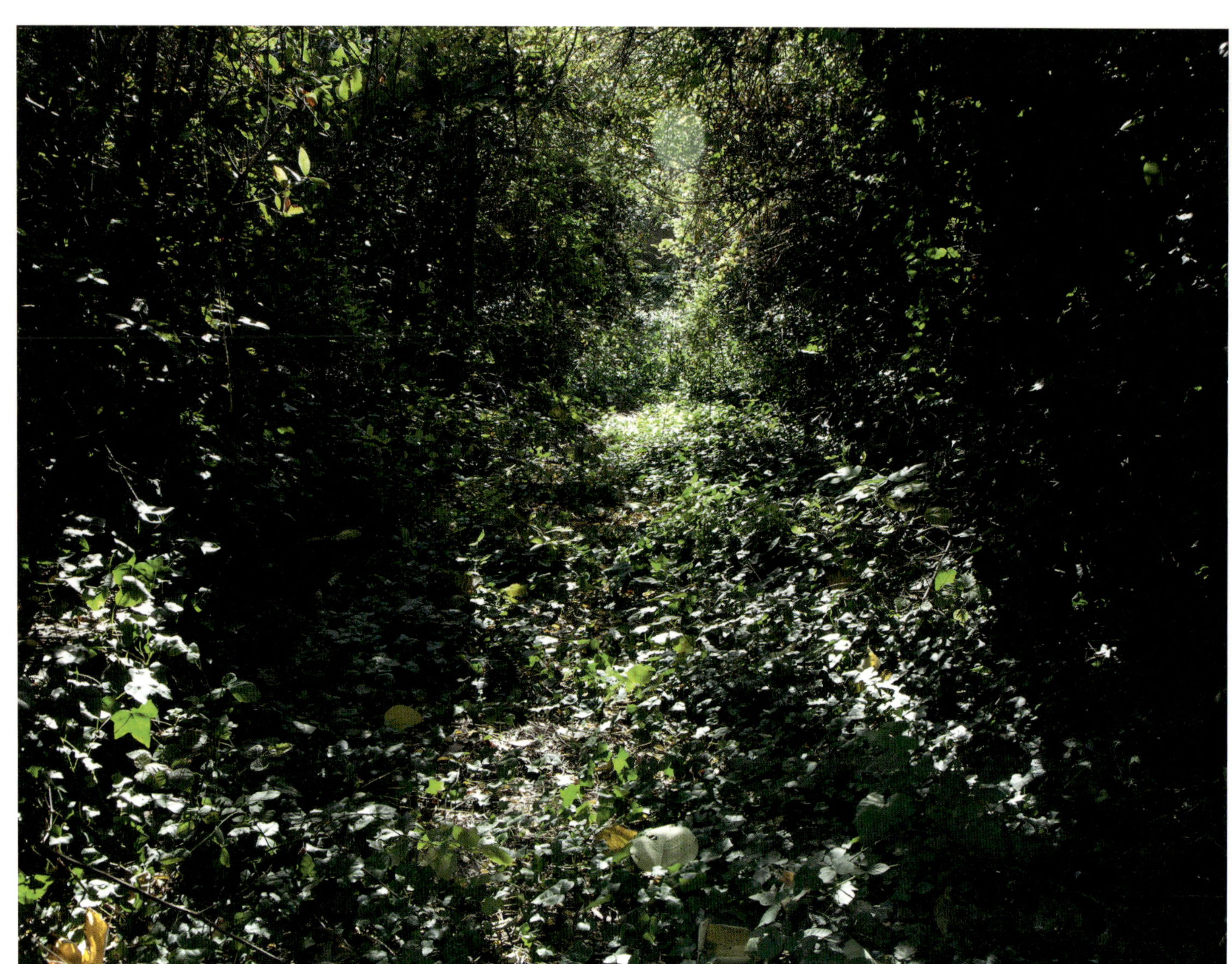

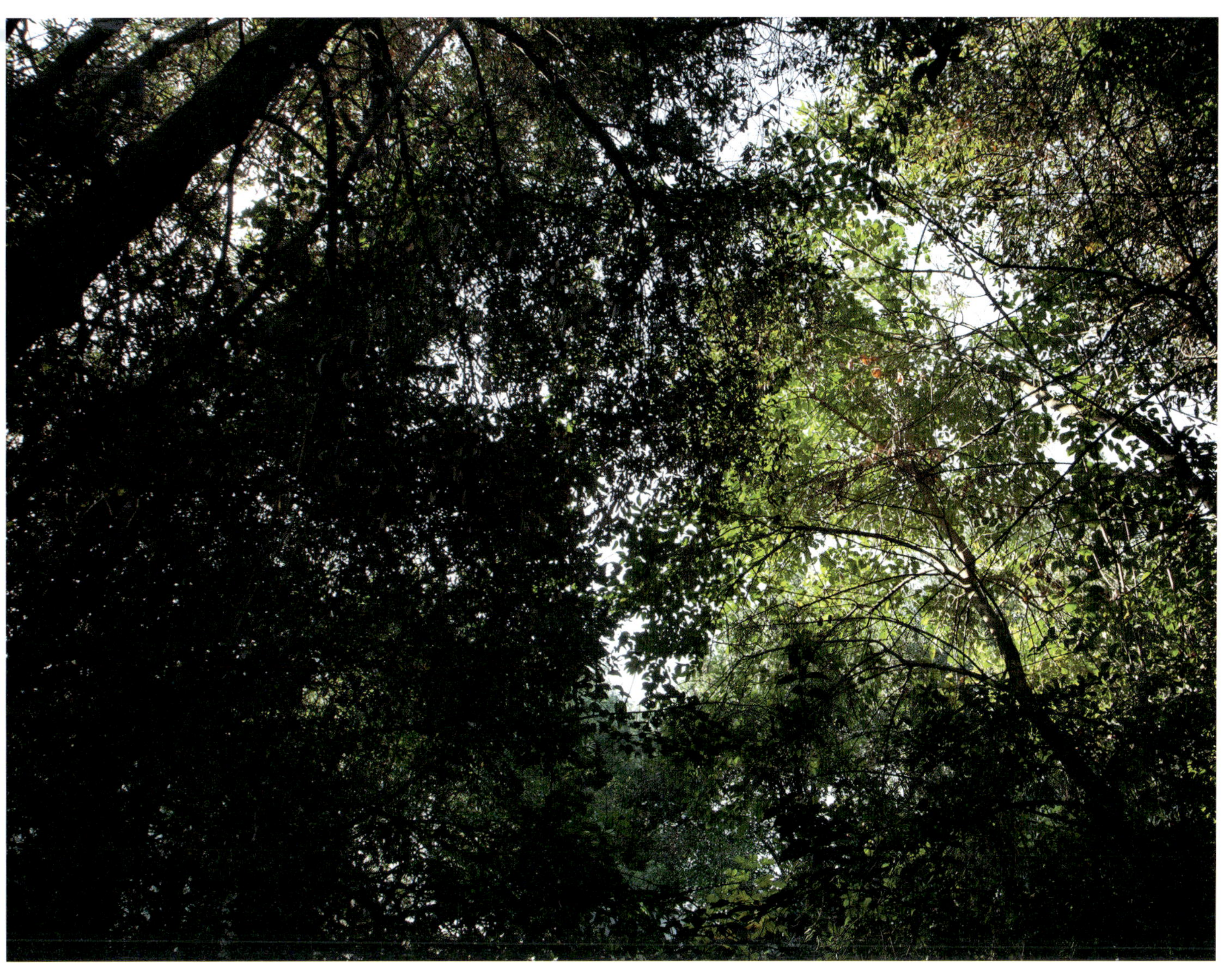

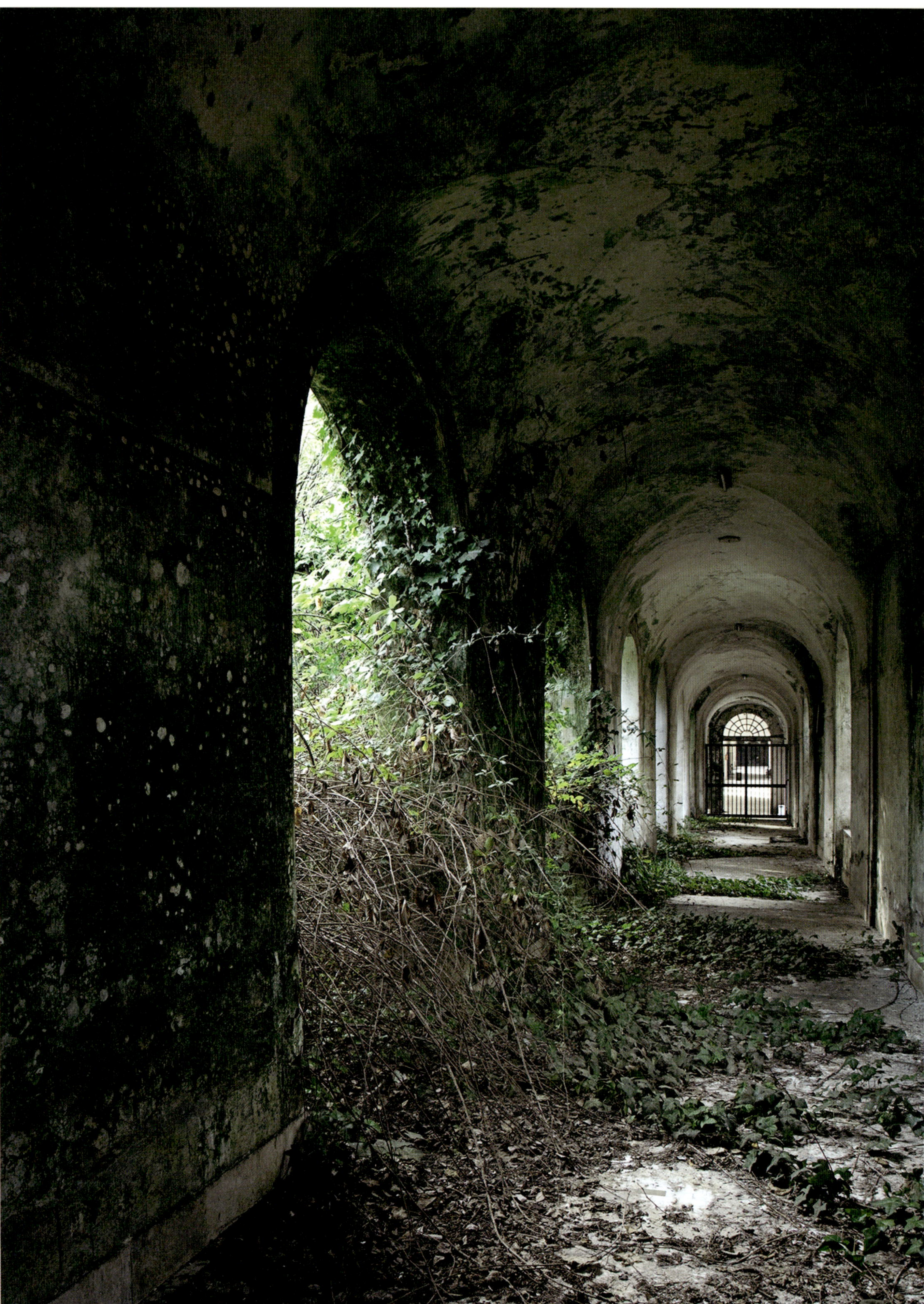

Libera Viva
Emanuela De Cecco

1

Gilles Clement, paesaggista o "giardiniere" come lui preferisce definirsi, introducendo l'edizione italiana del volume che raccoglie riflessioni ed esperienze del suo *giardino in movimento*[1], scrive delle aree incolte, solitamente associate con l'abbandono e il degrado, come di una sorta di modello a cui ha guardato per realizzare una particolare tipologia di giardino antitetica a quella tradizionalmente regolamentata da un principio di ordine. Osservando il comportamento delle piante in queste aree, egli rileva quanto in esse siano maggiori gli scambi e le contaminazioni rispetto a ciò che avviene in condizioni protette. In effetti, se prevale una logica interessata a conservare la purezza di ogni singola specie, la contaminazione è considerata una minaccia, ma se la preoccupazione principale è lo sviluppo fluido e diversificato del biologico, la contaminazione diventa una risorsa poiché tramite essa si moltiplicano le possibilità di sopravvivenza. Più precisamente: "L'abbandono di un suolo a se stesso è la condizione essenziale perché si inneschi il processo che porta una terra, prima destinata a una sola specie, a ricevere progressivamente decine e decine di specie diverse".

2

Libera Viva (2011) è l'esito di una relazione lunga un anno e a distanza ravvicinata tra Elisabeth Hölzl e gli spazi dell'ex ospedale psichiatrico Leonardi Bianchi di Napoli. Leggendo le parole di Gilles Clement, per caso in concomitanza con l'incontro con questo lavoro, ho avuto la sensazione che entrambi gli autori attribuissero lo stesso significato ai termini "abbandono", "disordine" e "probabilità" e alle conseguenze che la connessione tra di essi implica. Credo possa essere interessante assumere la percezione di questa sorta di sintonia a distanza, sia perché tanto per Hölzl, quanto per Clement, essa corrisponde a una precisa istanza progettuale messa al lavoro nei rispettivi ambiti di azione, sia perché entrambi condividono un atteggiamento dal carattere gentilmente sovversivo nei confronti di alcuni luoghi comuni che hanno avuto un peso significativo nell'ideologia dominante della nostra società e che a tutt'oggi persistono nonostante l'evidenza del loro fallimento e ancora perchè entrambi dimostrano come spostare il proprio punto di vista sia possibile e possa contribuire concretamente a modificare la percezione di una realtà che siamo soliti considerare esclusivamente in senso negativo. Questo atteggiamento è presente anche in altri lavori realizzati in questi anni dall'artista. Il riferimento è a quelli dedicati a luoghi sospesi tra la definitiva interruzione delle attività per cui erano stati pensati e l'incertezza del futuro: l'Hotel Bristol a Merano (*Hotel Bristol*, 2008) e l'area dove fino a qualche anno fa erano attive le acciaierie Ilva a Genova/Cornigliano (*Vacuum*, 2010).

3

L'ex Ospedale psichiatrico Leonardo Bianchi di Napoli occupa un'area di circa 300.000 metri quadri, oggi è uno spazio abbandonato, i piani per il futuro non sono ancora definiti: convivono ipotesi di riconversione a scopo sociale e culturale, rischio di speculazioni – come la stessa artista sottolinea nella nota introduttiva – preoccupazione per la necessità di fondi ingenti date le dimensioni e lo stato di degrado del complesso. Il lavoro di Elisabeth Hölzl è composto da una serie di fotografie e una raccolta di dati storici relativi alla gestione del manicomio: la pianta dell'area, le fotografie d'archivio, le dichiarazioni dei pazienti e il cosiddetto fardellario, ovvero il registro compilato per ogni paziente nel momento dell'ammissione dove si catalogano gli effetti personali consegnati e le motivazioni dell'internamento. Riprendendo una modalità introdotta anche in altri lavori, *Libera Viva* si sviluppa su un doppio registro: l'effetto complessivo è determinato dall'interazione tra di essi, sul piano del linguaggio utilizzato ma non solo. Le fotografie, a conferma della capacità dell'artista a entrare in sintonia con i luoghi, sono efficaci: i dettagli individuati negli spazi immensi del Leonardo Bianchi restituiscono il mistero attuale di un edificio un tempo potentissimo, ne mettono a nudo lo stato di abbandono dove la forza di un tempo trova una rispondenza nell'ampiezza della decadenza. La sospensione che le caratterizza si trasforma, allo sguardo, in sensazione fisica. In alcune Hölzl coglie le tracce essenziali attraverso le quali il passato di quel luogo emerge in tutta la sua brutalità: i letti, una sorta di ambulatorio, i graffiti, segni fisici sulla pelle dell'edificio, gesti di sopravvivenza. La polvere, a volte i calcinacci, attutiscono ma non eliminano l'eco dolente che emanano queste fotografie di spazi ora abbandonati. Dati e documenti storici non richiedono ulteriori spiegazioni: essi richiamano implacabilmente la realtà di questa come di altre analoghe istituzioni totali, dove le individualità sono spogliate di tutto e rese numero, dove le persone che entrano sono condannate, in molti casi per ragioni palesemente strumentali, a una vita reclusa, giorni, mesi, anni, decenni sempre uguali. Essi agiscono come una sorta di freno intenzionale che impedisce di cadere nella tentazione di abbandonarsi con malinconia all'incantesimo generato dalle fotografie. Essi sono un promemoria, mettono in luce le responsabilità storiche che hanno determinato la storia di questa e altre strutture analoghe: nomi, cognomi, oggetti, vissuti personali, ragioni dell'internamento. In *Libera Viva* l'interazione tra linguaggi differenti si articola oltre che nella coesistenza di fotografie e documenti, nella variazione di temperatura: il calore dallo sguardo empatico dell'artista presente nelle fotografie, il gelo dei dati storici. Gli effetti che i manicomi hanno prodotto fino a poco tempo fa sulla vita delle persone sono restituiti con due modalità diverse, impossibile restare indifferenti. Con questo lavoro Elisabeth Hölzl sembra spingerci al confronto con una questione complicata, che non si esaurisce nella preoccupazione per il futuro di quell'area. La percezione è di avere a che fare con una questione più ampia, delicata e decisiva per questo e altri futuri, di essere stati condotti, metaforicamente, in un luogo dove prendono forma le domande che riguardano la costruzione della memoria di intere parti della nostra società che in realtà cerchiamo di rendere invisibili. Là dove sono ancora aperte tutte le soluzioni, dalla tentazione di cancellare per sempre le tracce fisiche di un passato impresentabile, alla volontà di conservarle come monito e dovere civile di non dimenticare i danni prodotti dalle strategie di esclusione che strutture come i manicomi (oggi le carceri) hanno prodotto e come farlo.

4

Ancora a proposito delle fotografie. Se una parte mostra gli elementi che rimandano direttamente alle attività che caratterizzano il luogo, molte altre registrano la presenza della natura, in particolare la forza con cui essa si è riappropriata della struttura architettonica, invadendola, cambiandone i connotati. Elisabeth Hölzl torna più volte su questa potenza, la osserva da vicino e da lontano, le dà spazio, la rende evidente. Scrive l'artista, sempre nella nota introduttiva: "La riconquista degli spazi da parte della vegetazione è come una metafora della rivincita della vita sulla costrizione". È in queste parole che la risonanza con quanto scrive Clement a proposito dei giardini incolti sembra trasformarsi in una comunanza di sguardi che, partendo da diversi punti di vista, confluiscono in una visione che mette a nudo i limiti dell'azione umana. Non è in gioco la volontà di affermare una sconfitta assoluta ma entrambi ne sostengono la debolezza quando essa si manifesta come spinta alla conquista e al controllo, così come entrambi le contrappongono la maggiore efficacia dell'azione della natura nel reinventarsi, nel dare spazio alla diversità, nell'includere, traendo da questa attitudine la possibilità di continuare a vivere.

5

Tutti gli elementi messi in campo in *Libera Viva* concorrono a definire un equilibrio instabile, generato dagli effetti che producono la compresenza di temporalità diverse (la storia, il presente), registri emotivi diversi (i dati, l'empatia dello sguardo) e linguaggi diversi (le informazioni d'archivio, la fotografia). Ma questo equilibrio instabile, contrariamente a quanto siamo abituati a pensare, è la condizione perchè si produca una trasformazione intesa come rigenerazione. Solo provocandolo e accogliendolo si ottengono i benefici – la natura insegna – dati dall'inclusione della diversità. Con *Libera Viva* Elisabeth Hölzl aggiunge un contributo a sua volta inclusivo, innesca una relazione attiva con una storia che riguarda tutti noi e da vicino. Un contributo "vivo", radicalmente altro dalla fissità che troppo spesso caratterizza commemorazioni e celebrazioni. La serie di fotografie si chiude con l'immagine di un cielo.

1 Gilles Clement, *Il giardino in movimento*, Quodlibet, Macerata, 2011

Libera Viva

Emanuela De Cecco

1

Gilles Clement, the landscape designer (or simply "gardener" as he prefers to call himself), wrote about uncultivated land in his introduction to the Italian edition of his book in which he talks about and reflects on the experience of his *garden in movement* [1]. Uncultivated land is usually associated with abandonment and degradation, but Gilles Clement has used it as a sort of model to create a particular type of garden that is the antithesis of the traditional concept of nature regulated by principles of order. Observing the way the plants in these uncultivated areas behave, he has drawn attention to how much more exchange and contamination there is between species compared to what happens in protected conditions. In fact, if the prevailing logic is to preserve the purity of every single species, contamination is considered a threat. But if the main concern is to promote a fluid and biologically diversified development, contamination can become a resource. This is because it is through this process that we can see the possibilities of survival multiply. So, what Gilles Clement is saying is "it is the abandonment of the soil to itself which is the essential condition needed to trigger off the process which takes a type of earth, initially destined to support only one species, to receive little by little dozens and dozens of different ones".

2

Libera Viva (2011) is the result of a close, year-long relationship between Elisabeth Hölzl and the site of the ex-psychiatric hospital Leonardi Bianchi in Naples. By chance, I happened to have been reading Gilles Clement's book when I first saw these photographs, and I sensed that both of them were giving the same meaning to the words "abandonment", "disorder" and "probability", and to the consequences of the connection between them. It is interesting to be aware of this long-range empathy because for both Elisabeth Hölzl and Gilles Clement it corresponds to a precise moment in which the two projects, each in their respective field, took shape. This is because they both share a way of looking at things that is gently subversive towards some of the clichés that have dominated our society's ideology, many of which still persist today in spite of the obvious evidence of their failure. Also both of them show how it is possible to shift our point of view and help us modify our own perception of a reality that we usually only see as something negative. This can also be seen in other works by Elisabeth Hölzl of this period. These have all been dedicated to places suspended in time between the moment in which they no longer serve their original purpose and the uncertainty of the future: the Hotel Bristol in Merano (*Hotel Bristol*, 2008) and the area in Cornigliano near Genoa which was occupied until only a few years ago by the Ilva steelworks (*Vacuum*, 2010).

3

The ex-psychiatric hospital Leonardo Bianchi in Naples occupies an area of approximately 300,000 square meters. Today, it is abandoned and the plans for its future have still to be defined. There has been talk of reconverting the space here to provide social and cultural amenities, there is the risk of property speculation (just as the artist herself has underlined in her introductory note), and there are concerns for the vast sums of money needed given the size and state of decay of the site.

This work of Elisabeth Hölzl is made up of a series of photographs and a collection of historical data relating to the management of the mental hospital: the floor plan, the archive photographs, the testimonies of the patients themselves, and the so-called "Fardellario". This was the register filled in for each patient on admission in which the personal effects and belongings that they handed in were catalogued, and where the reasons for their commitment to the institution were recorded. *Libera Viva* picks up the style introduced in the other works and develops it on two levels: the overall effect is achieved by the interaction between them, and not only by the language used. The photographs clearly confirm the artist's skill in establishing a rapport with the places themselves. Small details are identified in the vast structural spaces of the Leonardo Bianchi, and these restore something of the mystery that still shrouds a building that was at one time so imposing and powerful. The state of abandonment is brought to the fore, a state in which the strength and power of the past are mirrored in the vastness of the decay. The suspension in time that characterizes this is transformed, as we look, into a physical sensation. In some photographs, Elisabeth Hölzl captures the essential traces through which the building's past emerges in all its cruelty: the beds, a sort of doctor's surgery, the graffiti, the physical signs on the skin of the building, gestures of survival. The dust, sometimes the broken bricks and plaster, all soften but do not deaden the painful echo which cries out from these photographs of abandoned spaces. The data and historical documents do not need any further explanation. They implacably remind us of the reality of this and other similar institutions, where the individual is stripped of everything and becomes a number, where people who enter there are condemned, in many cases for reasons that are clearly instrumental, to a life of reclusion: days, months, years, decades, always the same. The photographs act like a sort of brake to make sure we do not fall into the temptation of abandoning ourselves to the melancholy spell they cast. They act as a reminder, bringing to light the role of history in determining the story of this and other similar buildings: names, surnames, objects, personal effects, reasons for the commitment.

In *Libera Viva*, the interaction between the different languages is expressed not only in simply putting the photographs alongside the documents, but in the variations in temperature and tone: the warmth of the empathy in the artist's gaze which we can see so clearly in the photographs, and the icy coldness of the historical data. The effects that, until not so long ago, the mental asylums had on the lives of the inmates are represented in two different ways, and it is impossible not to be moved by them. With this work, Elisabeth Hölzl seems to want to push us to face something much more complicated than the relatively simple question of the future of the site itself. The perception is that we are dealing with a much wider question, and one that is both delicate and decisive for this and for other futures: to be condemned, metaphorically, to a place where the real question is about constructing the memory of entire aspects of our society that we are actually trying to hide. There, where anything is still possible. We could be tempted to wipe out for ever the physical traces of a past which we have not got the courage to face, or we could preserve it as a warning and a civil obligation so as not to forget the damage caused by the strategies of exclusion which structures like the mental hospitals (and today the prisons) have produced, and how we can achieve this.

4

To return once again to the photographs, if some of them refer directly to the activities that characterized the place, many others record the presence of nature. In particular, they show the force with which nature has taken over the architectural structure, invading it, changing its features. Elisabeth Hölzl comes back again and again to this power; she examines it both close-up and at a distance, and she makes it real. Again in her introductory note, the artist writes: "the vegetation takes back the space and becomes a metaphor of the victory of life over restraint". This resonates with Clement's words when he talks about uncultivated gardens that transform themselves into a collection of different pictures that, starting from different view points, meet in a single vision of man's limitations. Here we are not talking about the desire to declare absolute defeat, but to sustain the weakness in that defeat when it acts as a stimulus for conquest and control. Both victory and defeat are set one against the other in celebration of nature's greater efficiency in recreating itself, in making space for diversity, in inclusion rather than exclusion, and from this, making it possible that life continues.

5

Together, all the elements presented in *Libera Viva* define an unstable equilibrium generated by the effects of the juxtaposition of different times (history and the present), the different emotional levels (the dates and figures, the empathy of the artist's gaze), and the different languages used (the archive material, the photographs). But this unstable equilibrium, contrary to what we are used to thinking, is the reason why such an intense transformation as regeneration is produced. Only by provoking that equilibrium and welcoming it can we gain the benefits; nature teaches us about the inclusion of diversity. In *Libera Viva*, Elisabeth Hölzl offers us something which is in turn inclusive and all-embracing, and which creates an active relationship with a part of history that closely involves all of us. What she presents us with is something "alive", something completely different from the fixed approach that so often characterizes traditional commemorations and celebrations. The series of photographs closes with a picture of an open sky.

1 Gilles Clement, *Il giardino in movimento*, Quodlibet, Macerata, 2011

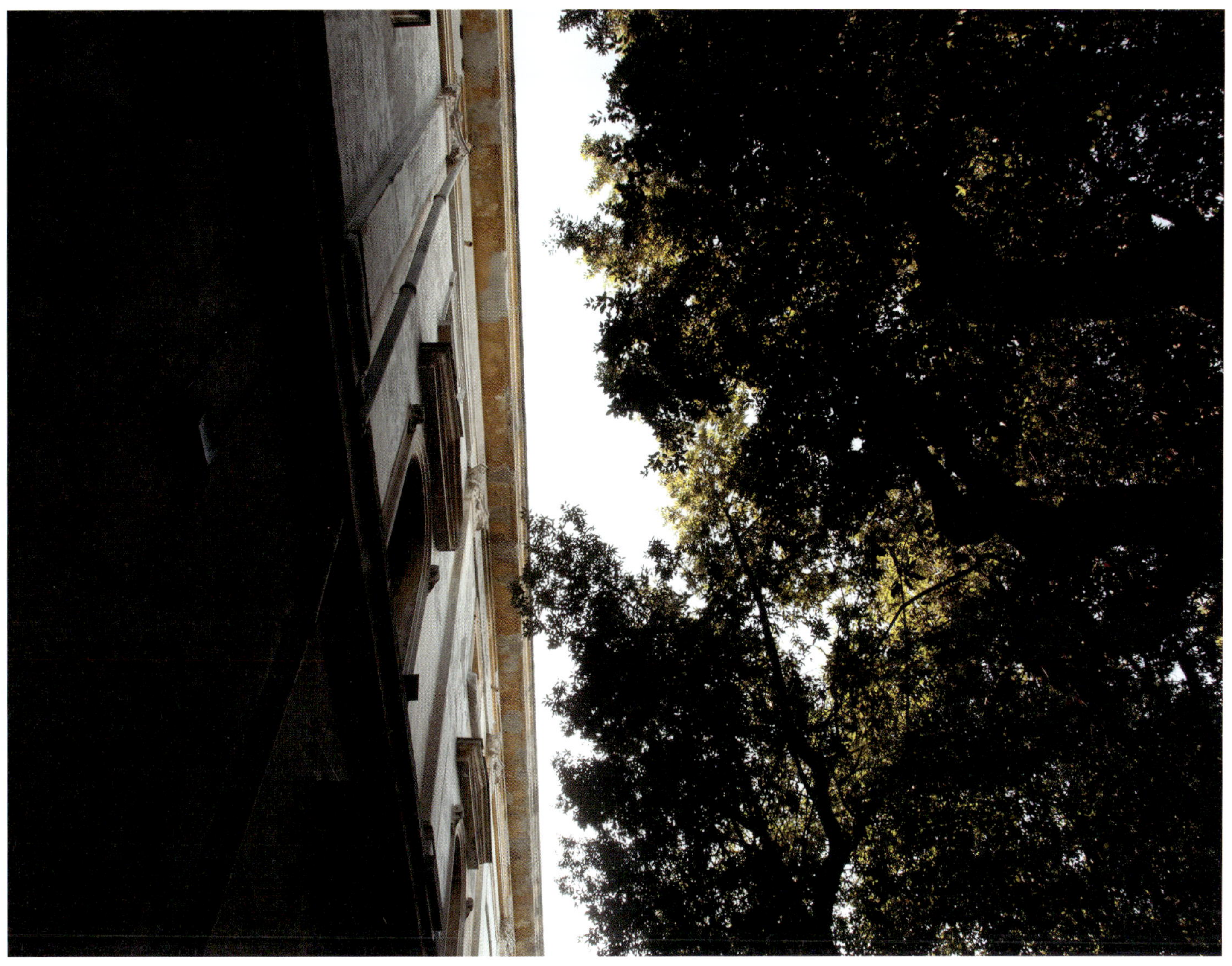

Haupteingang
Ingresso principale
Main entrance

nächste Doppelseite pagina successiva
next double page

Verwaltungsbüros, Garten
Uffici amministrativi, giardino
Administration block, garden

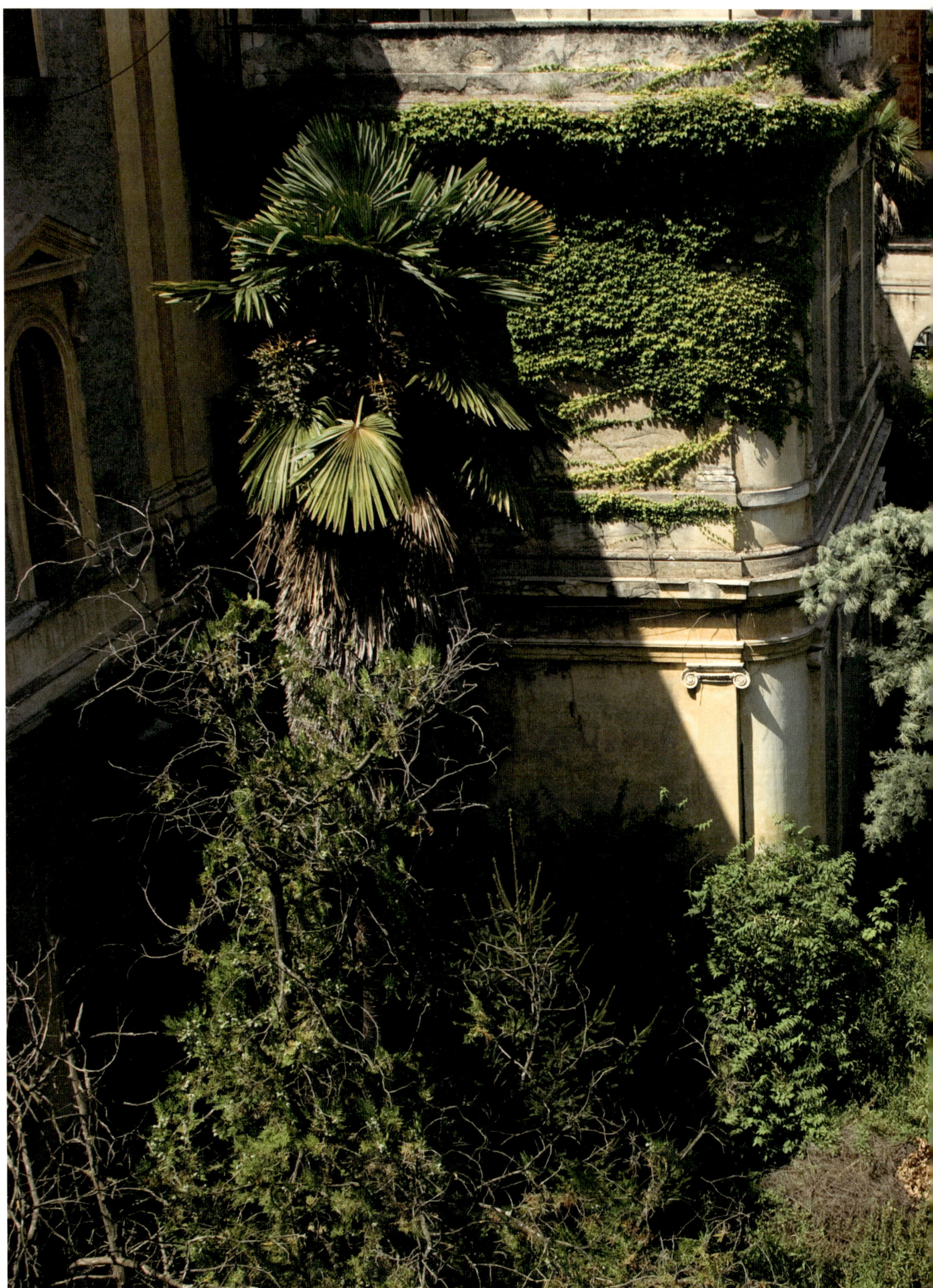

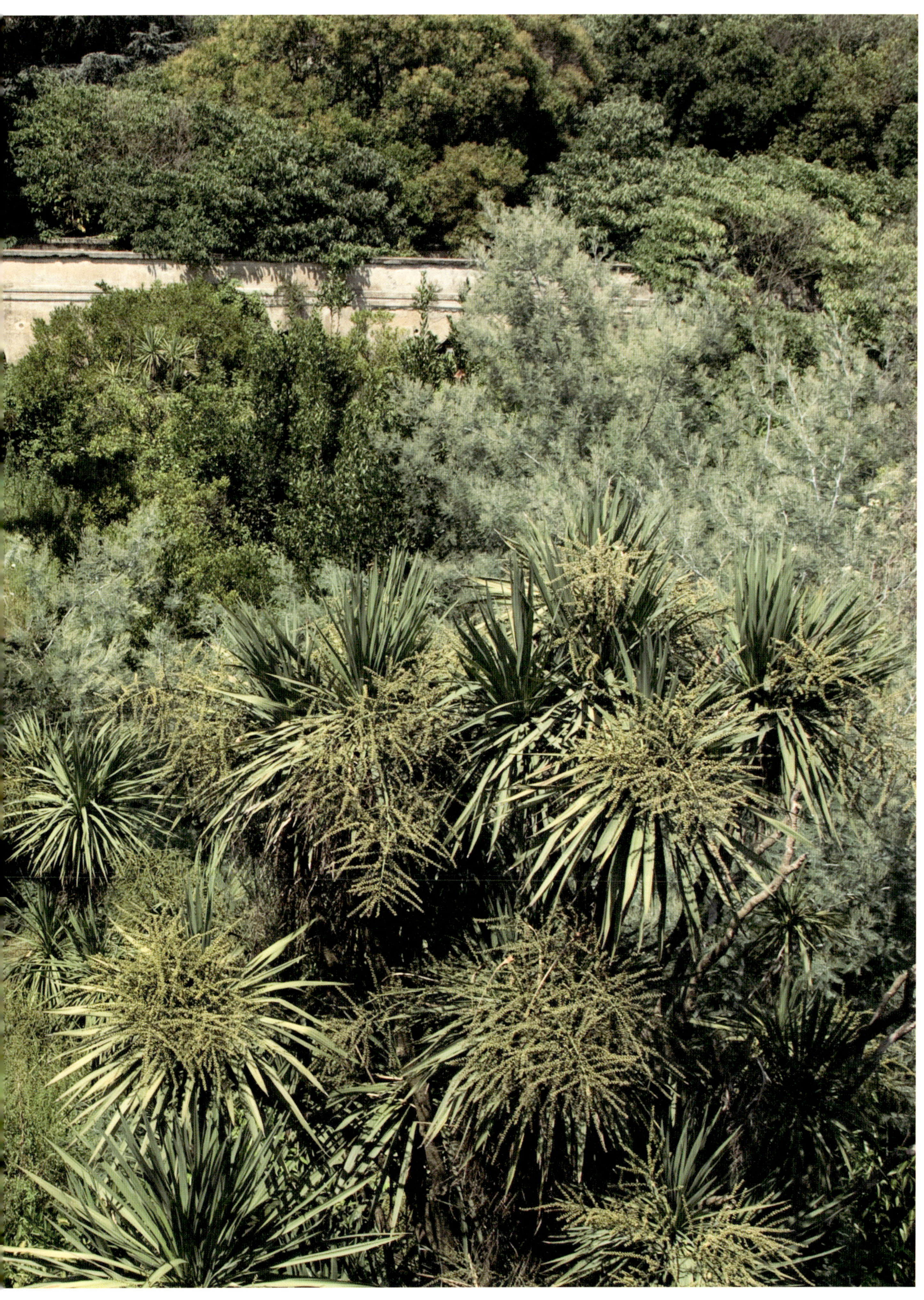

Kühlzelle
Cella frigorifera
Cold storage room

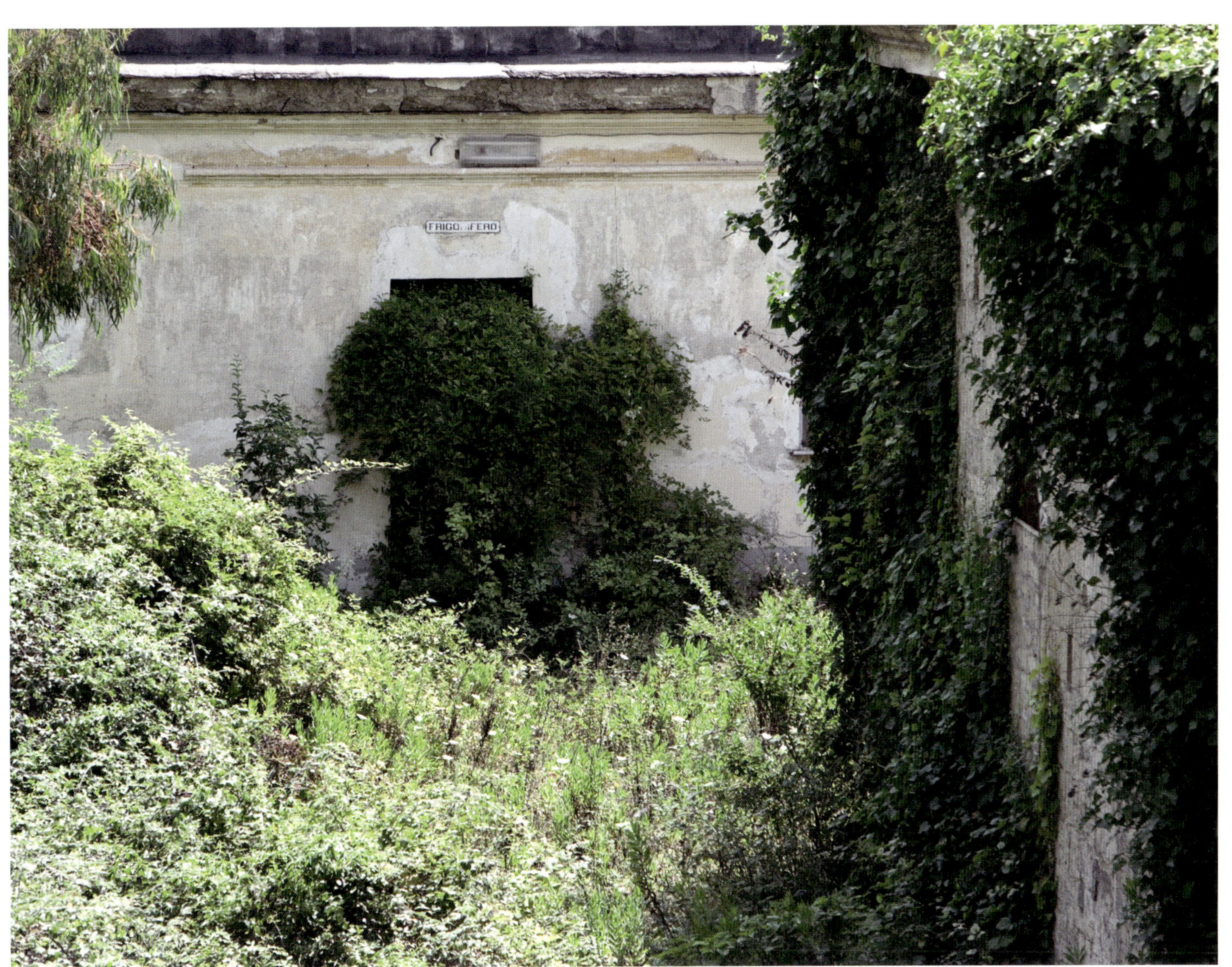

Dachpassage, vergittert
Passaggio pensile con grata
Overhead pathway with grated arch

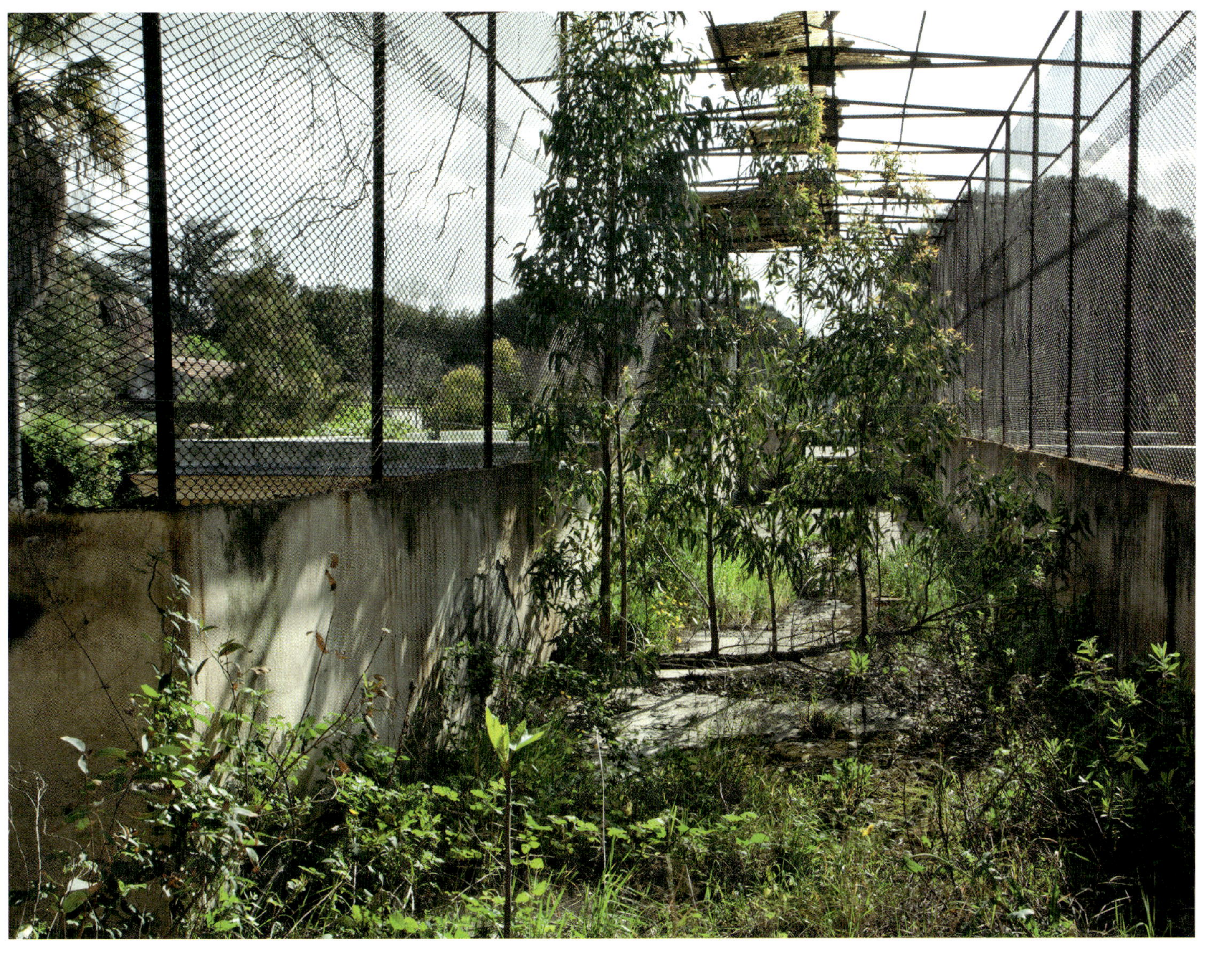

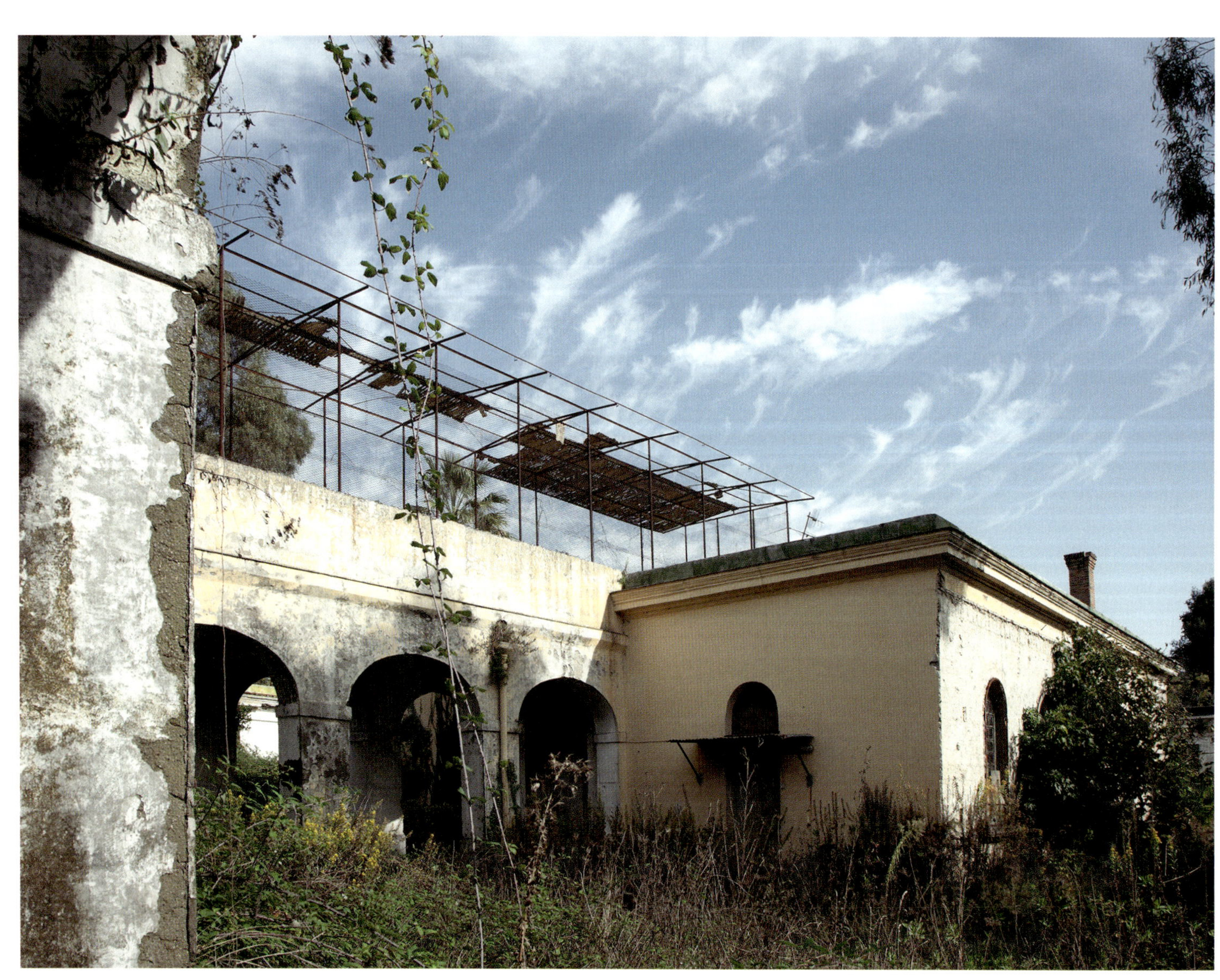

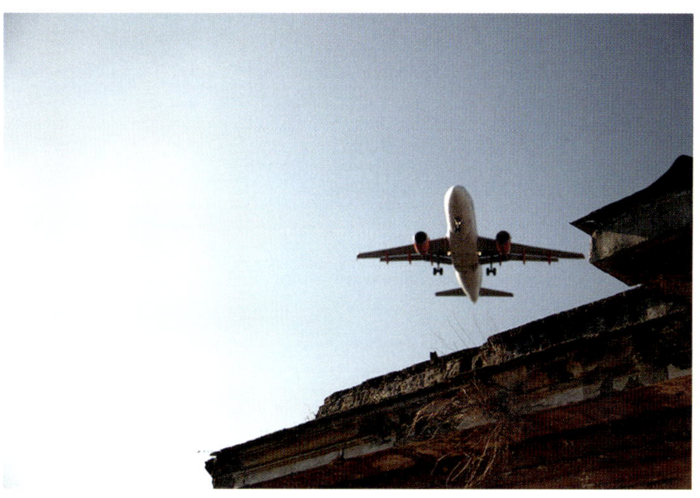

Dachpassage, vergittert
Passaggio pensile con grata
Overhead pathway with grated arch

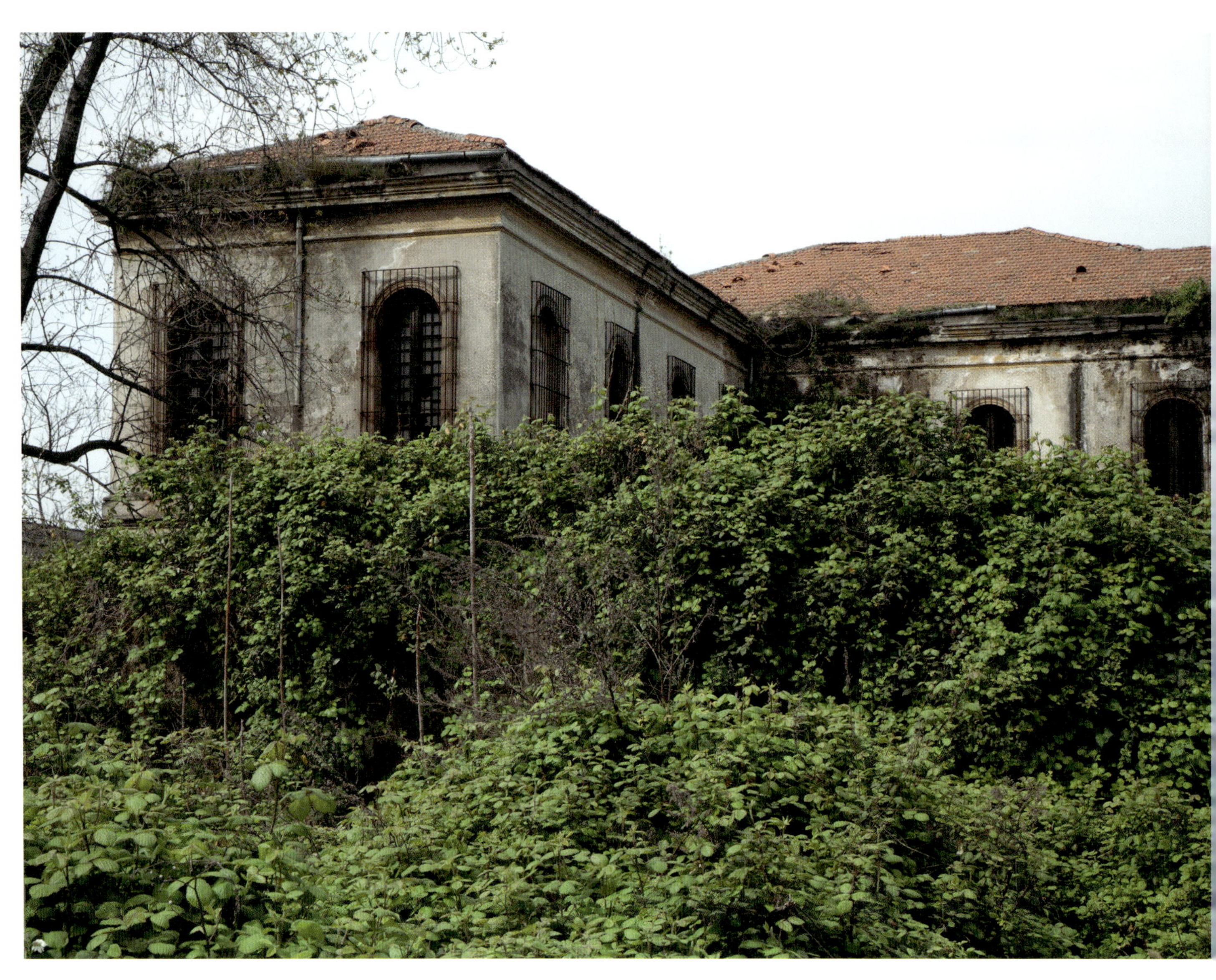

VI. Abteilung „gefährliche“ Männer
VI. Sezione uomini "pericolosi"
VI. Men's high security wing

Fardellario (1921 – 1973) *

* Registri nominativi dei folli con indicazione degli effetti ed oggetti costituenti il fardello consegnato al momento dell'ammissione e/o ritirato all'atto della dimissione, ovvero consegnato ai parenti in caso di morte. Secondo il regolamento del 1889, dopo la morte del folle all'interno del manicomio, doveva essere venduto il suo fardello a beneficio del manicomio se non veniva reclamato entro due mesi (*art. 200*).

Il folle aveva presso di sè i seguenti valori ed ogetti di corredo, ritirati tutti dall'Economo all'atto di ammissione.

Essi sono:

Uomini

Un vestitino da ragazzo.

Giacca, cappotto,
scarpe e cappello.

Cenci.

Giacca, gilet, pantalone
e cenci.

Giacca, gilet,
pantalone, camicia,
maglia, colletto,
cravatta, calze, scarpe,
cappello.

Cappotto, giacca, gilet,
pantaloni, camicia,
maglia, mutande,
colletto, cravatta,
bretelle, calze, scarpe
e cappello, orologio
di metallo falso con
catenina dello stesso
metallo, portafogli con
carte personali, fondo
caffè.

Cenci.

Giacca, pantaloni,
cappotto, due maglie,
mutanda, scarpe,
calze, cinghia di cuoio,
beretto.

Capotto, giacca,
pantaloni, gilet,
camicia, mutande,
maglia, calze, scarpe,
colletto, cravatta,
cappello, bottoni
gemelli per polsi di
metallo falso.

Giacca, cappotto,
scarpe e cappello.

Cappotto e pantalone.

Cappotto, giacca,
pantaloni, nr 2 calze,
scarpe, cravatta,
maglia, gilet, cappello,
mutanda, involto
con carte personali
e guanti, due lenti,
catenina di metallo
bianco, due carte valori
austriache da diecimila
corone e cento corone.

Cenci.

Camicia, due maglie,
mutanda, giacca,
pantalone, gilet,
bretelle, scarpe.

Cappotto, giacca, gilet,
pantaloni, camicia,
maglie due, mutanda,
calze, scarpe, bretelle,
beretto, due bottoni per
polsi di metallo falso,
anello di metallo giallo.

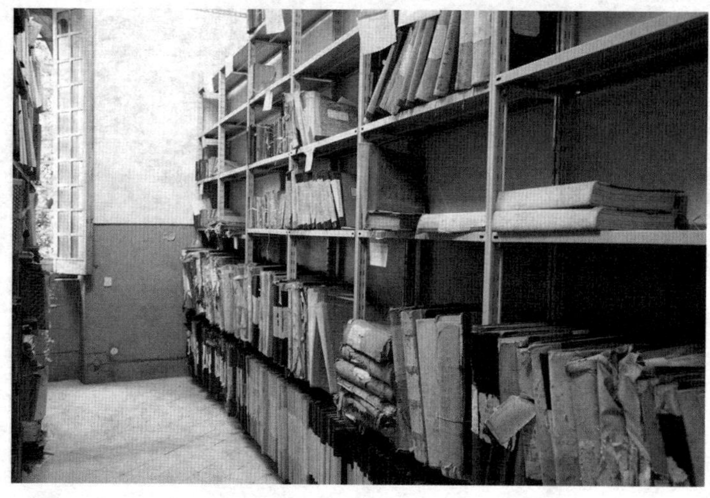

Cappello, giacca, gilet, pantaloni, camicia, maglia, mutande, calze, scarpe, giarrettiere, molle per camicia, cinghia, cappello, valigia con sei camicie, due maglie, due mutande, un asciugamani, una giacca e un pantalone, tre paia di calzini, un paio di scarpe, quattro colletti, tre fazzoletti, due cravatte, un pezzo di sapone, pennello per barba, una scatola con rasoio.

Cenci.

Giubba, gilet, pantaloni, camicia, due maglie, mutande, calze, scarpe, cappello.

Cenci.

Cappotto, giacca, camicia, mutanda, maglia, calze, scarpe, bretelle, scolla, cappello, anello di metallo giallo.

Cappotto, giacca, gilet, pantaloni, camicia, mutande, bretelle, giarrettiere, calze, scarpe, colletto, cravatta, cappello.

Giacca, gilet, pantalone, camicia, due maglie, mutande, calze, scarpe, cinghia, sciarpa e cappello.

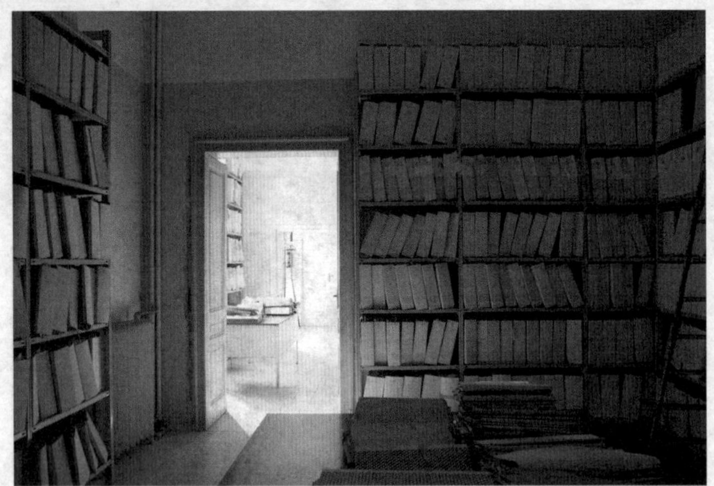

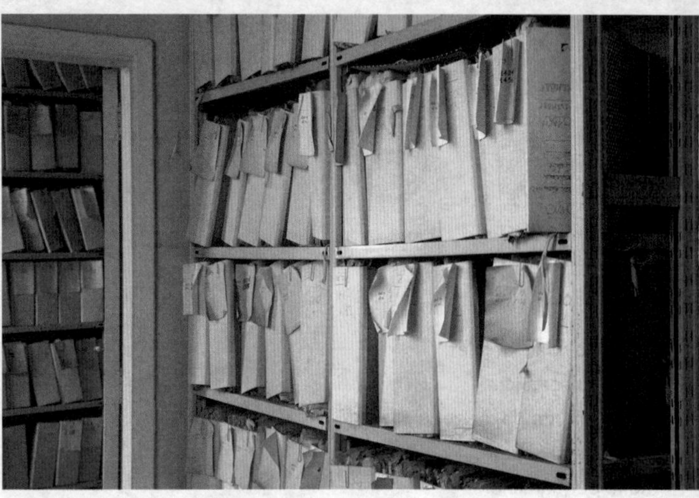

Historisches Archiv, Krankenakten, Liste der Habseligkeiten
Archivio storico, cartelle cliniche e “Fardellario”
Archives, patients’ records and “Fardellario” Register of Inmates’ Belongings

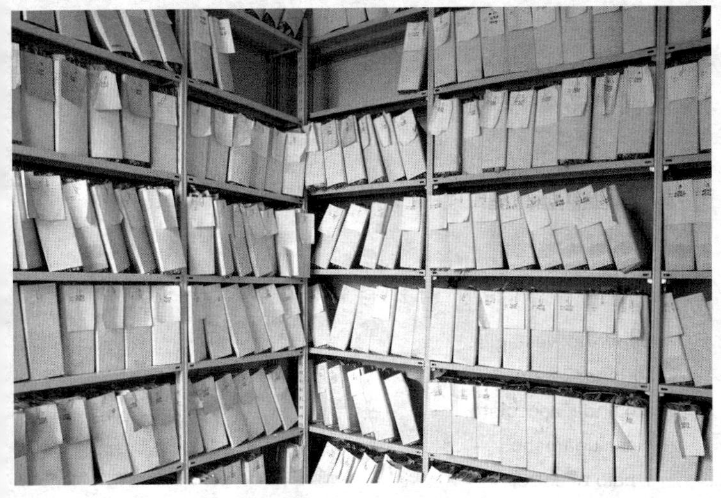

Cappotto, giacca, gilet, pantaloni, camicia, mutanda, maglia, calze, scarpe, cappello, bretelle, colletto, cravatta, due bottoni gemelli per polso di metallo bianco e giallo, una lente con astuccio (metallo bianco).

Cappotto giacca, gilet, pantaloni, camicie tre, mutande sei, maglie due, salviette due, fazzoletti due, cravatta, cappello, scarpe in cattive condizioni, una valigia con cenci, contanti lire nove e centesimi 95 (L 9.95), bolletta N.27.

Cenci.

Camicia, due maglie, mutanda, giacca, pantalone, gilet, bretelle, calze, scarpe.

Cappotto, giacca, gilet, maglia, pantaloni, camicia, mutanda, maglione, scarpine, calze, cinghie, cappello, colletto, portafogli con tessera, portasigarette di metallo falso. Il tutto al fardello.

Giubba e pantalone di tela, camicia, mutanda, calze e scarpe.

Cappotto, giacca, gilet, pantaloni, camicia, mutanda, calze, scarpe.

Donne

Camicia, mutanda,
due sottane, vestaglia,
cappotto, scarpe e
calze.

Cenci.

Camicie tre, maglie
due, mutande due,
vestaglie due, pannolini
tre, cappotto, scialle,
sciarpa, calze paia tre
e scarpe.

Camicia, maglia,
mutanda, sottana, due
vestaglie, scialletto,
calze e pantofole.

Camicia, maglia,
mutanda, vestaglia,
cappotto, calze e
scarpe, sciarpetta.

Vestaglia, cappottino,
camicia, maglia,
blousetta, mutande,
scarpe, due paia di
calze, un fazzoletto, una
borsa di pelle.

Camicia, maglia,
mutanda, sottana, due
vestaglie, scialletto,
calze e pantofole.

Vestaglia, camicia,
mutande, zoccoletti.

Giacca, vestaglia,
camicia, mutande,
sottana, scarpe,
fazzoletto.

Cappotto, vestaglia,
sottana, 3 camicie,
mutande, zoccoletti,
1 asciugamano,
1 paio di calze,
L 102,10 (centodue
e centesimi 10).

Vestaglia, camicia,
mutande, sottana,
zoccoletti.

Camicia, giacca.

Vestaglia, camicia,
sottana, mutande,
zoccoletti.

Gonna, blusetta,
giacca, reggiseno,
sottoveste, calza,
scarpe, una fedina di
metallo giallo.

Gonna, maglia, sottana,
maglietta, reggiseno,
reggicalze, calze,
scarpe, una borsa,
otto buoni fruttiferi di
lire centomila e tre da
lire cinquantamila, un
libretto del Banco di
Napoli col rimanente
credito di L 50.143,
5 chiavi, una catenina
di metallo giallo, un
paio di orecchini di
metallo giallo.

Veste, giacchettino,
sottoveste, mutande,
reggiseno e scarpe.

Veste, gonna,
giacca, 3 blusette,
2 sottovesti, mutande,
scarpe.

Vestaglia, giacca,
blusa, gonna, sottana,
reggiseno, maglietta,
mutanda, fazzoletti,
2 calze, scarpe.

Una maglia.

Veste, giacchettino,
sottoveste, canottiera,
3 fazzoletti e scarpe.

Camicia, mutande,
giacca.

Due cappelli, sei
fazzoletti, due fazzoletti
di seta, una panciera,
due sottane, due
camicie, tre mutande,
una maglia, reggipetto,
otto pannolini, tre
vestaglie, tre paia di
scarpe, cappotto, calze,
cinghia e guanti, un
cesto con effetti per
neonato, un anello
di metallo giallo, due
chiavette, cerchietti di
metallo falso, una rosa
di madreperla.

Camicia, maglia,
vestaglia, cappottino,
calze e scarpe, un paio
di orecchini di metallo
giallo con pietre
bianche, un anello di
metallo giallo.

Camicia, mutande, busto sottovita, vestaglia, calze e scarpe, una borsetta vuota, una borsa con carte inutili, un anello e cappello, un paio di orecchini con pietre bianche di metallo giallo, una spilla di metallo giallo, 28 chiavette, contanti lire duemilatrecentoottantaquattro e centesimi 65- (L 2384,65), sul fondo caffè, e L 2000 (duemila) sul fondo personale giusta bolletta N. 6.

Camicie due, mutande tre, sottanini 4, maglie 4, camiciette due, cappotto, cappello, vestaglie otto, pelliccia, asciugamani 4, faverette 4, salviette 2, pannolini due, lenzuola 1, sciarpa, impermeabile, valigietta di paglia, borsette di pelle due, due lenti, scarpe due paia, calze.

Camicia, sottanino, maglia, gonna, camicietta, grembiale, calze e pantofole, un paio di orecchini di metallo giallo senza pietre.

Camicia, mutanda, sottana, vestaglia, calze, scarpe, un cappello.

Orecchino di metallo giallo con pietre false, un orologetto di metallo falso.

Camicia, maglia, mutanda, vestaglia, giacca, cappotto, cappello, guanti, calze, scarpe, nove chiavette.

Camicia, vestaglia, cappotto, calze, scarpe, un anello di metallo giallo senza pietre.

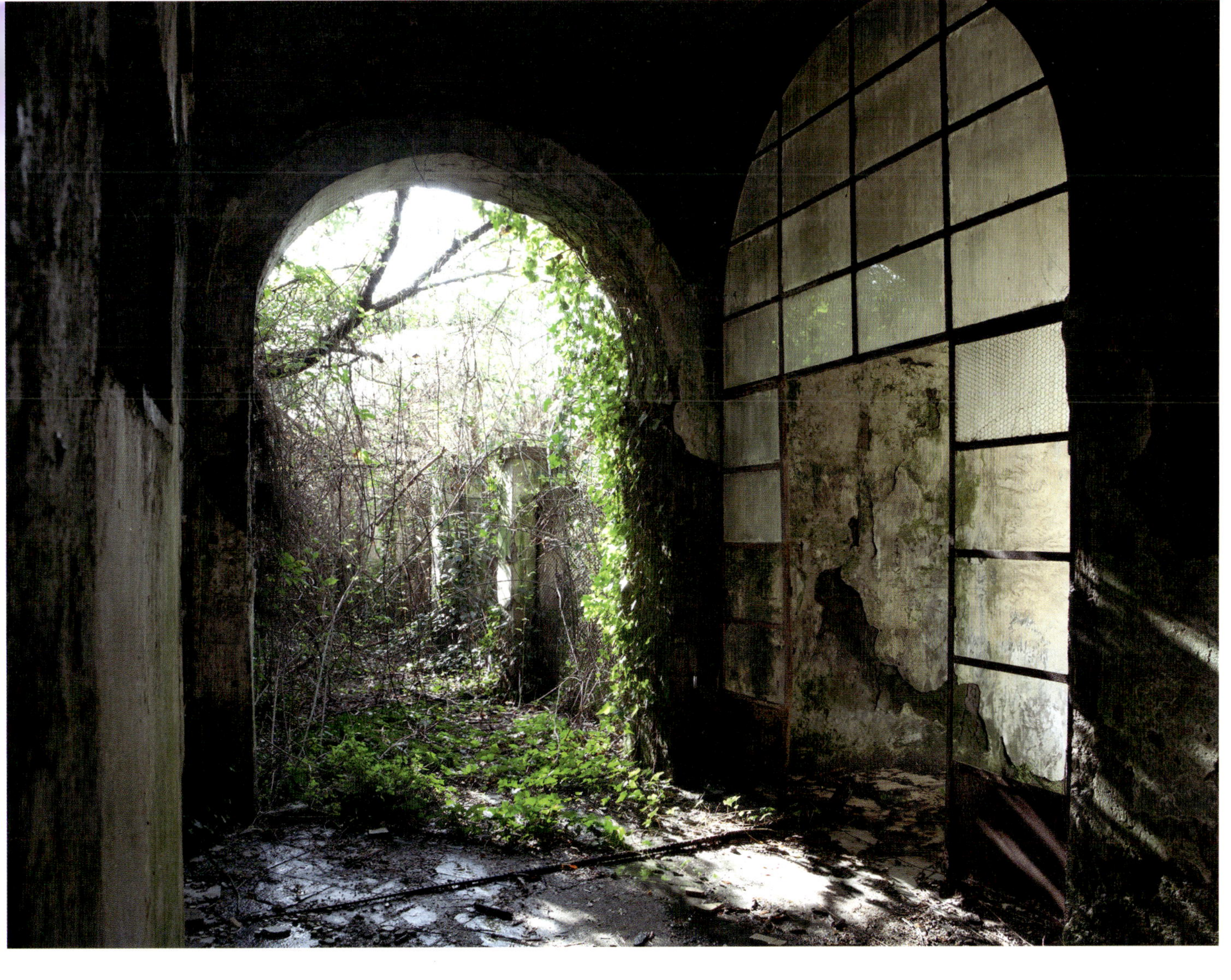

Bogengänge, Verbindung zwischen den einzelnen Abteilungen
Porticati, passaggio tra le singole sezioni
Covered passageway, connection between individual wings

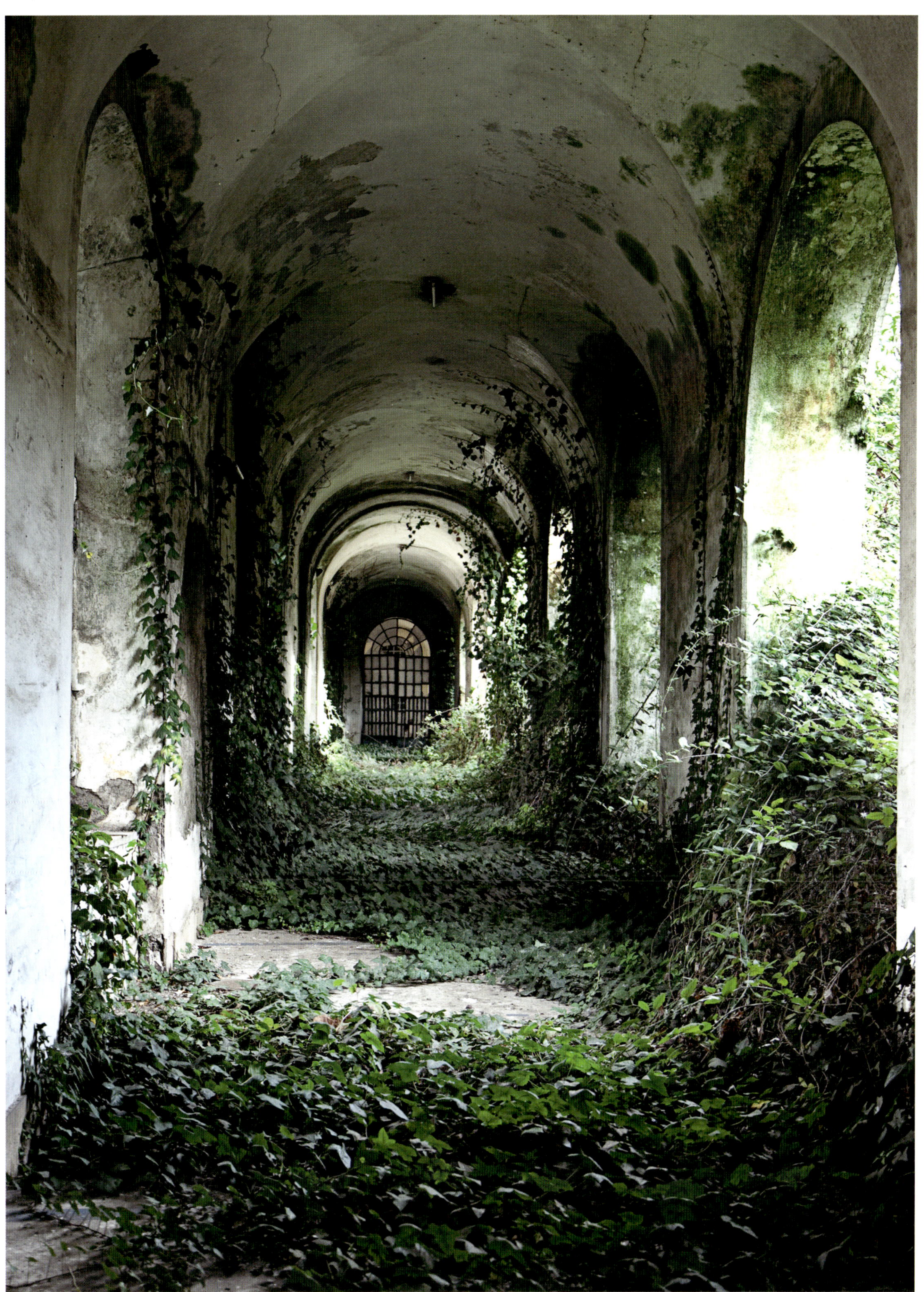

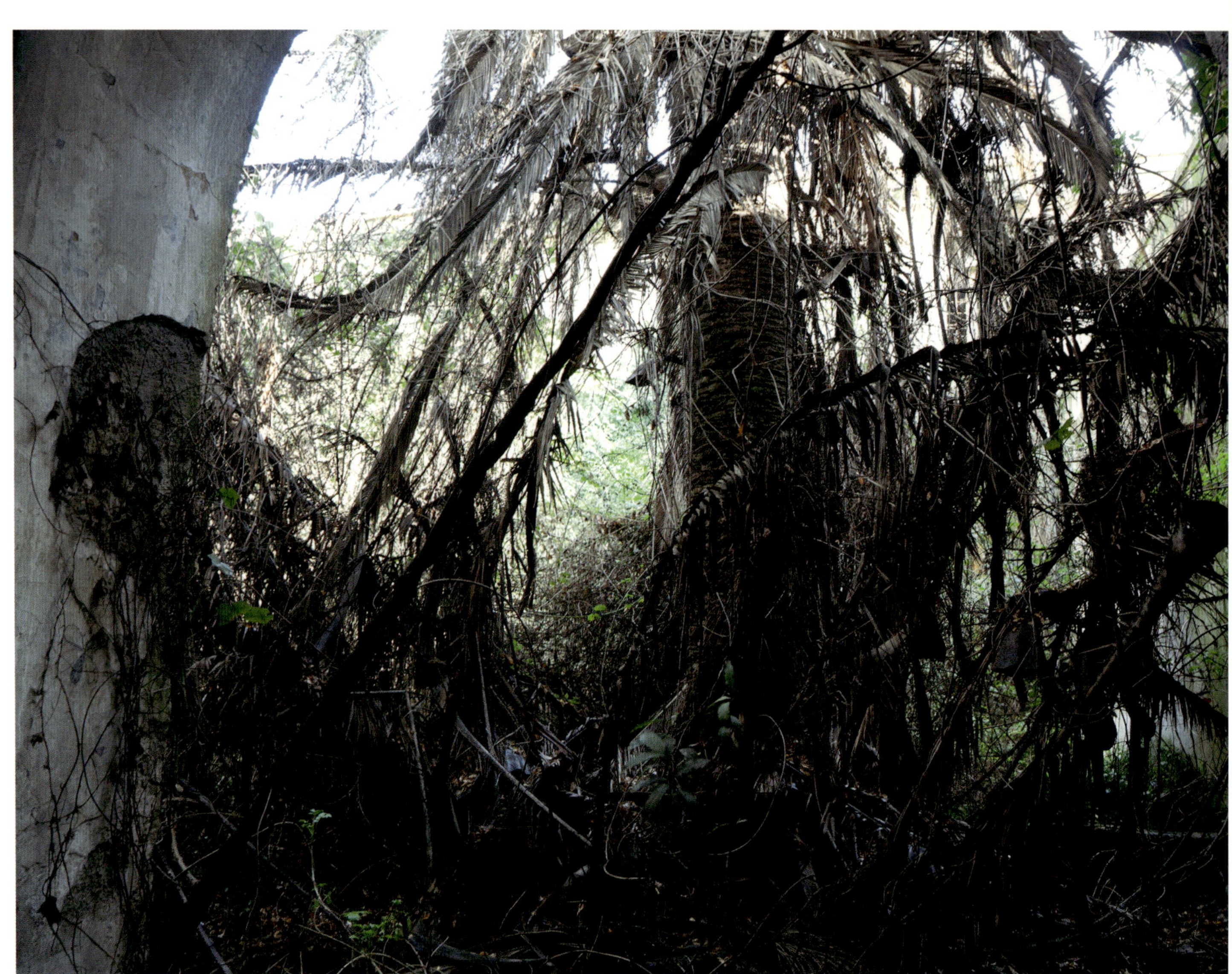

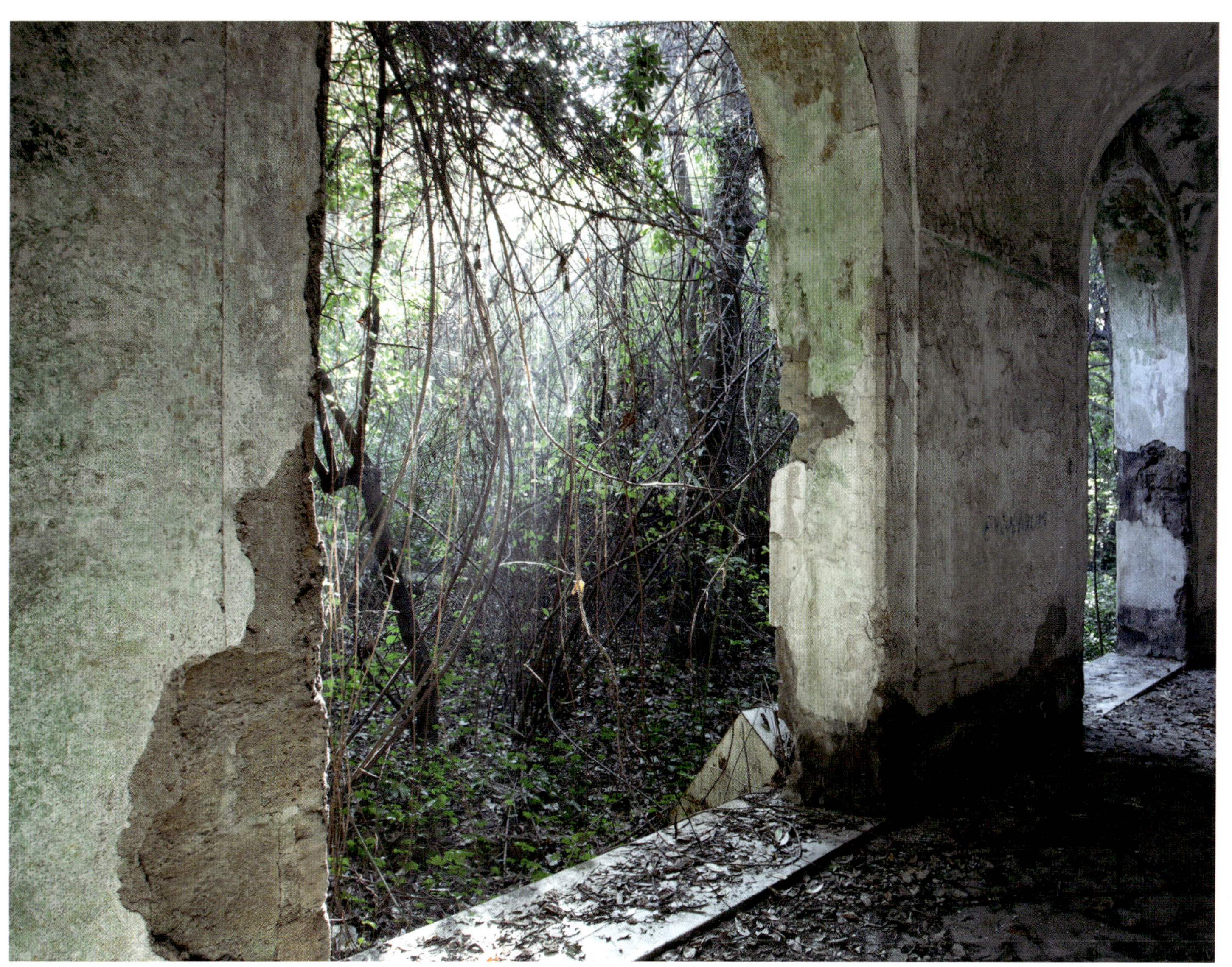

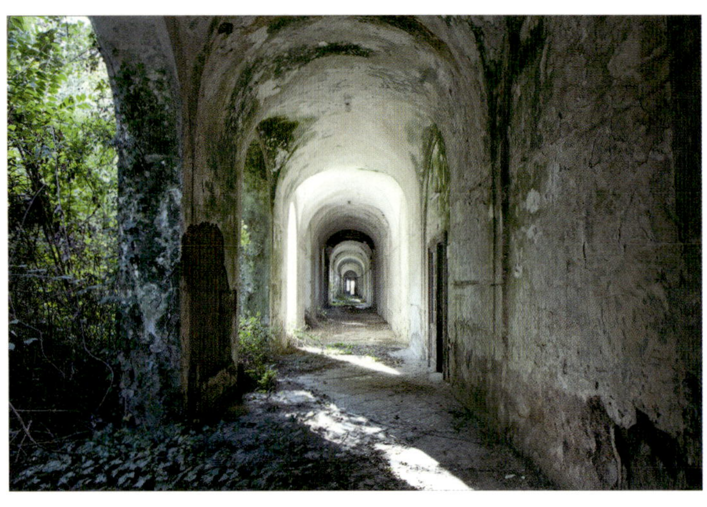
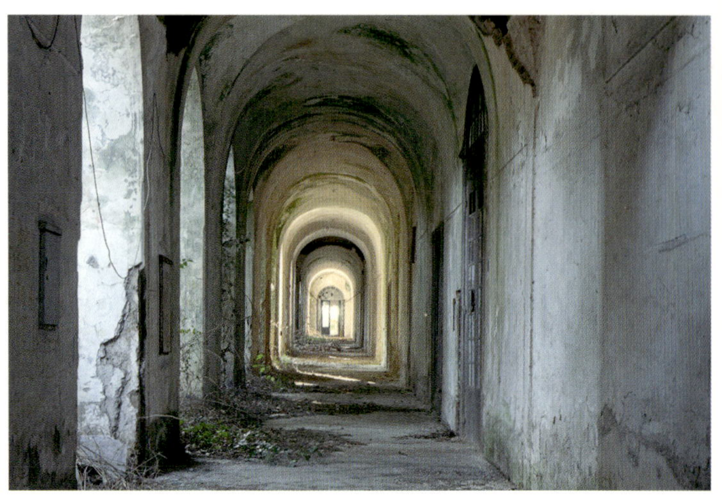
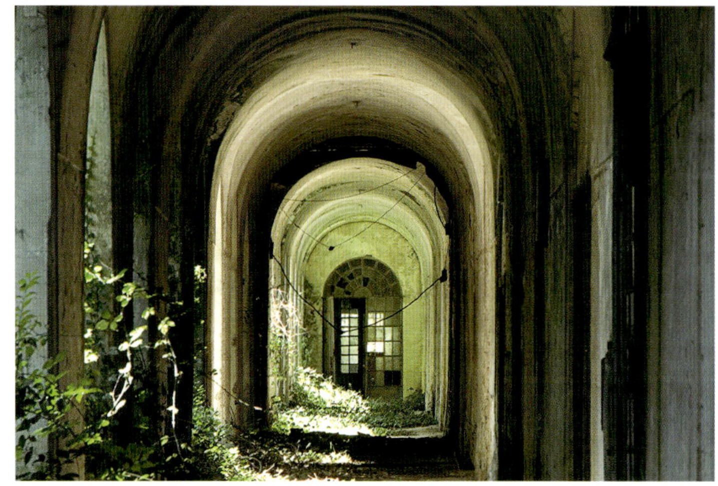

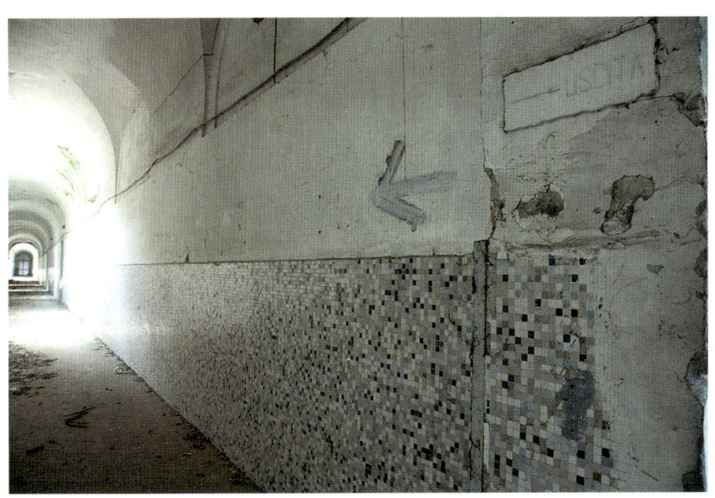

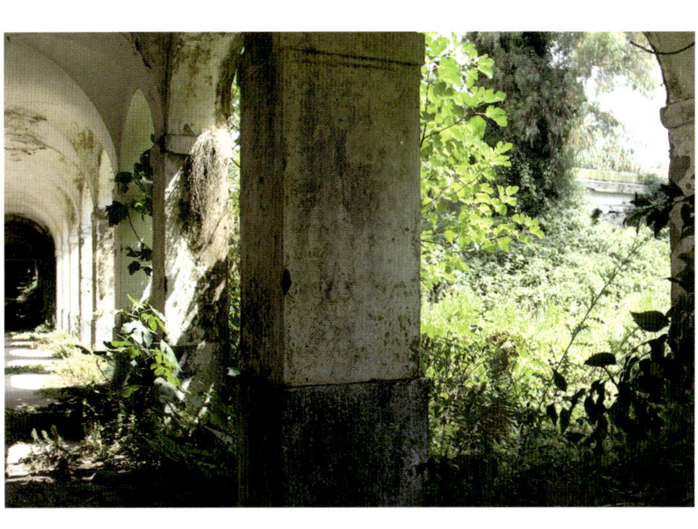

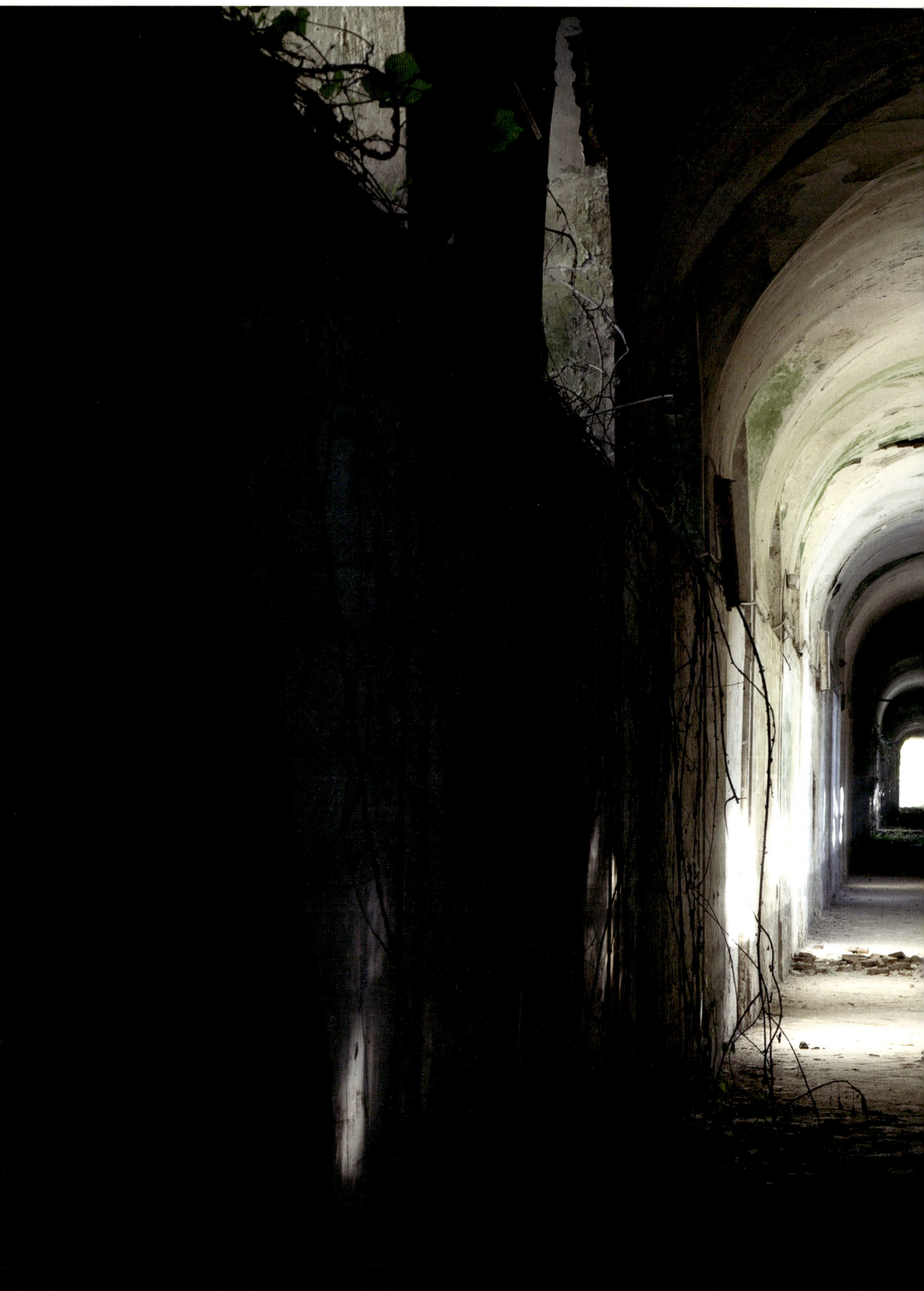

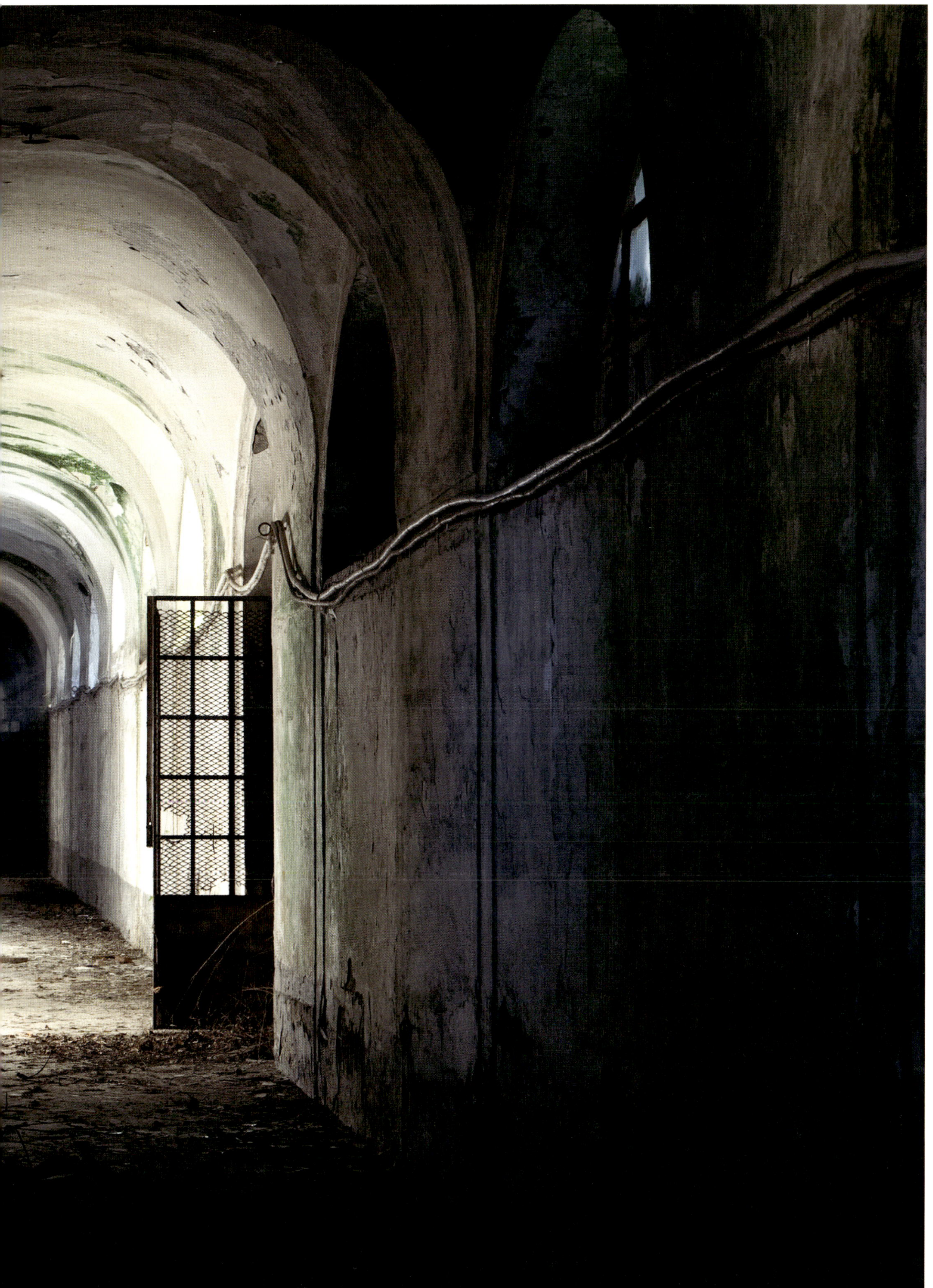

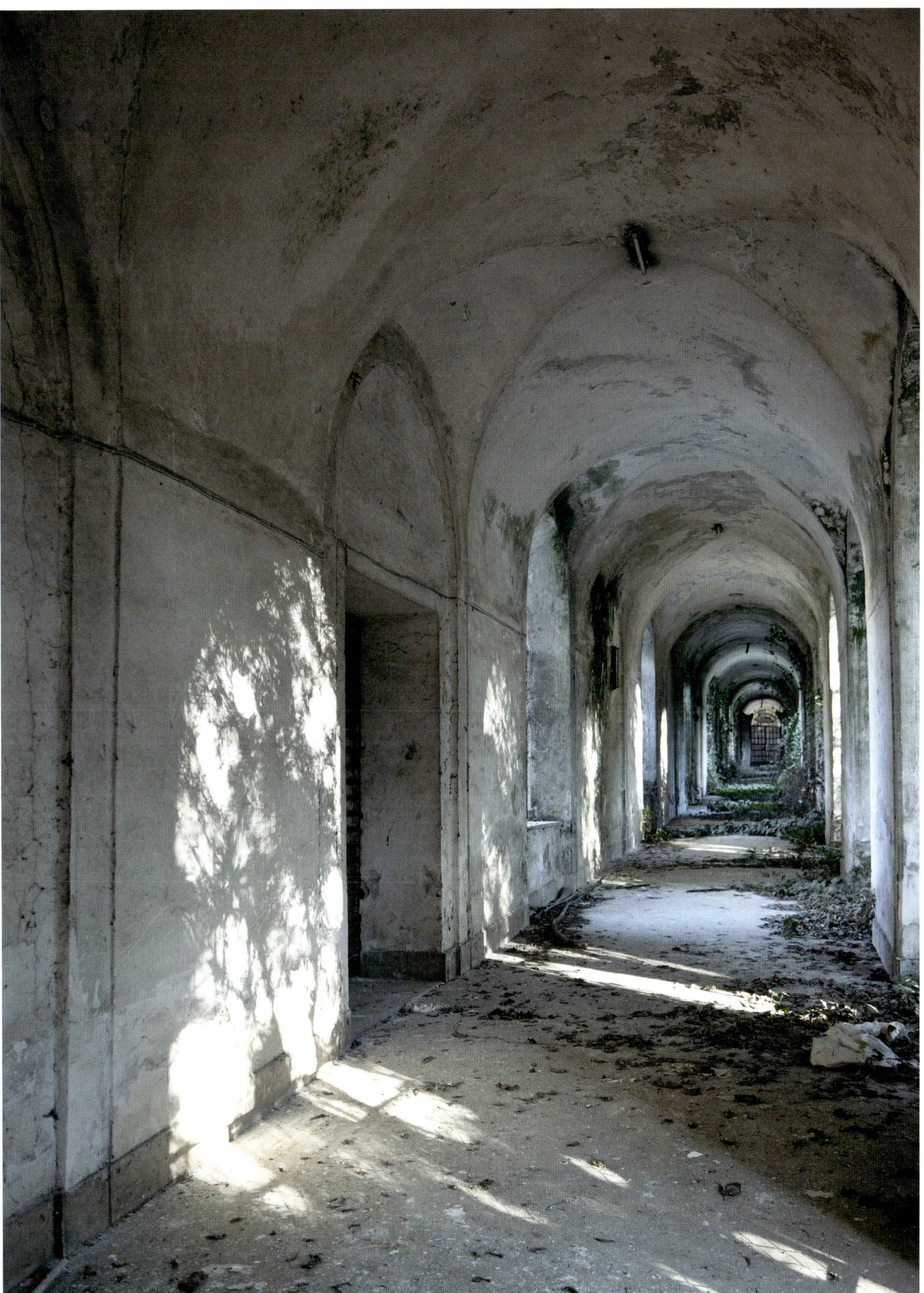

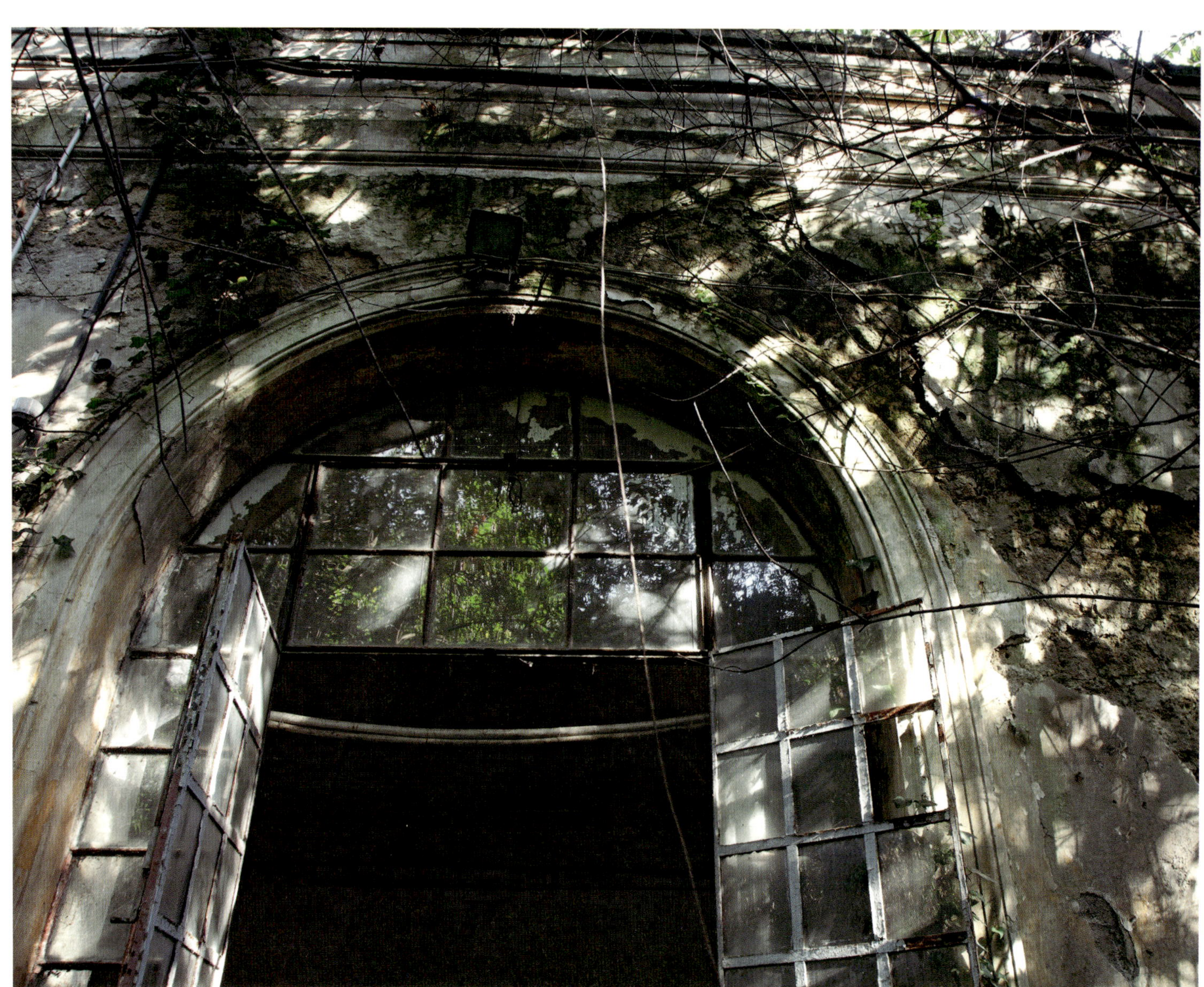

Ospedale Leonardo Bianchi
Silvie Aigner

„Das Leben ist ein Gefangener seiner Darstellung. Dabei ist das Leben prallvoll, ungeduldig, es möchte aus dem Viereck ausbrechen“, schrieb der italienische Schriftsteller Antonio Tabucchi. Seine Äußerung steht im Zusammenhang mit dem Versuch, die Wirklichkeit fotografisch einzufangen, die, so Tabucchi, nichts von der „wahren Wahrheit“ preisgebe.[1] Ähnlich diskutierte auch Umberto Eco in *Das offene Kunstwerk* die Frage, warum die Kunst überhaupt den Versuch unternimmt, die Wirklichkeit über das Bild zu verhandeln, „das doch viel ärmer an Möglichkeiten ist als der reale Sand, als die Unendlichkeit der natürlichen Materie, die uns zur Verfügung steht.“[2] Er beantwortete diese Frage selbst, indem er anmerkte, dass „nur das Bild es ist, das diese rohe Materie organisiert“. So gesehen ist die Fotografie von Elisabeth Hölzl an einer besonderen Schnittstelle angesiedelt. Dort, wo die beiden Systeme, jenes der Realität und jenes der Kunst zusammentreffen. Innerhalb dieses Kontextes hat die Fotografie, gemessen an der Malerei, eine kürzere Tradition, ist jedoch längst zu einem wichtigen und etablierten Feld der Kunstpraxis geworden, in dem diese Fragen ebenso verhandelt werden. Wie die Malerei hat auch die Fotografie im besonderen Maße die Möglichkeit, ein Begreifen des nicht Beschreibbaren bzw. die Ahnungen von den inneren Zusammenhängen des Lebens sinnlich und visuell darzustellen. Dass dies vor allem in der Reduktion der Form am besten gelingt, ist evident, da hier die Priorität eindeutig auf dem Dialog zwischen Wahrnehmung und Form beim künstlerischem Schaffensprozess liegt. So stellt sich auch Elisabeth Hölzl in ihrer Fotoserie über das *Ospedale Leonardo Bianchi* in Neapel nie in den Dienst der reinen Narration oder Dokumentation, sondern benutzt die Möglichkeiten von Bildausschnitt, Abstraktion, Perspektive, um einerseits eine gewisse Distanz zur Realität zu schaffen und den Ort aus einer zeitlichen Ordnung herauszuheben, und andererseits in gewisser Weise, auch wenn dies paradox erscheint, um eine räumlich-topografische Verortung herzustellen. Erst die Kombination der Fotografien mit den Textteilen des Buches erschließt die gesamte Komplexität der konzeptuellen Arbeit von Elisabeth Hölzl.

Die Hochzeit der psychiatrischen Anstalt lässt sich in ihren Bildern nicht einmal mehr erahnen, vielmehr überwiegt die melancholische Grundstimmung, die über dem verfallenen Gebäude liegt. Elisabeth Hölzl arbeitet an einer reinen Wiedergabe des Sichtbaren und einer sozialen Studie, wobei das künstlerische Interesse an der Architekturruine überwiegt und der Fokus auf der autonomen künstlerischen Handschrift liegt. Die Behutsamkeit, die Elisabeth Hölzls Methode auszeichnet, verbindet ihr Werk nicht nur mit der Geschichte der klassischen Fotografie, sondern – durch das Befragen der Techniken der fotografischen Bildrepräsentation – ebenso mit der zeitgenössischen Kunst. Ihre Werke sind stets mit einem wachsamen Auge arrangiert. Dies zeichnete schon ihre Fotoserie über das Hotel Bristol aus. Die Bilder wirken durchkomponiert wie ein Gemälde, nie entdeckt man ein störendes Element, etwas, das irritiert oder ablenkt. Dennoch: Elisabeth Hölzl arbeitet mit vorgefundenen Situationen und insbesondere mit den unterschiedlichen Lichtsituationen zu den verschiedensten Tages- und Jahreszeiten. Im Idealfall trägt alles, was man sieht, zur Bildwirkung bei. So sind ihre Architekturfotografien auch nicht mit der kühlen Sachlichkeit eines Thomas Struth oder dem Minimalismus von dessen Lehrern Bernd und Hilla Becher zu vergleichen. Es ist zu hinterfragen, ob ihre Arbeiten in diese Tradition überhaupt einzuordnen sind. Elisabeth Hölzls Bildserie zeigt Gänge, in denen Farbe und Putz abblättern, sowie Fenster und Arkadenbögen, die von der üppig wuchernden Pflanzenwelt des Spitalsgartens nach und nach in Besitz genommen werden – wie gleichsam die gesamten Gebäude des Spitals.

Diese Bilder lassen den Betrachter vergessen, dass sich die Anlage inmitten der Großstadt Neapel befindet. Man wähnt sich an einem verlassenen Ort in Südamerika. Andere Bilder jedoch holen den Betrachter jäh in die Realität zurück, sie zeigen Behandlungs- oder Schlafräume, in denen die spärlichen Möbelstücke wie stumme Zeugen der Vergangenheit wirken. Durch einen zuweilen sehr eng gesetzten Bildausschnitt sowie die Modulation des Lichts besticht die Bildserie auch durch einen gewissen Abstraktionsprozess. Die wechselnden Lichtverhältnisse tauchen die Räume je nach Jahreszeit in das warme gleißende Licht des Sommers oder in das kalte blaue Licht des Winters, das die linearen Strukturen der Architektur stärker betont. Die Sommerbilder wirken zuweilen fast impressionistisch und spielen mit einer gewollten Unschärfe. Vor allem dort, wo das üppige von Sonnenflecken durchbrochene Grün des wuchernden Dickichts auf die blau-grüne Bemoosung oder auf den farbenprächtigen Schimmelbefall des Mauerwerks trifft. Diese Ausschnitte bringen die Oberfläche in die Nähe der Malerei. So wirken die Farben der Fotografie wie transparente lasierende Schichten und verändern die Lesbarkeit des Sichtbaren. Der zunehmende Verfall verleiht dem Gebäude eine neue Ästhetik – jene individuelle Schönheit des Vergänglichen. Das Spielerische der vielen Möglichkeiten der Fotografie überwiegt in diesen Bildern ebenso wie in den nahsichtigen Darstellungen des Grünbewuchses und lässt die Bilder frei im Raum stehen. Andererseits erzählen diese auch von der Poesie geheimnisvoller Zusammenhänge, jenseits einer mimetischen Assoziation. Wir betrachten das Unendliche im Staubzustand, beschrieb Umberto Eco die Präsenz der Farbmaterie im Bereich des Informellen, die zugleich auch eine neue Art des „In-Beziehung-Tretens“ von Raum und Zeit ermöglicht, vor allem in Hinblick auf eine neue Verbindung von Zufall und Kausalität.[3] Wie weit Umberto Eco hier relevant ist, bleibt abzuwägen, doch haben die Bilder Elisabeth Hölzls neben dem Aspekt des Dokumentarischen und des Thematischen auch mit der Auseinandersetzung mit den Möglichkeiten fotografischer Bildkomposition zu tun. Darüber hinaus stehen sie in einer Dialektik zwischen dem Erzählen von Geschichte – indem sie Erinnerungen und die damit verbundenen Emotionen aufgreifen und somit die Vergangenheit einbeziehen – und der Sinnlichkeit der Farbmaterie. „Wie weit reicht die Kunst in das Innere der Welt?“, fragte schon Friedrich Nietzsche.[4] Auf diese von ihm angeschnittene Differenz von Kunst und Leben bezieht sich später der deutsche Soziologe Georg Simmel in seiner posthum erschienenen Aufsatzsammlung *Philosophie der Kunst*. Er beschrieb die innere

Geschlossenheit als Charakteristikum einer Autonomie des Kunstwerkes, das keiner Beziehung zu einer äußeren Welt bedürfe.[5] Doch wie verhält sich dies nun mit den scheinbar gegensätzlichen Ansprüchen der Künstlerin: Einerseits bewusst einen bestimmten Ort einschließlich seiner Geschichte aufzunehmen, und andererseits diese auch als Basis rein selbstreferenzieller medialer Prozesse zu vereinnahmen? Doch auch Simmel schränkte später ein, dass ein Kunstwerk eine Welt sui generis darstellen und gleichzeitig in einen Kontext eingebunden sein kann. So finden sich in den komponierten Bildern und engen Bildausschnitten von Elisabeth Hölzl sowohl der rein künstlerische Anspruch als auch die Intention, den Bezug zur Geschichte des *Ospedale Leonardo Bianchi* zu dokumentieren oder vielmehr zu interpretieren und festzuhalten, den Ort für einen kurzen Moment vor seiner endgültigen Zerstörung wieder in den Mittelpunkt unserer Wahrnehmung zu rücken. Von einer äußeren Wirklichkeit ausgehend, stehen das subjektive Erleben und die Darstellung einer konzeptuellen Idee im Mittelpunkt. Elisabeth Hölzl geht darüber hinaus noch einen Schritt weiter und versucht, in ihrer Fotoserie auch jene elementaren Erfahrungen einzubeziehen, die nicht eindeutig fassbar sind und im Bereich des Nichtsprachlichen erlebt werden. Dies unterscheidet die künstlerische Fotografie von der medialen Bilderflut. Sie erfasst wie auch die Malerei eine länger andauernde Gegenwart und impliziert ein Davor und Danach und die Möglichkeit der Reflexion und Verknüpfung von mehreren Informationen und Assoziationen. Elisabeth Hölzls Bilder geben dem Betrachter die Zeit, den Ort tatsächlich auch in seinen vielfältigen Dimensionen wahrnehmen zu können und vielleicht sogar zu begreifen und holen das Hospital wohl zum letzten Mal erfolgreich aus dem Bereich des Ephemeren. Der Ort ist menschenleer und doch übermitteln die Bilder menschliche Spuren: Das Archiv mit Schränken voll mit Ordnern, in denen die Krankengeschichten der Menschen, die hier gelebt haben, dokumentiert sind, in die Mauer gekratzte Wörter, Sätze – Botschaften an die Außenwelt vielleicht? Es sind Spuren der Hoffnungen, die nie erfüllt wurden, von Schmerzen und Leid, die auf den Behandlungstischen erduldet werden mussten.

Weitere Überreste sind die Listen der Kleidungsstücke, die den Patienten bei ihrem Eintritt abgenommen wurden. Diese Aufzeichnungen wurden von 1921 bis 1973 geführt und geben Auskunft über die Biografien der Patienten, deren Herkunft und sozialen Verhältnisse. Auf berührende Weise wird, ohne dies näher ausführen zu müssen, schlagartig klar, welchen Einschnitt im Leben die Einweisung in das Hospital bedeutete. Mit dem Ablegen der eigenen Kleider war auch der Verlust der Individualität verbunden. Die Patienten wurden zu anonymen Nummern in den Archivordnern des Spitals. Die Rezeption der Fotoarbeiten, die von diesen ausgehende lyrische Poesie wird von diesen Dokumenten jäh durchbrochen. Doch selbst dort, wo Elisabeth Hölzl narrativ wird und den Betrachtern einen kurzen Einblick in ein anderes Leben gewährt, ist die Darstellung nicht voyeuristisch, sondern äußerst sensibel. Bilder können die Zeit überspringen, und Elisabeth Hölzls Arbeiten können das im Besonderen, indem sie die Vergangenheit in die Gegenwart einschreibt und damit eine Art Zwischenwelt entwickelt. Die Fotografie ist eine Konstruktion desjenigen, der hinter der Kamera steht, meinte der Fotokünstler Thomas Struth in einem Interview.[6] Die Realität der Bilder ist daher jene des Fotografen und bringt dessen Reflexion mit ein. Die Autorenschaft des Fotografen, der hinter der Kamera steht, ist zwangsläufig ein das Bild konstituierender Faktor. Denn die Fotografie zeigt nicht nur das vordergründig Sichtbare, sondern ist zumeist mit einem konzeptuellen Arbeiten im Umfeld des Sujets verbunden. So gesehen ist das Bild nie nur ein Abbild des Gesehenen, sondern ein Bild der Gegenwart im Umfeld des Dargestellten und im Umfeld der Künstlerin. Solcherart zeigt sie auch das Verborgene und wird zum Faktum des Fragmentarischen – doch realisiert sich die Kunst nicht gerade im Hinweis auf die jeweiligen Lücken dazwischen? Gerade weil die Realität eine wichtige Rolle in der Fotografie spielt und diese zum Modell des jeweiligen Bildes wird, steht die Frage nach dem *Wie* der Umsetzung in das Medium stets im Zentrum der künstlerischen Arbeit und wird später zu einer der Distribution von Daten und ihrer Konsumation durch den Betrachter. So wird auch bei Elisabeth Hölzl durch das Ausloten der Grenzen zwischen Deskription und Abstraktion die Illusion von Wirklichkeit destabilisiert und gleichzeitig das Medium Fotografie einmal mehr in den Mittelpunkt gestellt. Der Bildausschnitt und die Setzung der Motive in der Bildkomposition ermöglichen der Künstlerin eine Verdichtung der Atmosphäre und Intensivierung der Szene. Und wenn Nietzsches Annahme zutrifft, dass die Kunst dem Menschen hilft, sich das Ganze des Daseins bewusst zu machen, so ist die Konstruktion der Wirklichkeit in der Fotografie allemal ein Mittel einer sensiblen Annäherung an die kaum fassbaren Zwischenräume des Lebens.

1 Antonio Tabucchi, *Es wird immer später*, München 2004.
2 Umberto Eco, *Das offene Kunstwerk*, Frankfurt am Main, 1973.
3 Umberto Eco, *Das offene Kunstwerk*, Frankfurt am Main, 1977, S. 179.
4 Friedrich Nietzsche, *Nachgelassene Fragmente 1882 – 1884, Sämtliche Werke, kritische Studienausgabe*, Hrsg. G. Colli u. M. Montinari, München, Berlin 1980, Bd. 10, S. 563.
5 Georg Simmel, *Zur Philosophie der Kunst, Philosophische und kunstphilosophische Aufsätze*, Potsdam, 1922, S. 46.
6 Matthias Dusini, *Interview mit Thomas Struth*, Der Falter, Wien, 2008.

Ospedale Leonardo Bianchi
Silvie Aigner

"Life is a prisoner of its own representation. Life is filled to bursting, impatient, it wants to break out of the square", wrote Italian author Antonio Tabucchi, in connection with trying to capture reality by means of photography, it would give nothing away of the real truth.[1] Similarly Umberto Eco also discussed in *The Open Work* the question as to why art even makes the attempt to negotiate reality through the image, "which is much poorer in possibilities than real sand, than the infinity of natural matter that is available to us"[2] He answered this question himself by noting that it is "only the image that organizes this raw matter". Seen in this light, the photography of Elisabeth Hölzl is situated at a particular interface, at the point where the two systems, that of reality and that of art, come together. Within this context photography has a much shorter tradition compared with painting, and yet has long become an important and established field of art practice in which these issues are equally dealt with. Like painting, photography also has the possibility in a special way of sensually and visually representing an understanding of what cannot be described or the premonitions of inner connections of life. The fact that this succeeds best above all in the reduction of form is evident, because here the priority lies in the dialog between perception and form in the artistic creative process. And it is true that in her photo series about the *Ospedale Leonardo Bianchi* in Naples, Elisabeth Hölzl never puts herself at the service of pure narrational documentation but uses the possibility of composition, abstraction, perspective to on the one hand create a certain distance to reality and also to lift out the location from a chronological order and in a certain way, even if this may seem to be a paradox, from its spatial-topographical localization. It is only when the photographs are combined with a text section of the book that the full complexity of the conceptual work of Elisabeth Hölzl becomes apparent.

It is difficult even to guess what the heyday of the psychiatric institution would have been like, instead there is a general melancholy mood that prevails over the derelict building. In this photo series, positioned between a pure reproduction of the visible and a social study, the artistic interest in the architectural ruins and the focus on the autonomous artistic signature predominate. The caution that distinguishes Elisabeth Hölzl's method combines her work not only with the history of classical photography but – through querying the techniques of photographic image representation – equally with contemporary art. Her works are always arranged with a watchful eye. This was already a characteristic of her photo series about the Hotel Bristol. The pictures are fully composed, like a painting, you never find a disruptive element, something that irritates or distracts. Nevertheless: Elisabeth Hölzl works with existing situations, and in particular with varying light at different times of the day and in different seasons. Ideally everything that you can see contributes to the effect of the picture. Thus her architectural photographs cannot be compared with the cool objectivity of someone like Thomas Struth or the minimalism of his teachers Bernd and Hilla Becher, it must be questioned whether her works can even be classified in this tradition. Elisabeth Hölzl's picture series show corridors in which paint and plaster is peeling, window and arcade arches through which the vegetation of the park grows exuberantly, and yet the building of the hospital reasserts itself, as it were.

Here at the latest you are no longer in an institution in the middle of a big city, you feel as if you are in the middle of a remote location in South America. Some pictures, however, bring the viewer abruptly back to reality. They show treatment rooms, bedrooms in which the spartan furnishings appear to be silent witnesses of the past. And yet the picture series also stands out because of a certain process of abstraction achieved by the artist by an at times very closely arranged image composition and through the modulation of light. Depending on the season this bathes the rooms in the warm flowing to glowing light of the summer and in the cold blue light of winter, more strongly emphasizing the linear structures of the architecture. The summer pictures seem at times almost impressionistic and play with a deliberate haziness of the colours. In particular where the luxuriant sun-speckled green of the undergrowth running wild meets the bluish-green growing moss or the flamboyant mould infestation of the brickwork. These details bring the surface into a dialogue with the painting. The colours of the photograph are like transparent, glazed layers and alter the interpretation of what is visible. Through its increasing state of disrepair the building acquires a new aesthetic – that individual beauty of the transient. The playful element in the many possibilities of photography predominates in these pictures as well as in the closer portrayals of the weeds and allows the pictures to stand freely in the space. On the other hand they also tell of the poetry of secret correlations that go beyond a mimetic association. We observe the infinite in a state of dust, Umberto Eco described the new presence of the colour material in the area of the informal, which at the same time enables also a new type of "establishing a relationship" of space and time, above all with regard to a new connection of chance and causality.[3] It must be weighed up as to what extent Umberto Eco is relevant here, but apart from the aspect of the documentary and the thematic, the pictures of Elisabeth Hölzl also have a lot to do with the analysis of the possibilities of photographic picture composition. In addition, they also stand in a dialectic between the narration of stories in which they seize on memories and the emotions connected with them – and thus integrate the past and the sensuality of the colour material, and this directly in the present. "How far into the inner world does art reach?" Friedrich Nietzsche asked.[4] This difference between art and life broached by Nietzsche is later referred to by German sociologist Georg Simmel in his posthumously published collection of essays, "Philosophie der Kunst". He postulated internal cohesion as a characteristic of an autonomy of the work of art and believes that the work of art is an entity in itself, requiring no reference to an external world.[5] But how does this now relate to the apparently contradictory claims of the artist: on the one hand deliberately recording the story of a specific location, one loaded with history, and squaring this as the basis of purely self-referential media processes? But Simmel also later qualified his position that an artwork on the one hand can be a world of its own and on the other is always integrated into a context. Thus in the composed images and closely cropped scenes there can be found both the purely artistic claim and the intention of documenting the relationship to the history of the *Ospedale Leonardo Bianchi*, or rather to interpret this, and to position the location at the centre of our perception for a brief moment before it it finally destroyed. Starting off with an external reality, the focus is on a subjective experience and the presentation of a conceptual idea. Elisabeth Hölzl goes a step further and in her photo series tries to include those elements which she experiences which are not unambiguously definable and which are felt in the area of the non-verbal. This distinguishes artistic photography from the media flood of images. As with painting, it involves a present that lasts longer and implies a before and after, and the possibility of a reflection and combination of several layers of information and associations. Elisabeth Hölzl's pictures give the viewer the time to really take in the location, to be able to perceive it in its wide variety of dimensions and perhaps even to comprehend it and successfully remove the hospital, probably for the last time, from the field of the ephemeral. The place is deserted and yet the pictures convey traces of the presence of people. Cupboards full of files, revealing the archives of the hospital, containing the medical histories of the people who lived here, words scratched onto the walls, sentences – messages to the outside world, perhaps? Hopes that will never be fulfilled, pain and suffering undergone on the treatment tables.

The lists of clothing taken from patients on their arrival. This documentation was maintained from 1921 to 1973 and gives an insight into the biographies of the patients, their origins and social circumstances. In a moving way it suddenly becomes clear, without having to go into this in more detail, what a radical change this must have been for those who were admitted to the hospital. Discarding their own clothes is also associated with a loss of individuality. The patients become anonymous numbers in the archive files of the hospital. The reception of the photo works is modified by these text passages, their lyrical poetry is abruptly interrupted. But even in those places where Elisabeth Hölzl takes up a narrative in her photo works and allows the viewer a short insight into a different life, the portrayal is not voyeuristic, but extremely sensitive. Pictures can jump across time and Elisabeth Hölzl's can do this especially so, as she inscribes the past into the present, developing a kind of intermediary world. Photography is a construction of the person behind the camera, said photo artist Thomas Struth in an interview.[6] The reality of the images is therefore already that of the photographer and thus already incorporates his reflections. The authorship of the photographer who stands behind the camera is inevitably a factor that constitutes the picture. Because photography shows not only what is visible in the foreground, but is usually associated with a conceptual working in relation to the subject. Seen in this light, a picture is never just a reproduction of what can be seen, but is a picture of the present in relation to what is portrayed and in relation to the artist. In such a way she also shows hidden elements and becomes a fact of the fragmentary – but is not art realised in terms of the respective gaps in between? Particularly because reality plays an important role in photography and thus becomes the model of the respective picture, the question as to how is always at the centre of the artistic work in the implementation in the medium and later becomes a question of the distribution of data and of the consummation by the viewer. Thus in the case of Elisabeth Hölzl through the sounding out of the borders between description and abstraction, the illusion of reality is destabilized and at the same time the focus is placed once more on the medium of photography. The image detail and the setting of motifs in the picture composition allow the artist to compress the atmosphere and intensify the scene. And if Nietzsche's assumption is true, that art helps people to become aware of the entirety of existence, then the construction of reality in photography is once and for all a means of a sensitive approach to the hardly tangible intermediary spaces of life.

1 Umberto Eco, *The Open Work*, Harvard University Press, 1989.
2 Umberto Eco, *The Open Work*, Harvard University Press, 1989.
3 Umberto Eco, *Das offene Kunstwerk*, Frankfurt / Main, 1977.
4 Friedrich Nietzsche, *Nachgelassene Fragmente 1882 – 1884, Sämtliche Werke, kritische Studienausgabe*, eds. G. Colli and M. Montinari, Munich, Berlin 1980, Vol. 10, p. 563.
5 Georg Simmel, *Zur Philosophie der Kunst, Philosophische und kunstphilosophische Aufsätze*, Potsdam, 1922, p. 46.
6 Matthias Dusini, *Interview mit Thomas Struth*, Der Falter, Wien, 2008.

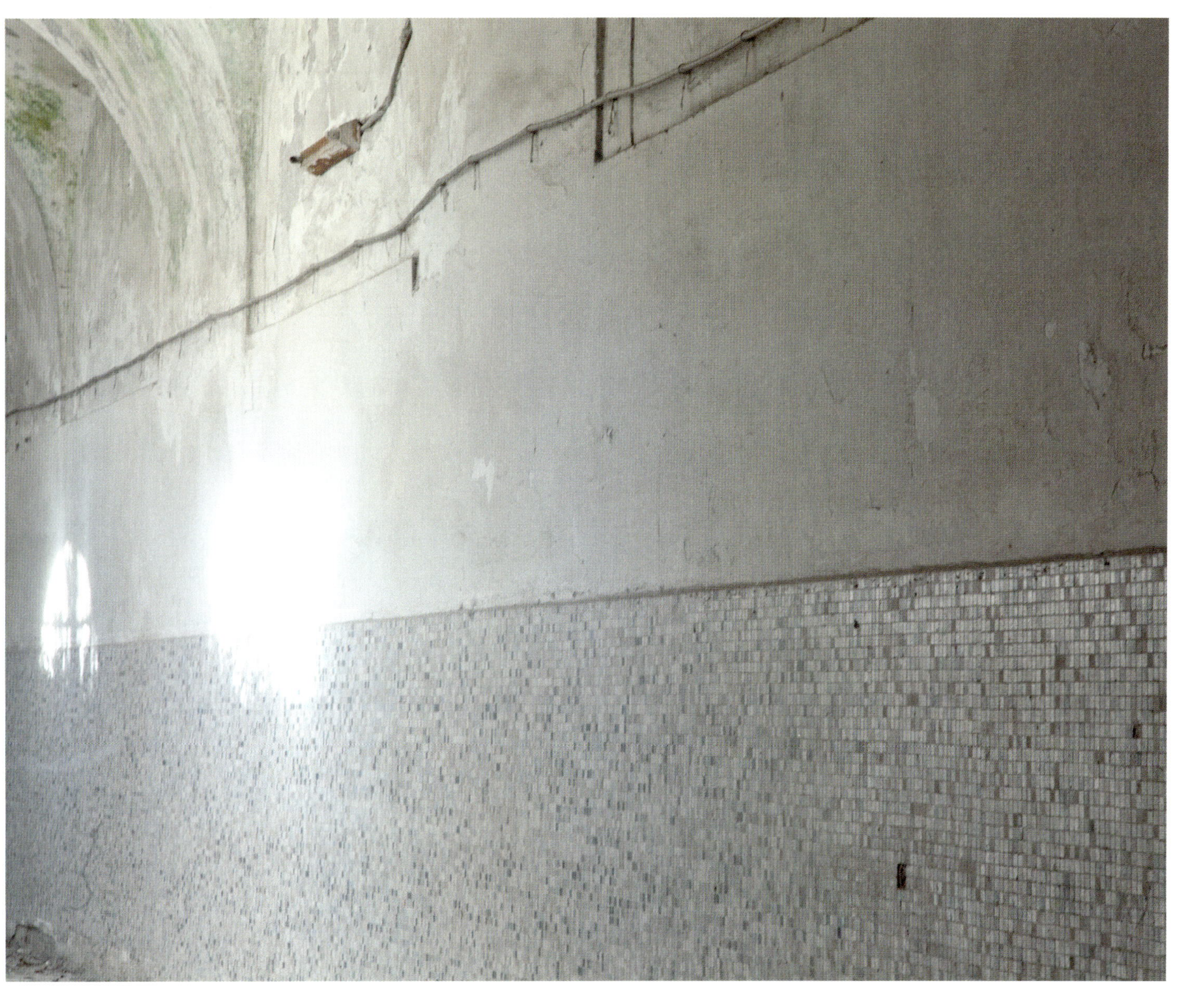

nächste Doppelseite pagina successiva
next double page

Gang, Krankenabteilung
Corridoio, reparto degenza
Corridor, ward

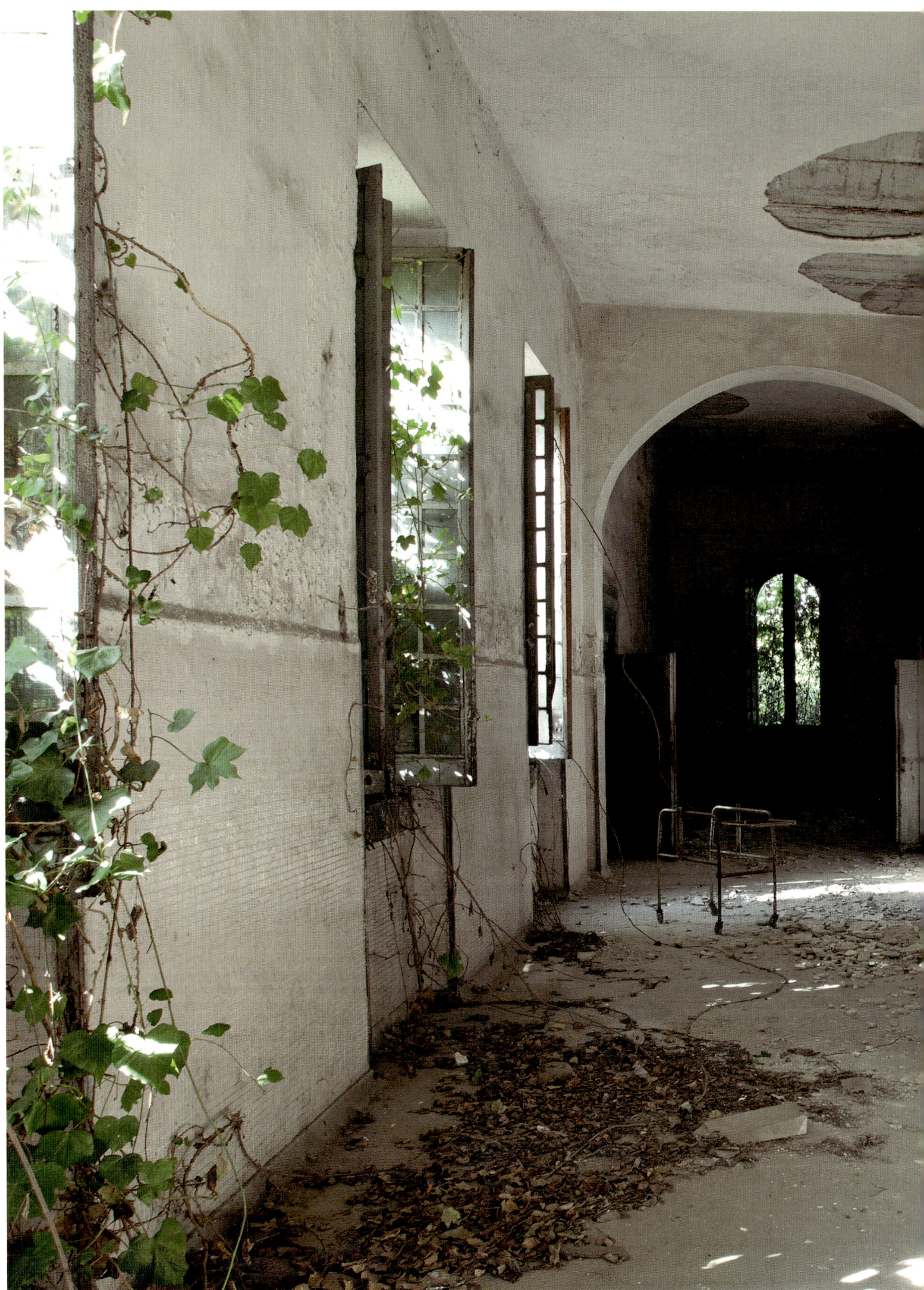

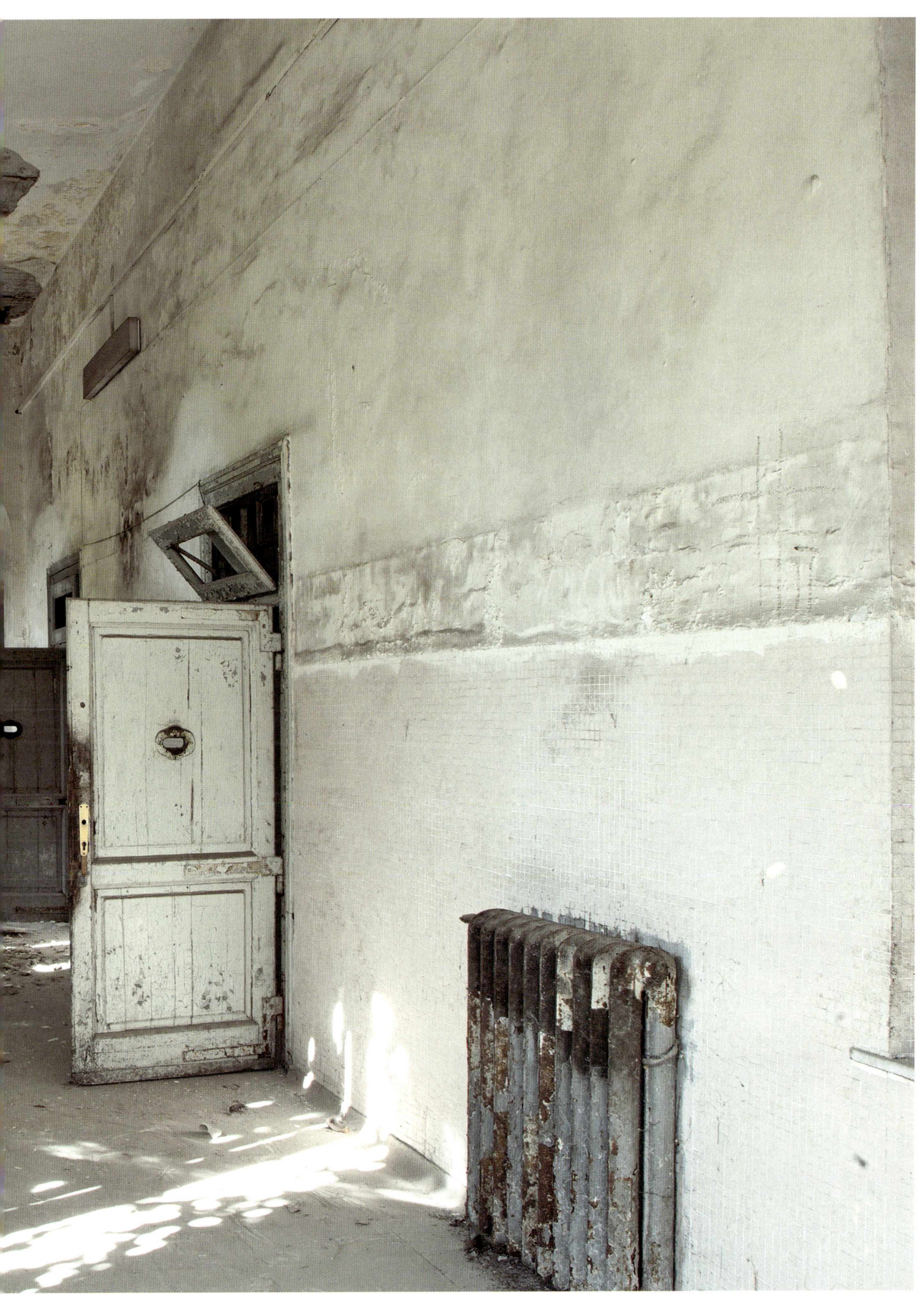

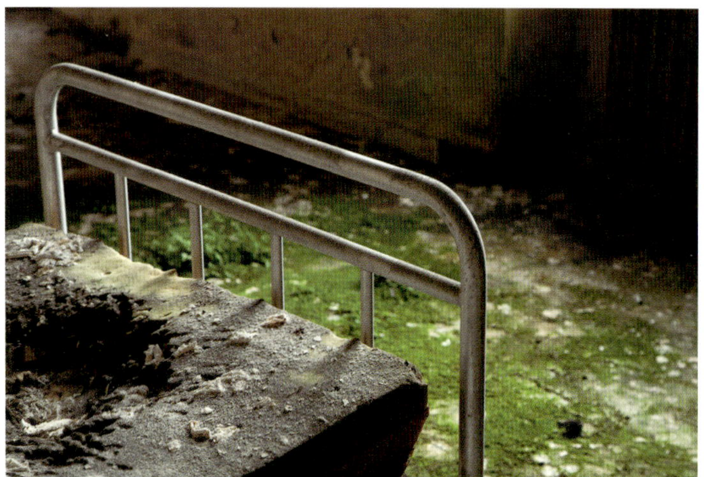

I. Abteilung Männer, Schlafsaal
I. Sezione uomini, dormitorio
I. Men's wing, dormitory

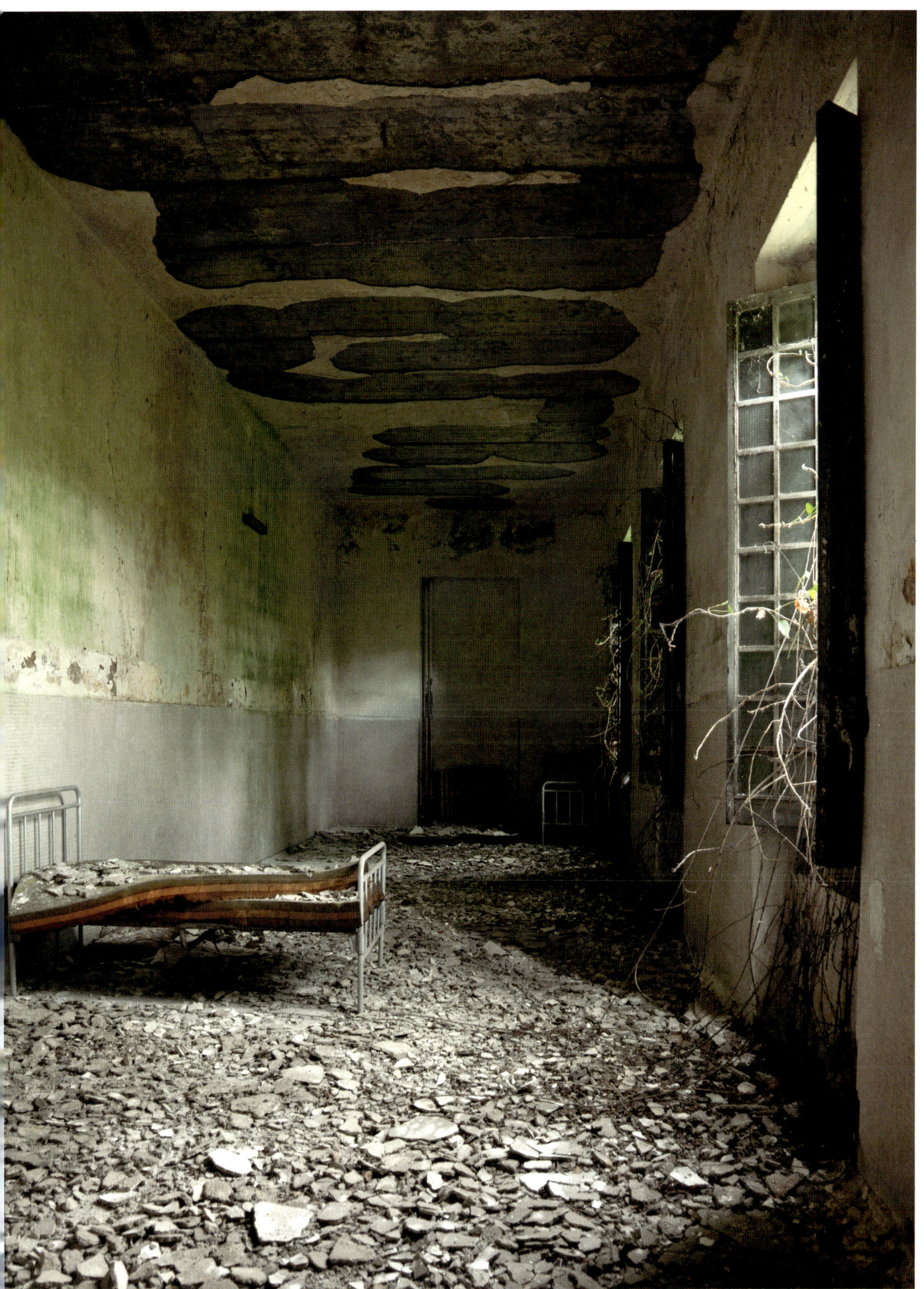

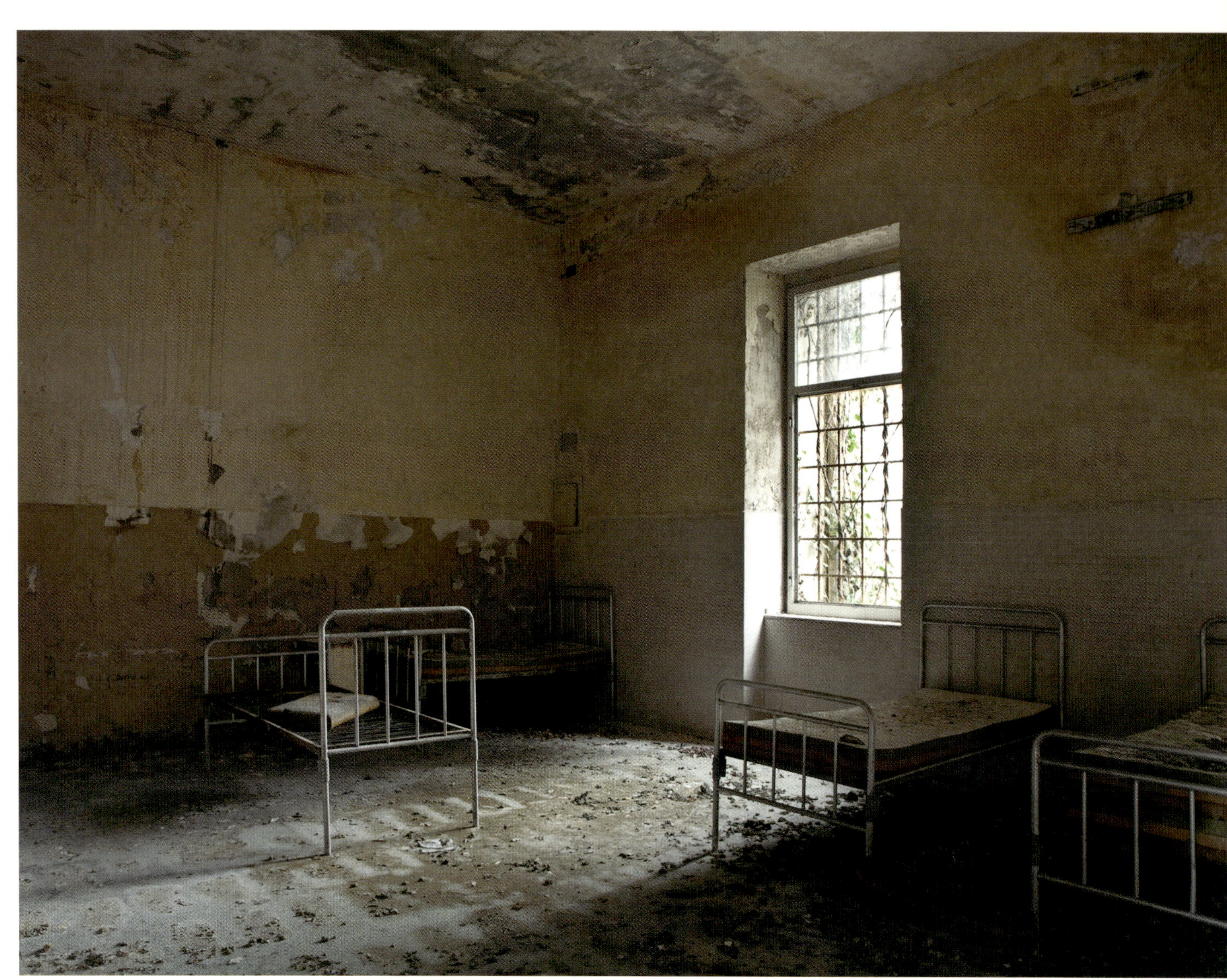

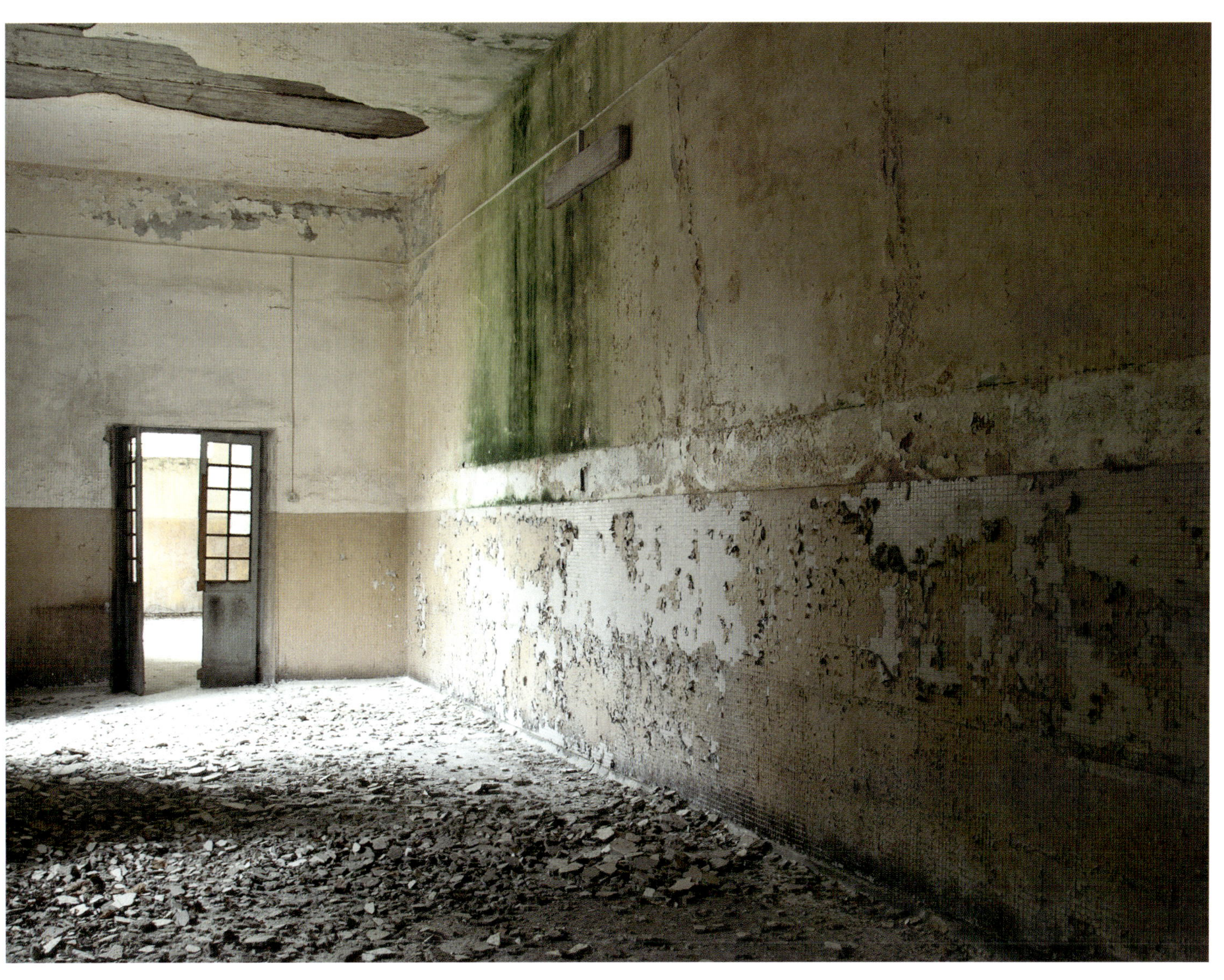

nächste Doppelseite pagina successiva
next double page

VII. Abteilung Frauen, Schlafsaal
VII. Sezione donne, dormitorio
VII. Women's wing, dormitory

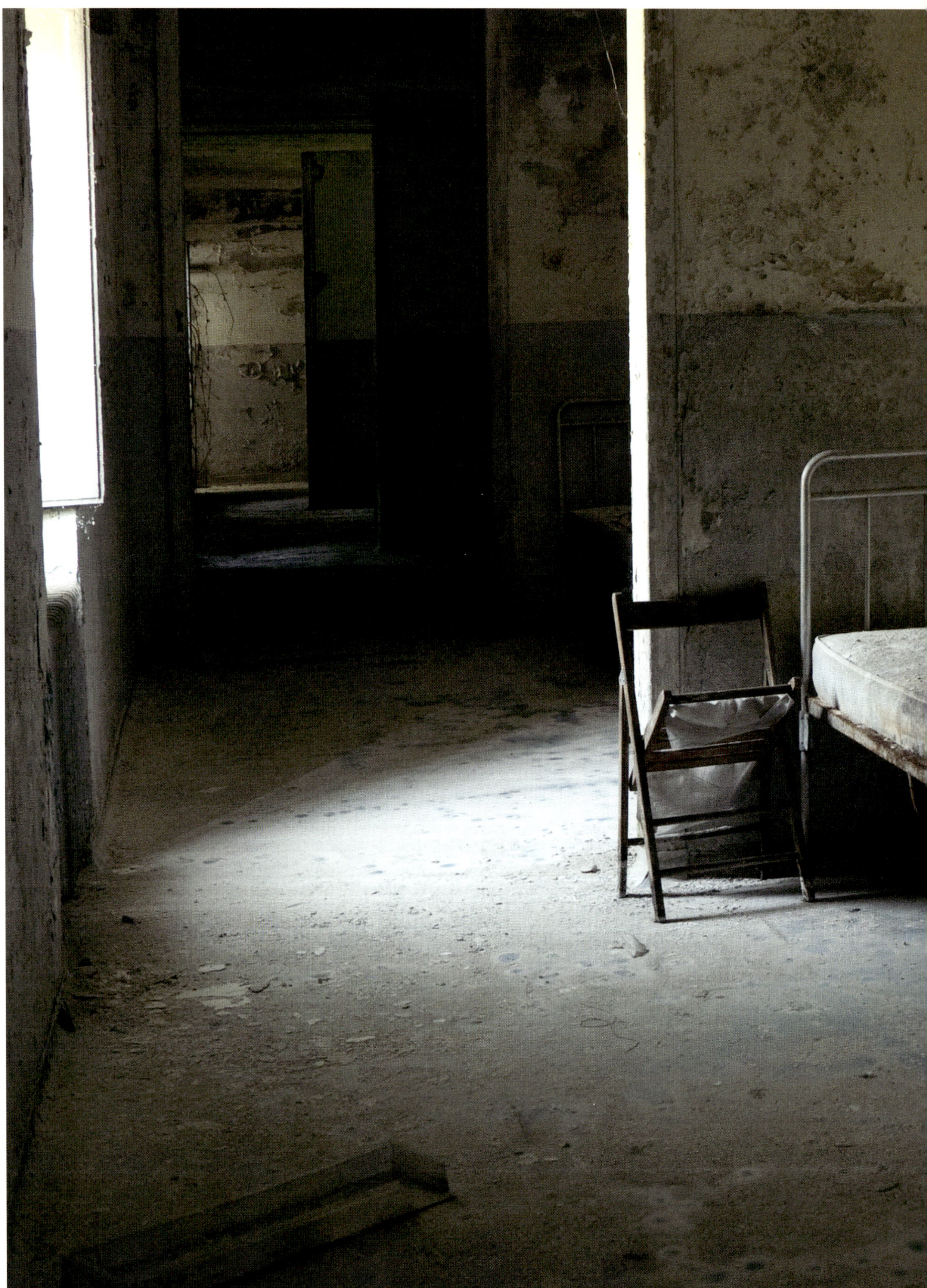

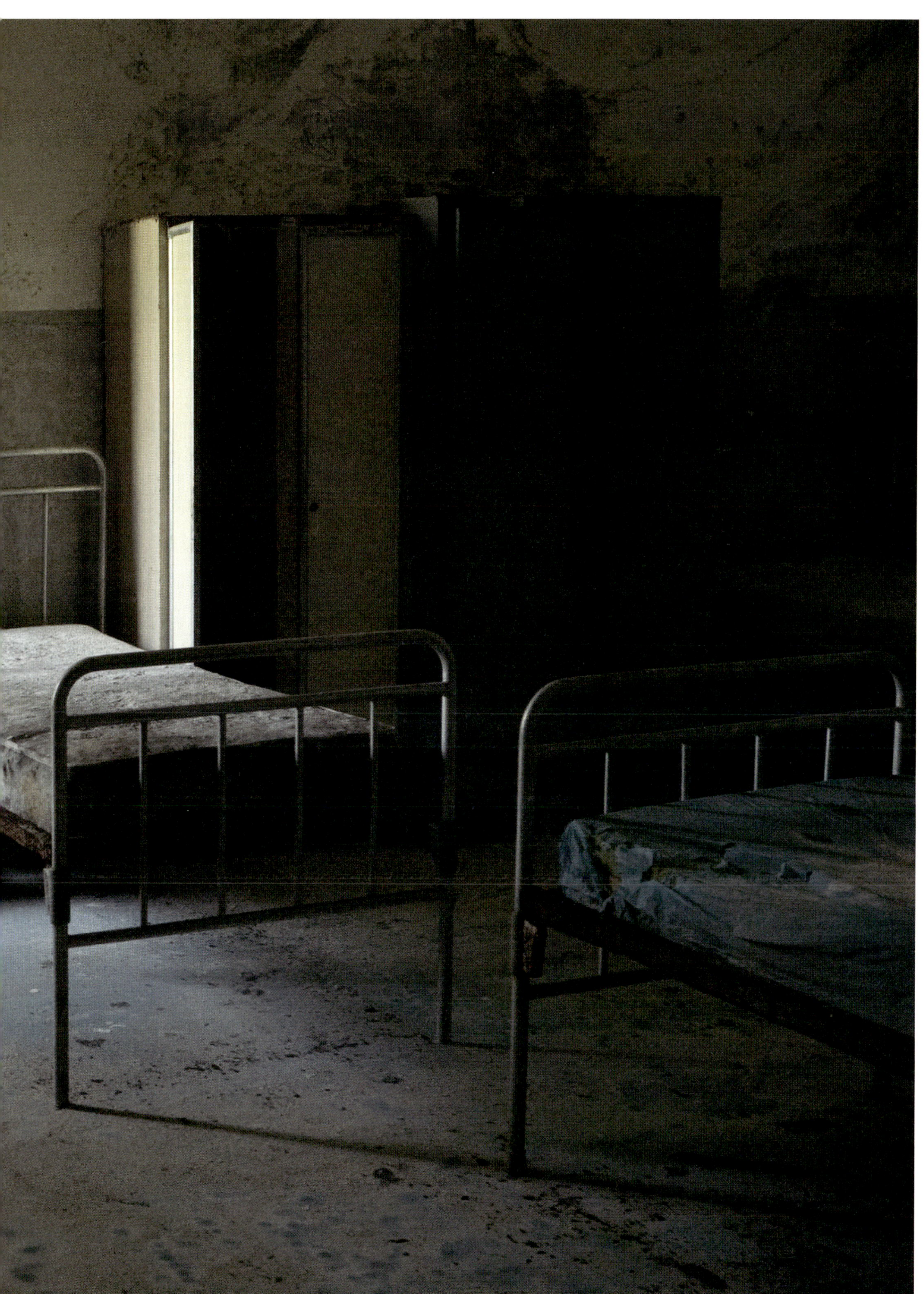

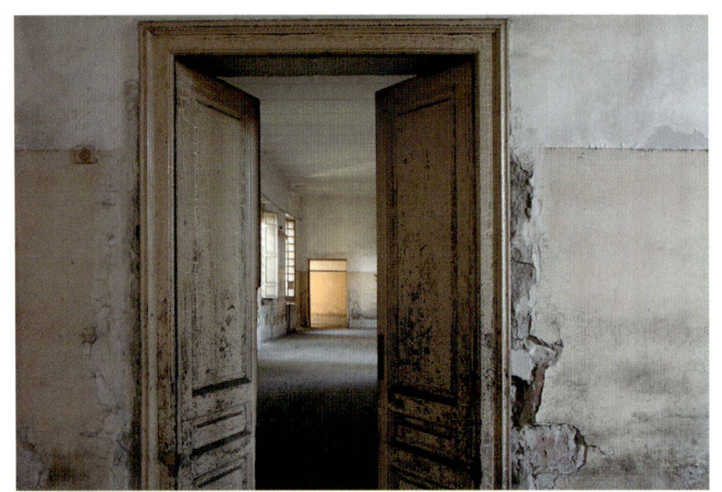

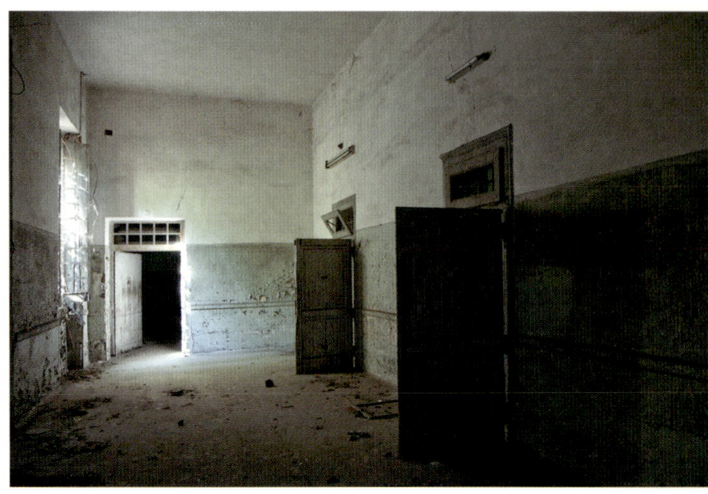

Innenansichten
Interni
Interiors

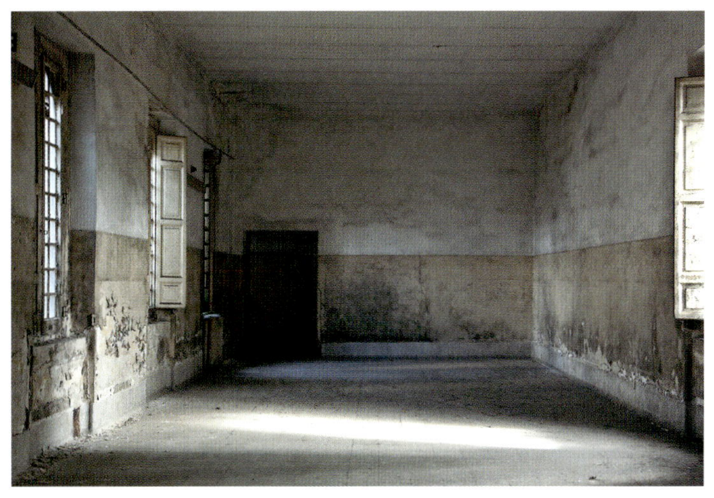

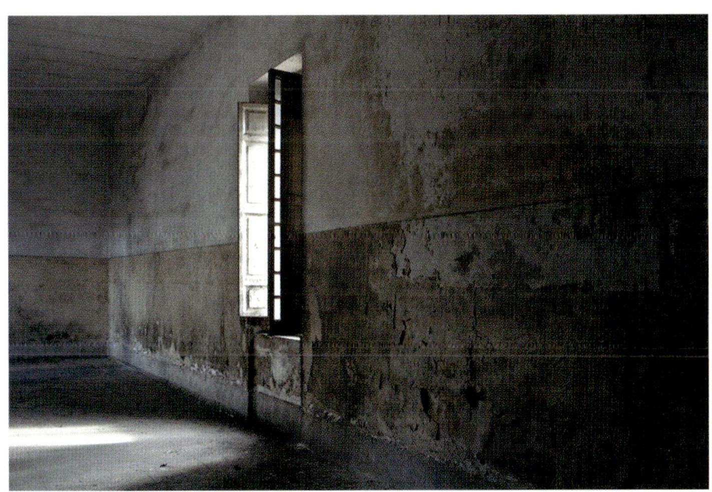

VI. Abteilung Frauen, Speisesaal
VI. Sezione donne, sala pranzo
VI. Women's wing, dining room

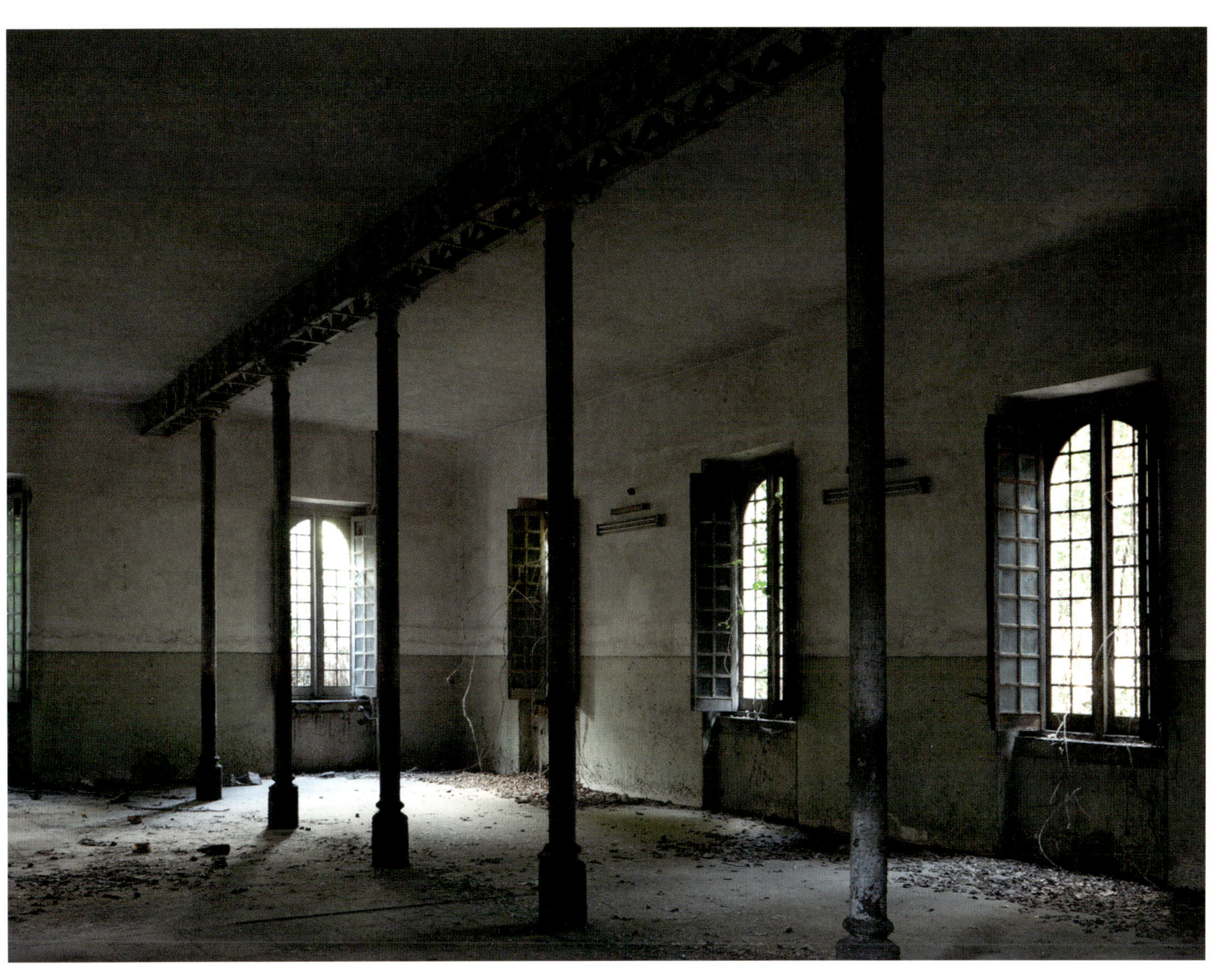

Nächste Doppelseite pagina successiva
next double page

VII. Abteilung Frauen, Krankenabteilung
VII. Sezione donne, reparto degenza
VII. Women's wing, ward

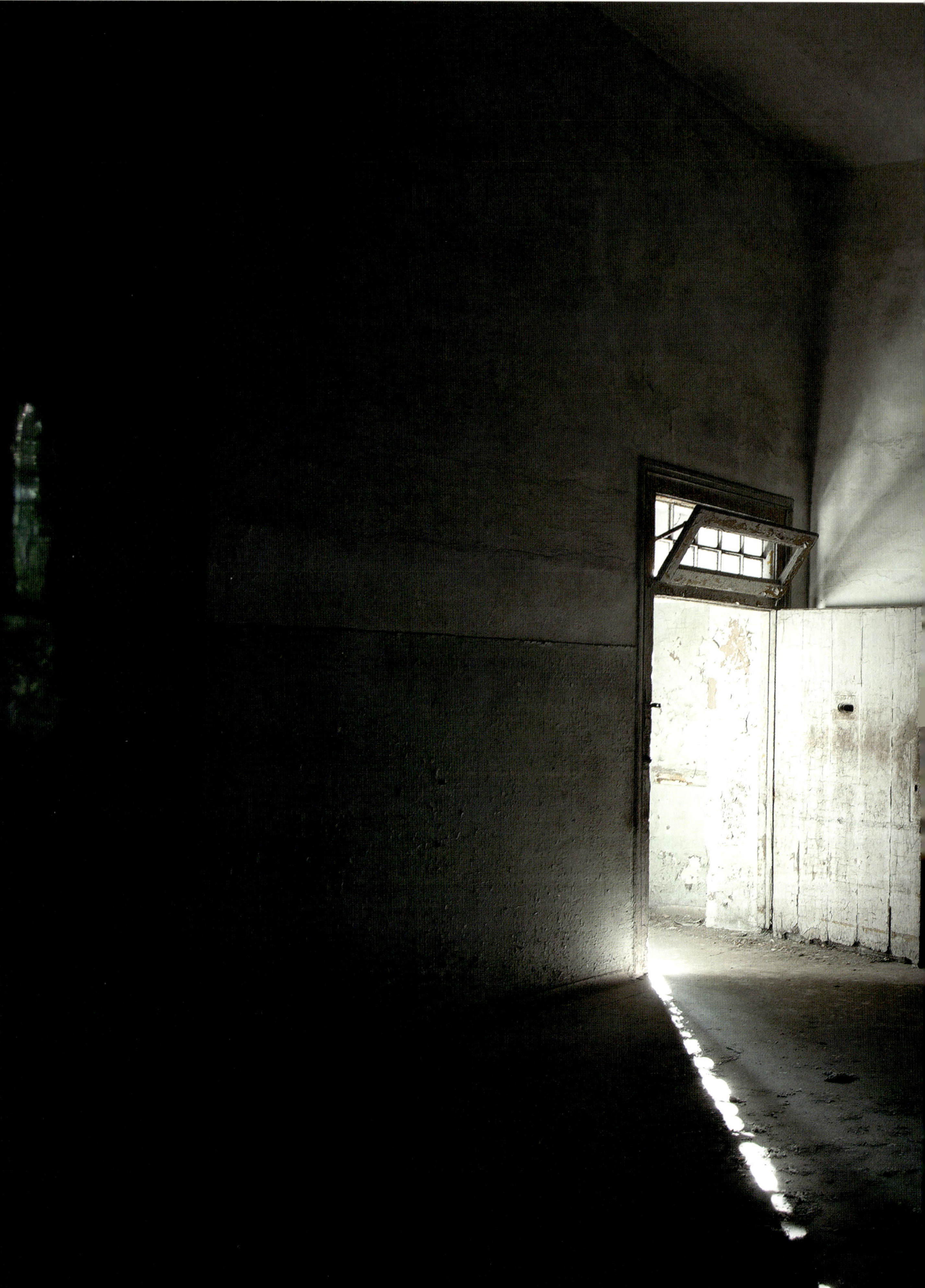

I. Abteilung Männer, Fernsehraum
I. Sezione uomini, sala tv
I. Men's wing, TV room

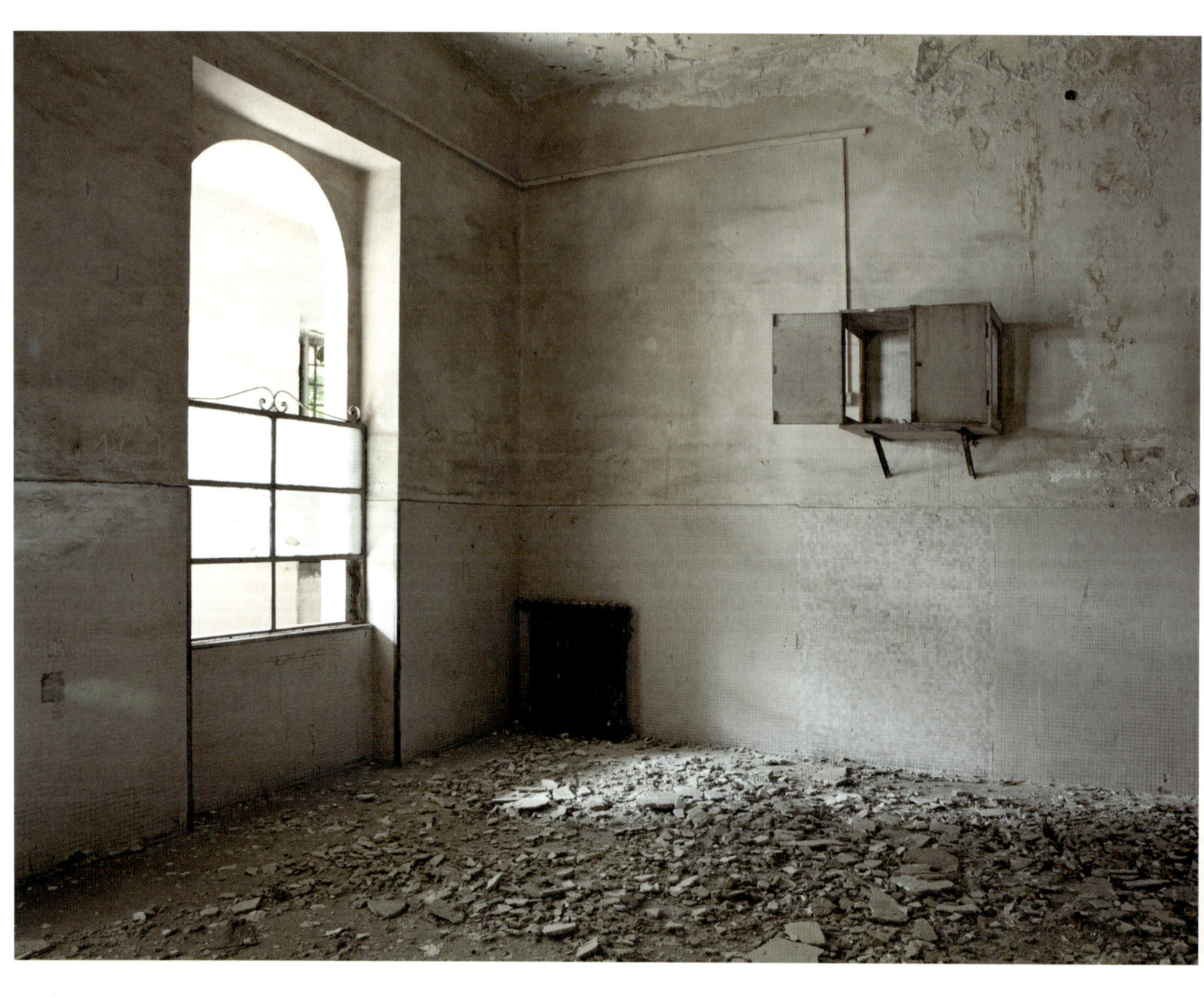

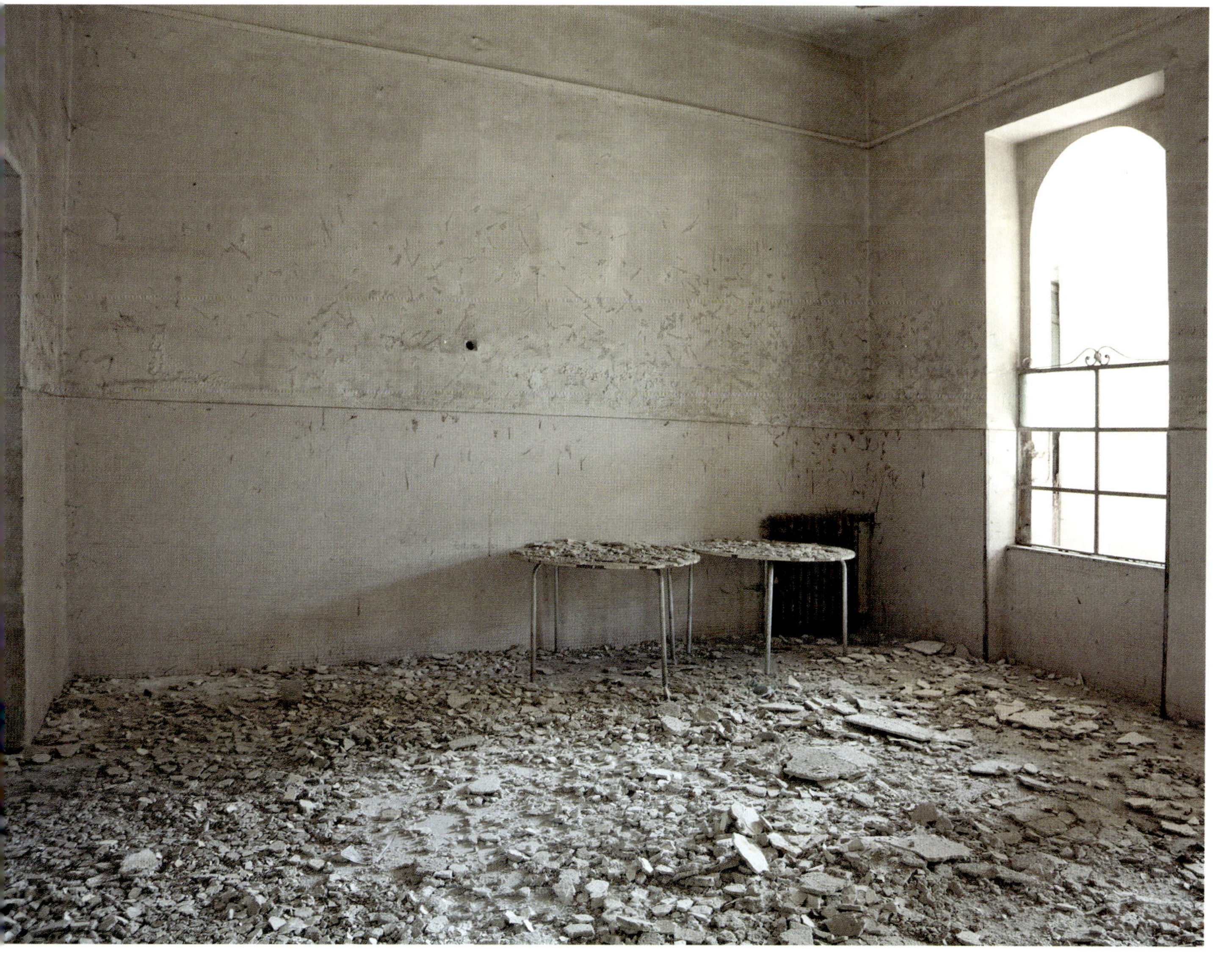

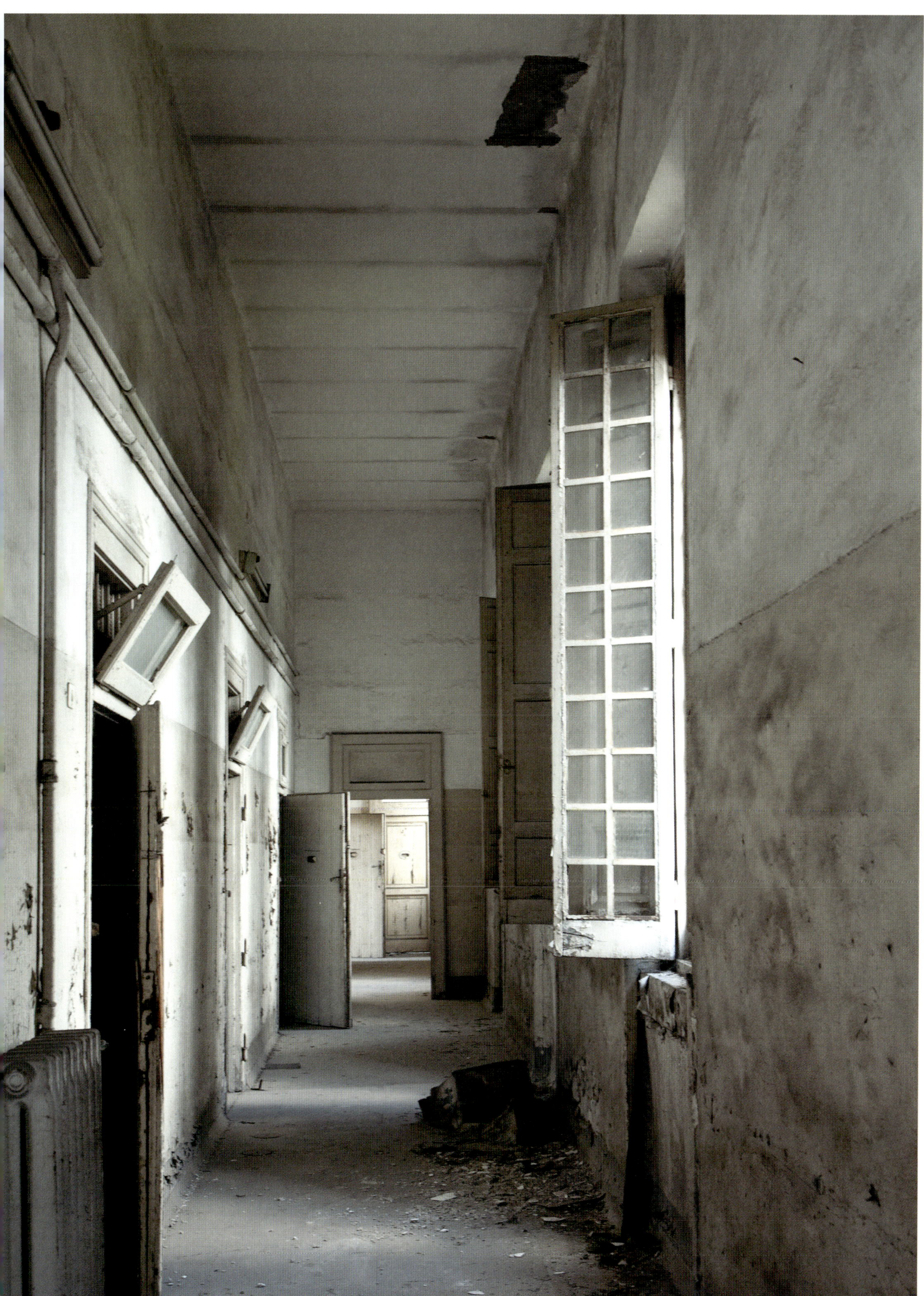

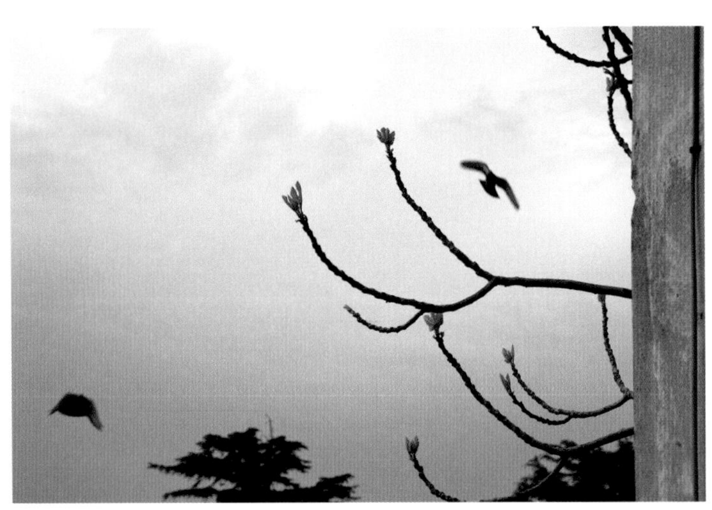

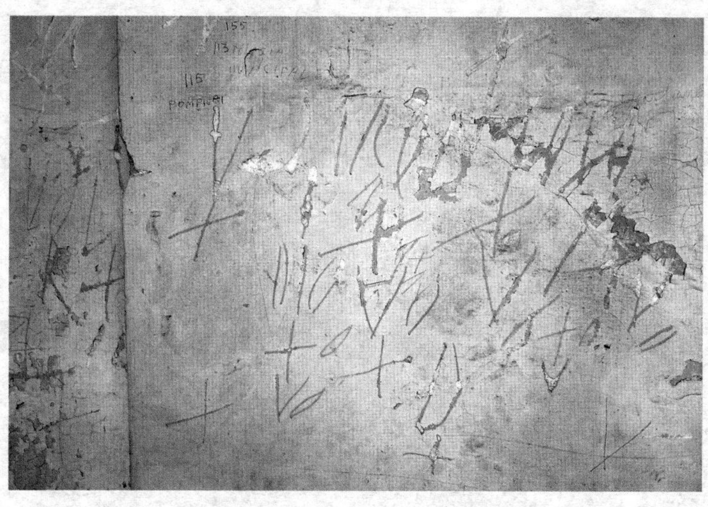

Graffiti der Insassen
Graffiti dei ricoverati
Inmates' graffiti

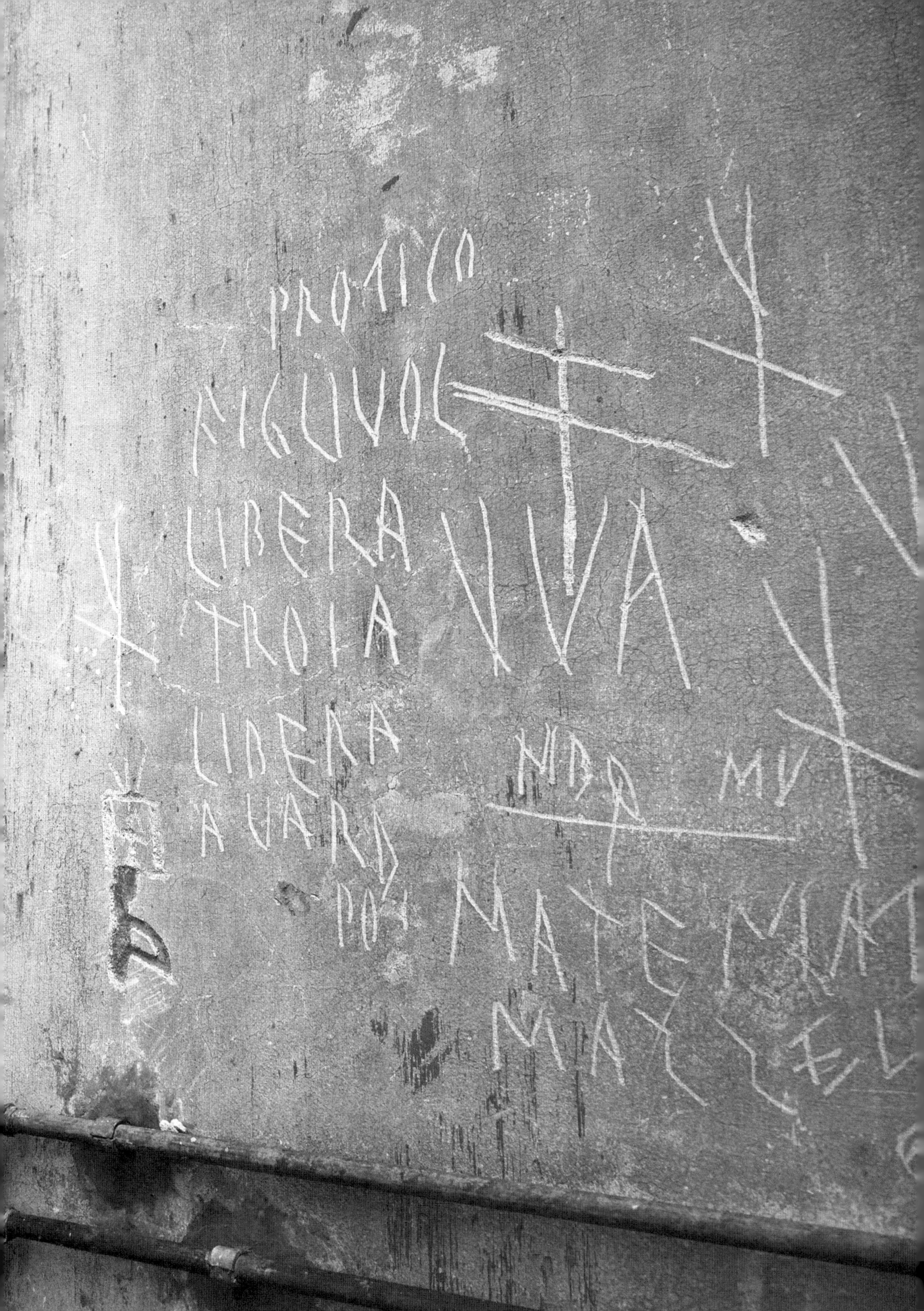
PROTICO
LIBERA
TROIA
VVA
LIBERA

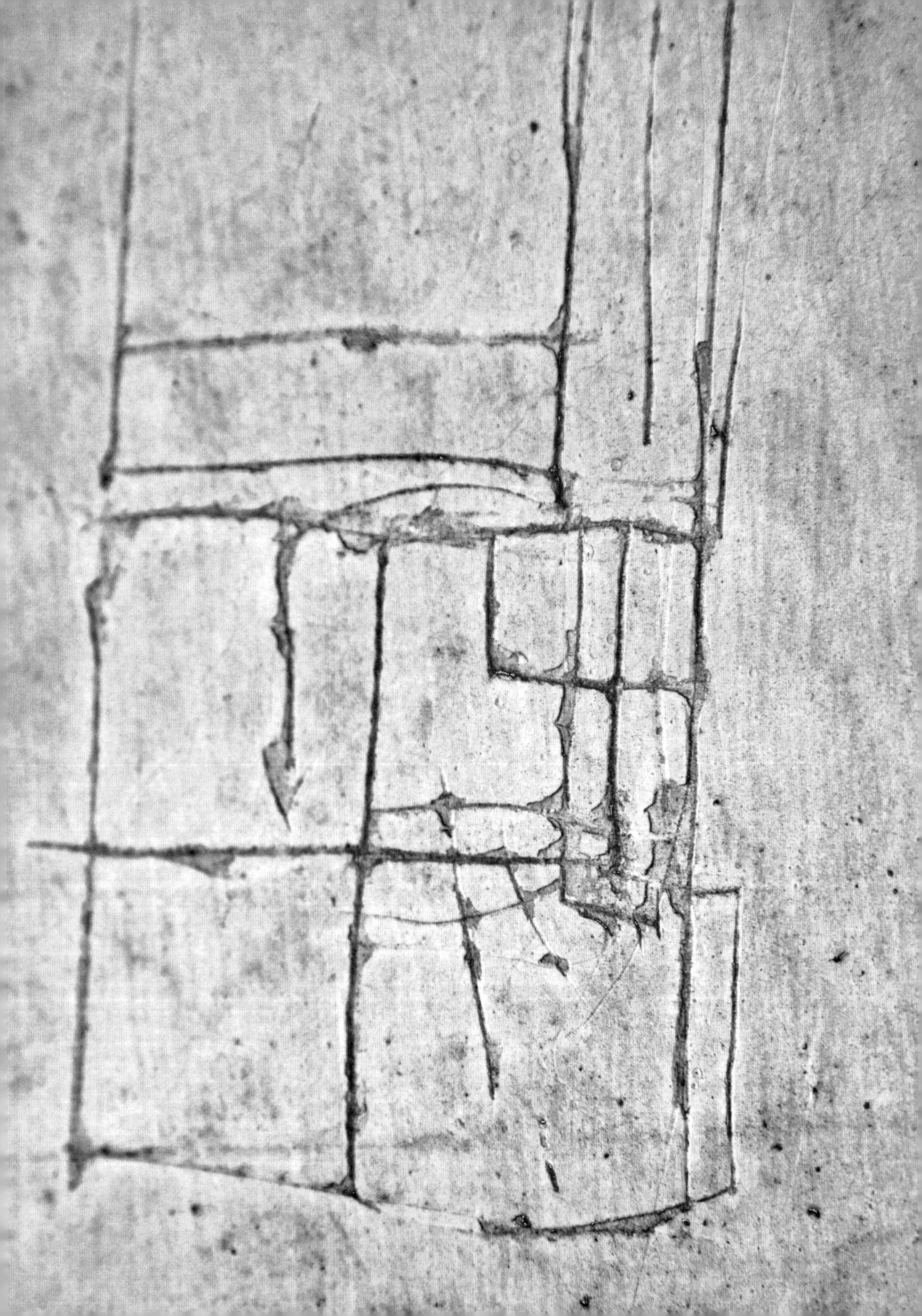

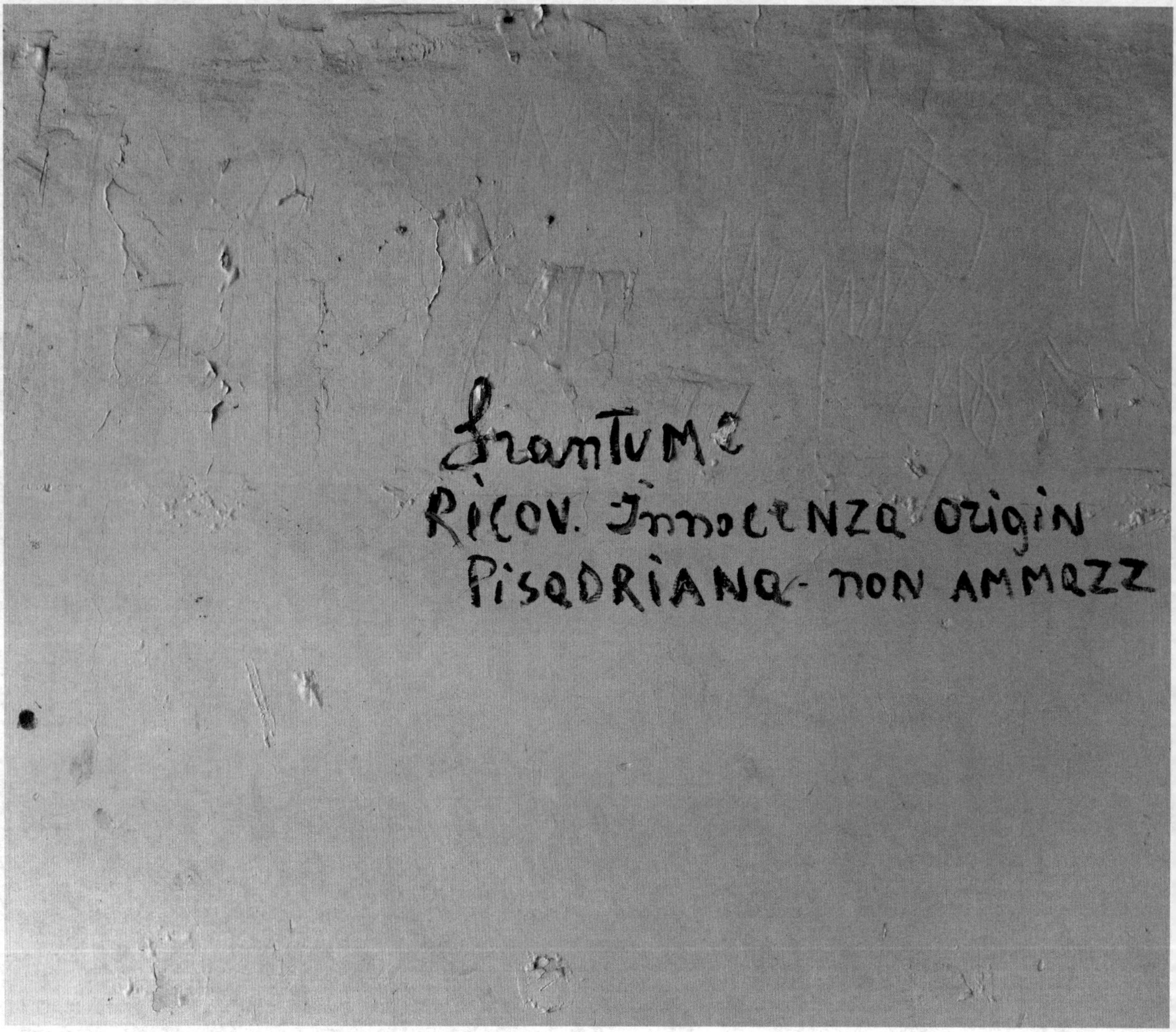

frantume
Ricov. Innocenza origin
Pisadriana - non ammazz

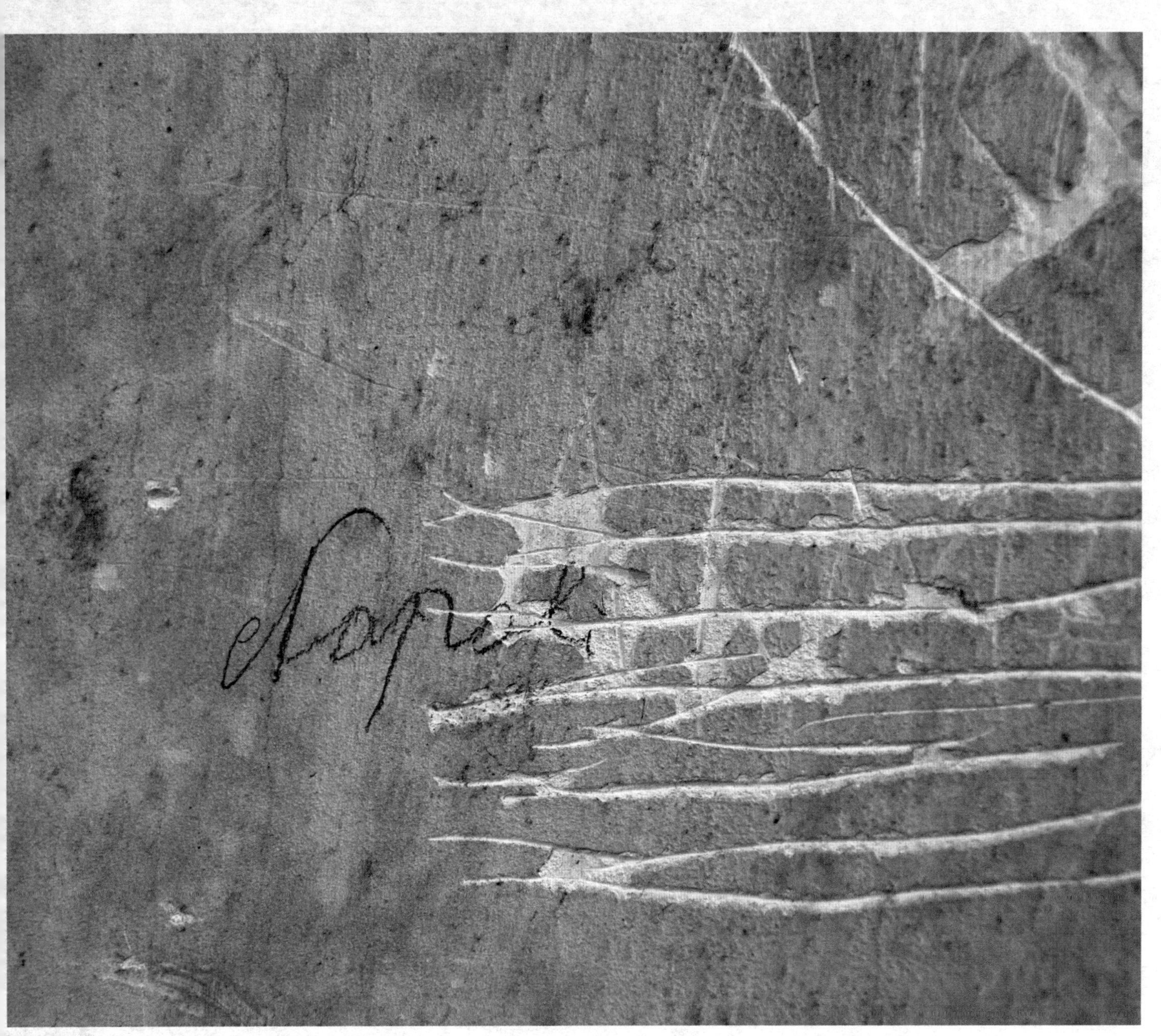

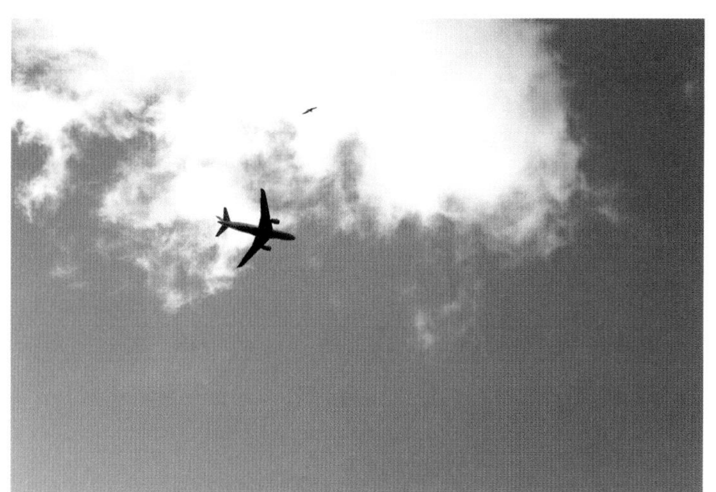

Stiegenhaus, vergittert
Giro scale con grata
Staircase with protective wire netting

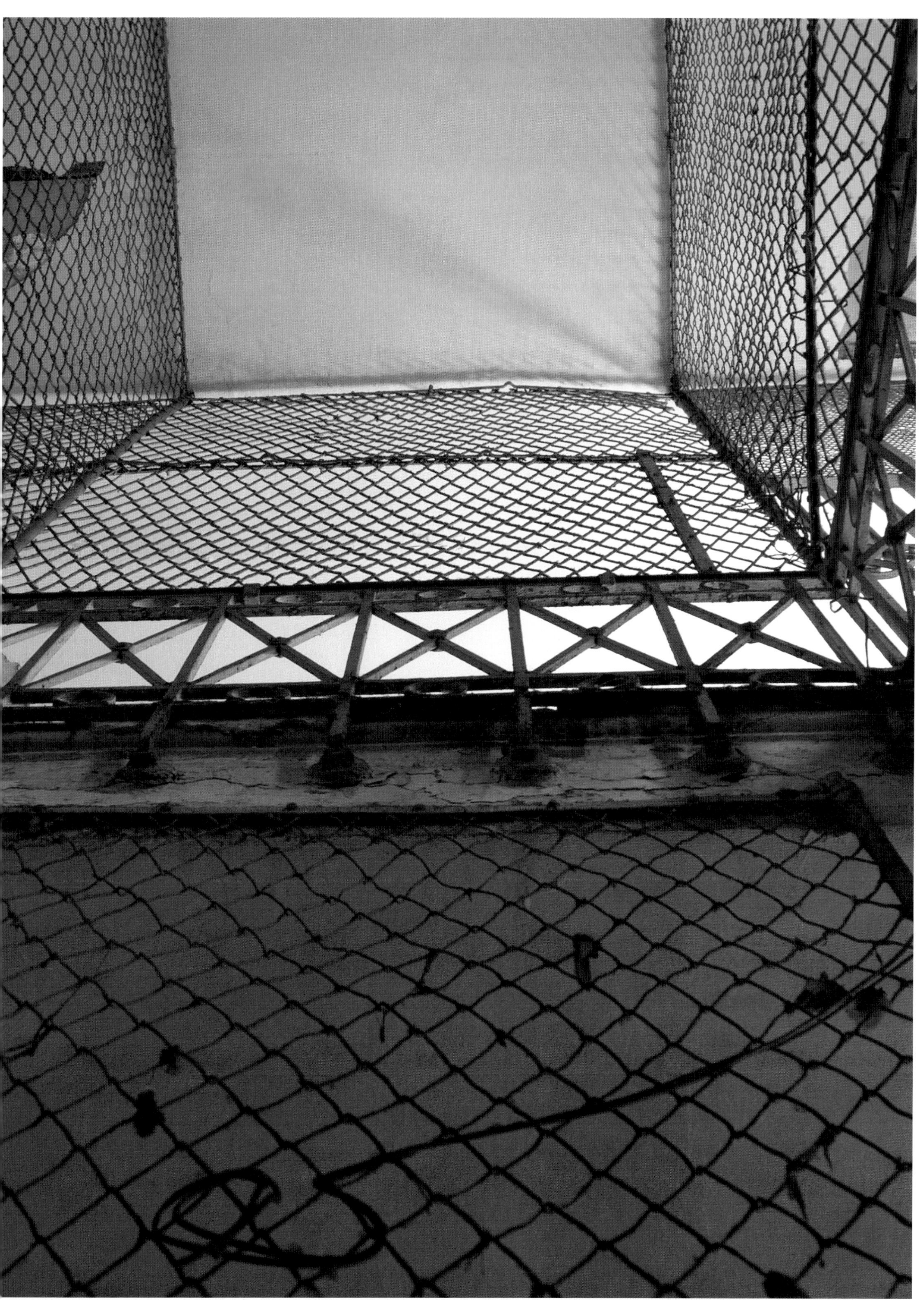

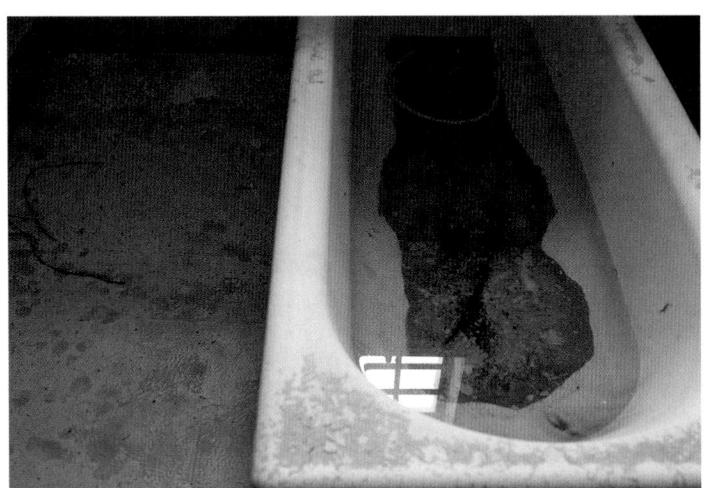

Badewannen
Vasche da bagno
Bath tubs

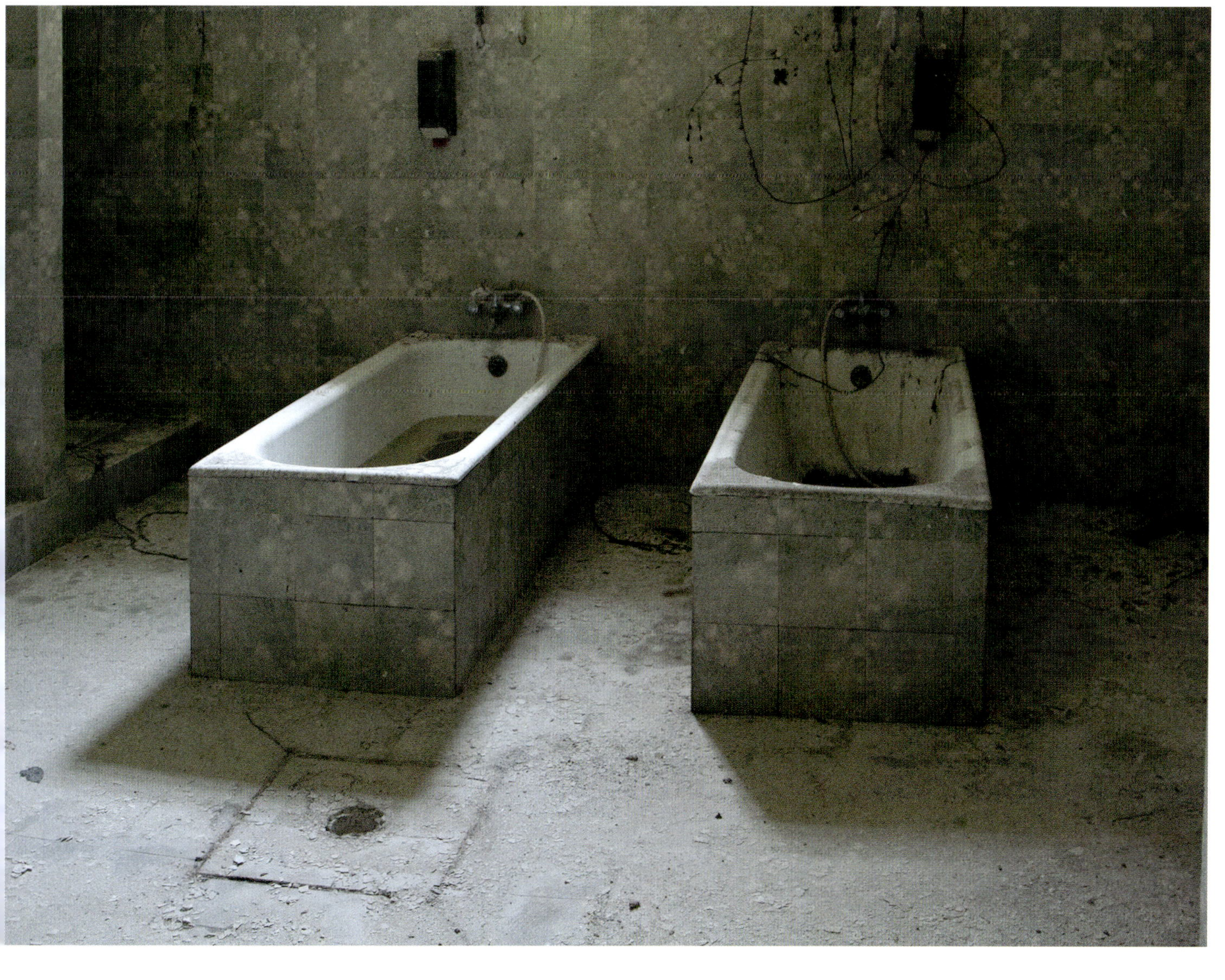

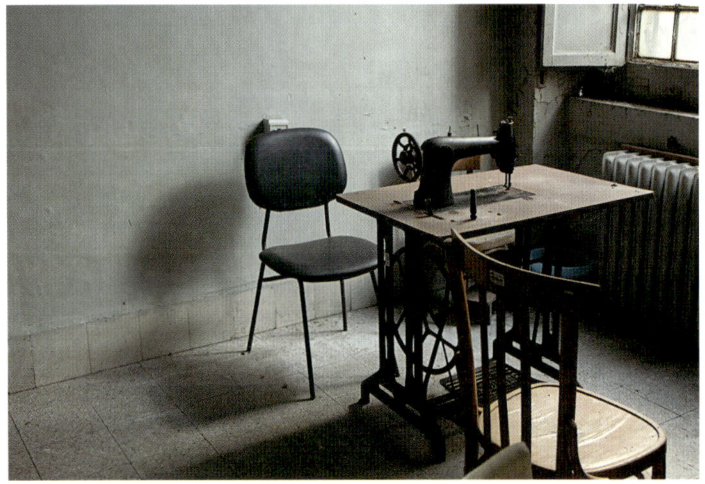

Nähstube, Stofflager
"Rattoppineria" e magazzino stoffe
Sewing room and storeroom

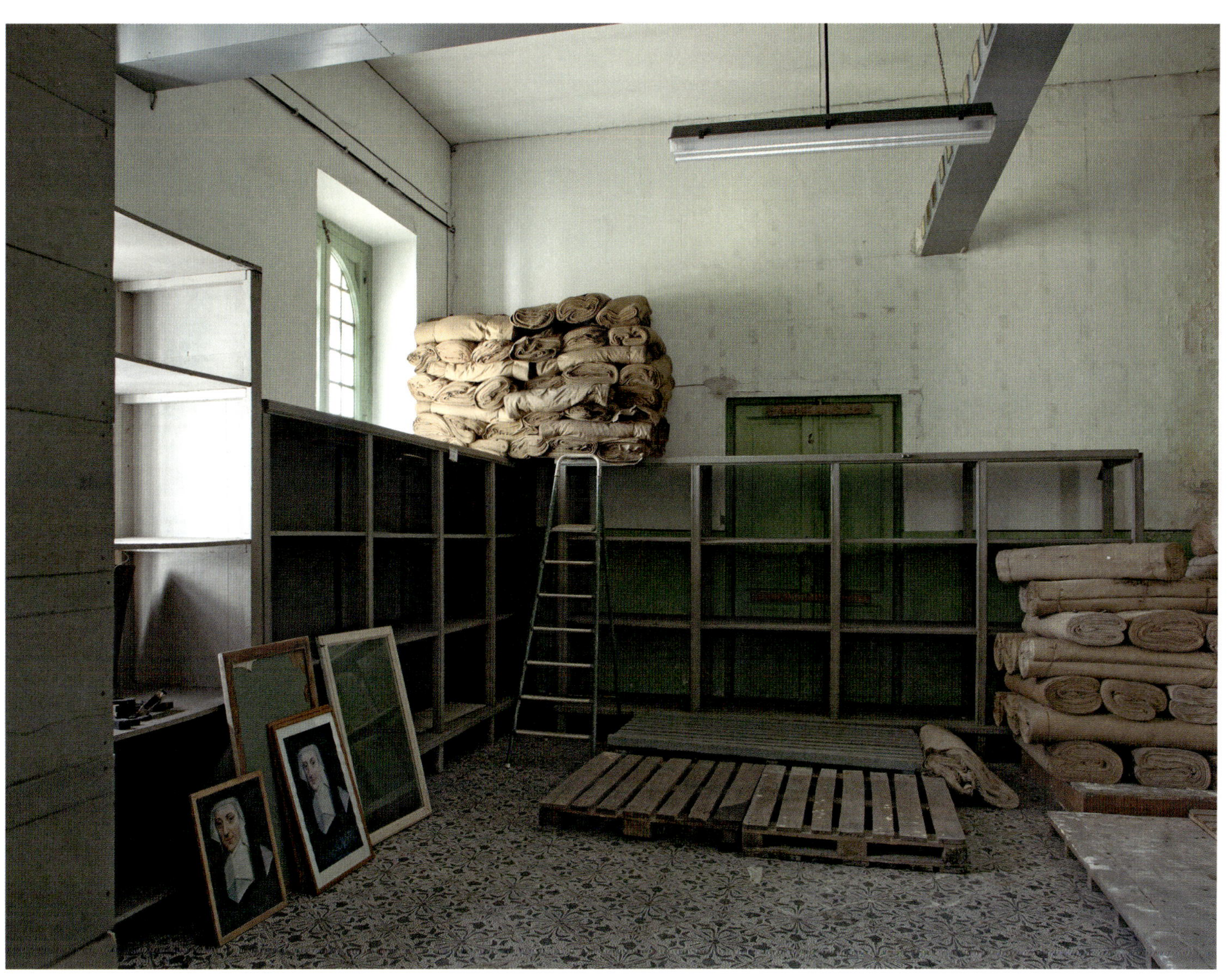

Nächste Doppelseite pagina successiva
next double page

Küche
Cucina
Kitchen

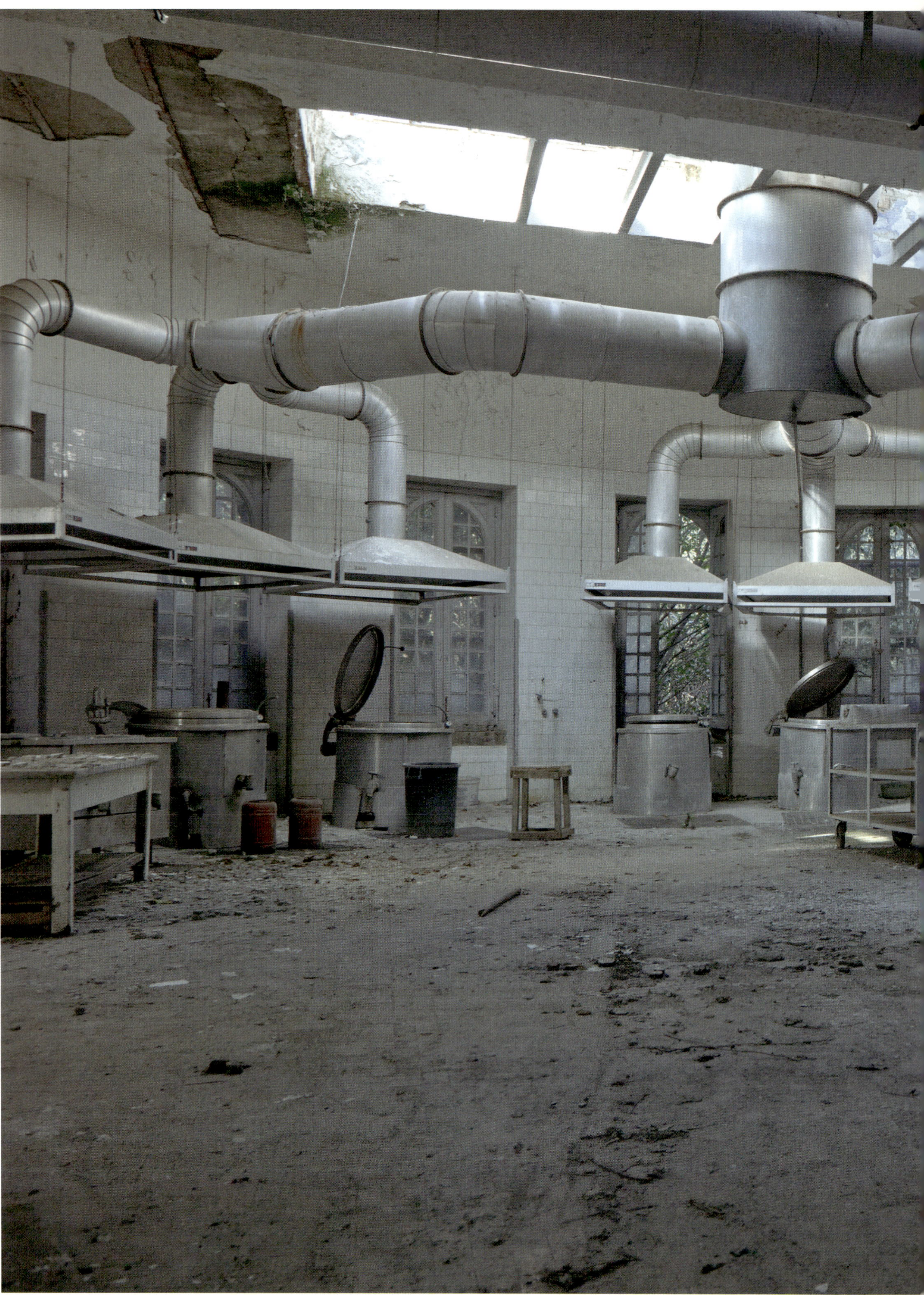

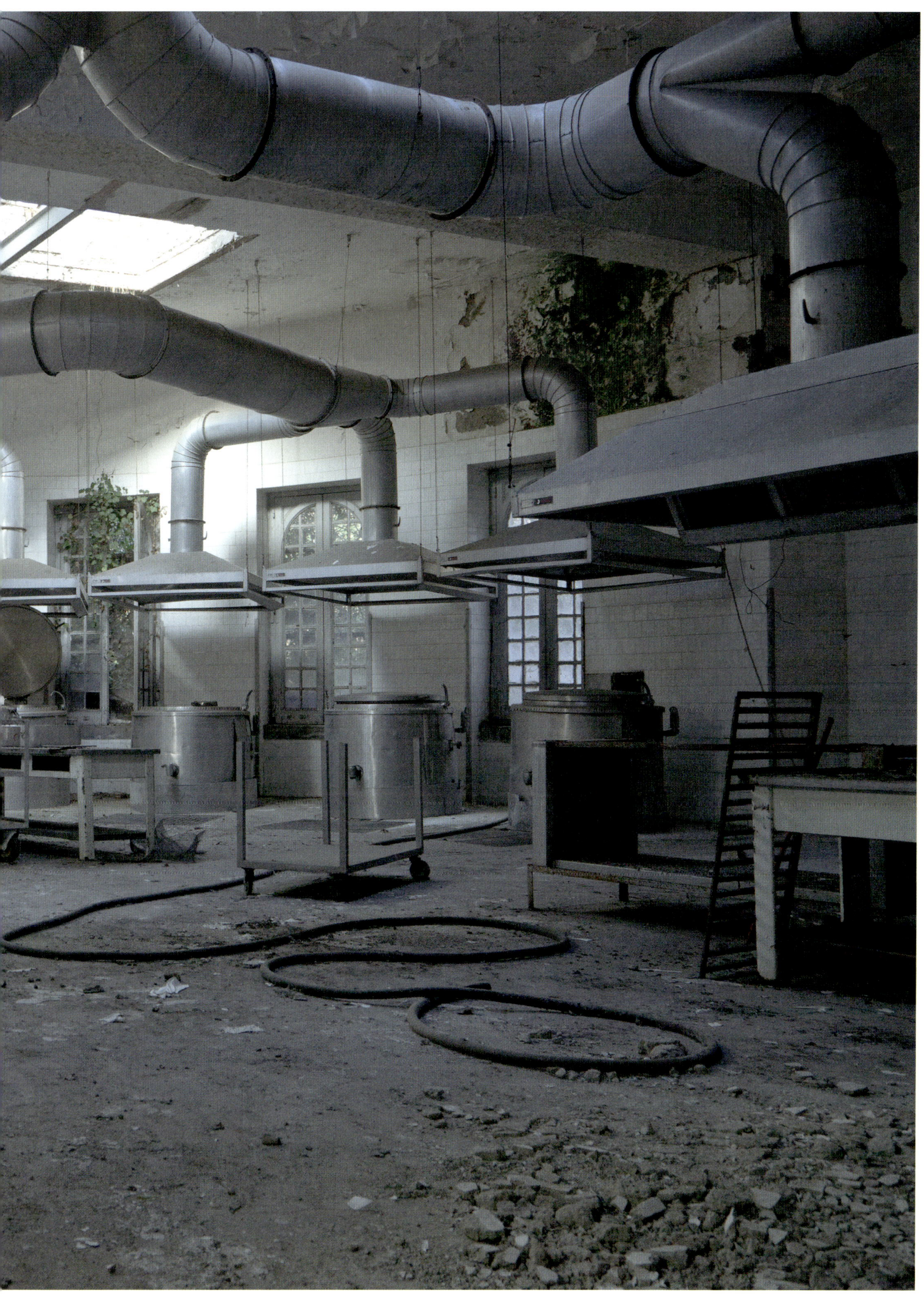

Nächste Doppelseite pagina successiva
next double page

Druckerei
Tipografia
Printer's

Schmiede
Officina del fabbro
Blacksmith's workshop

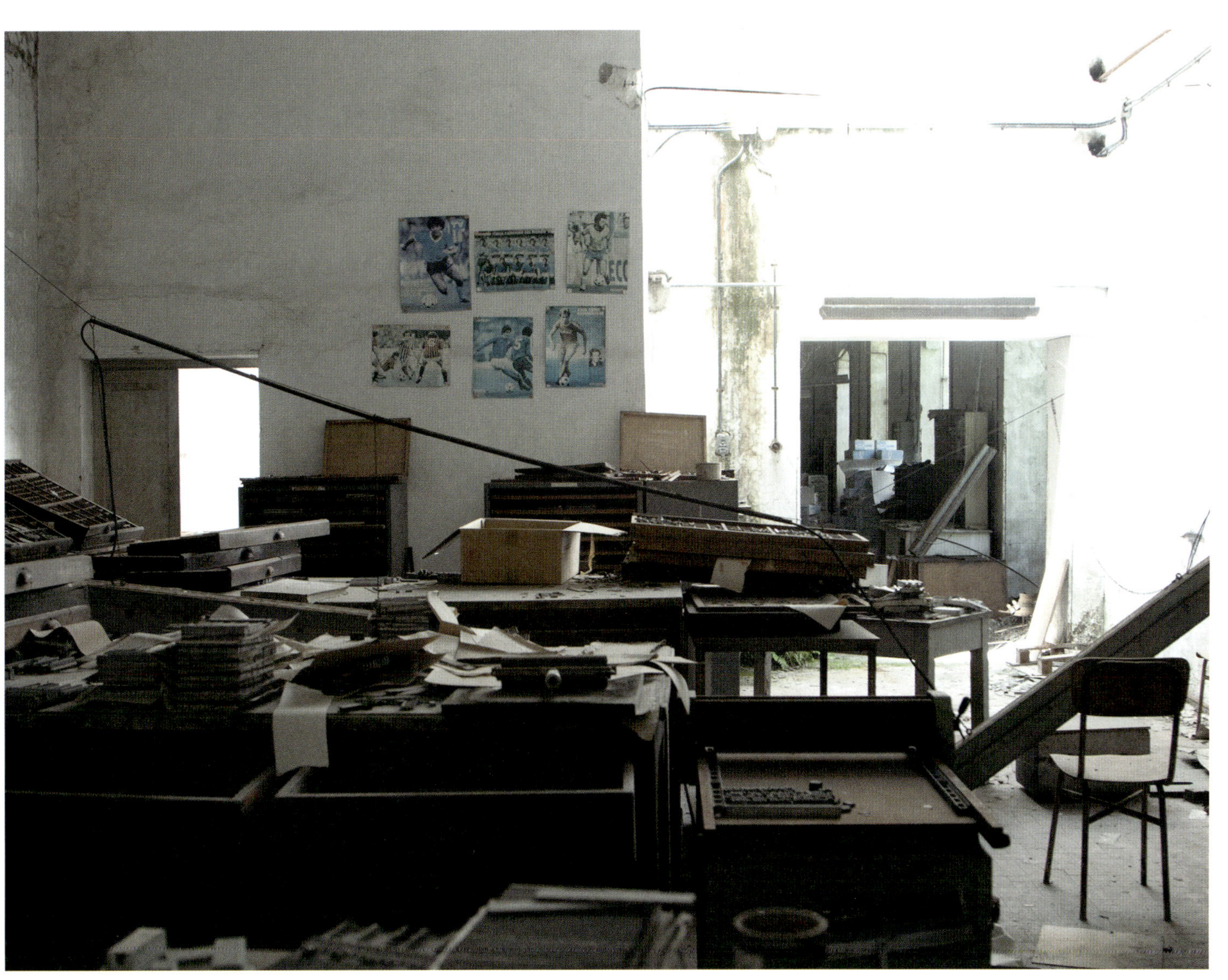

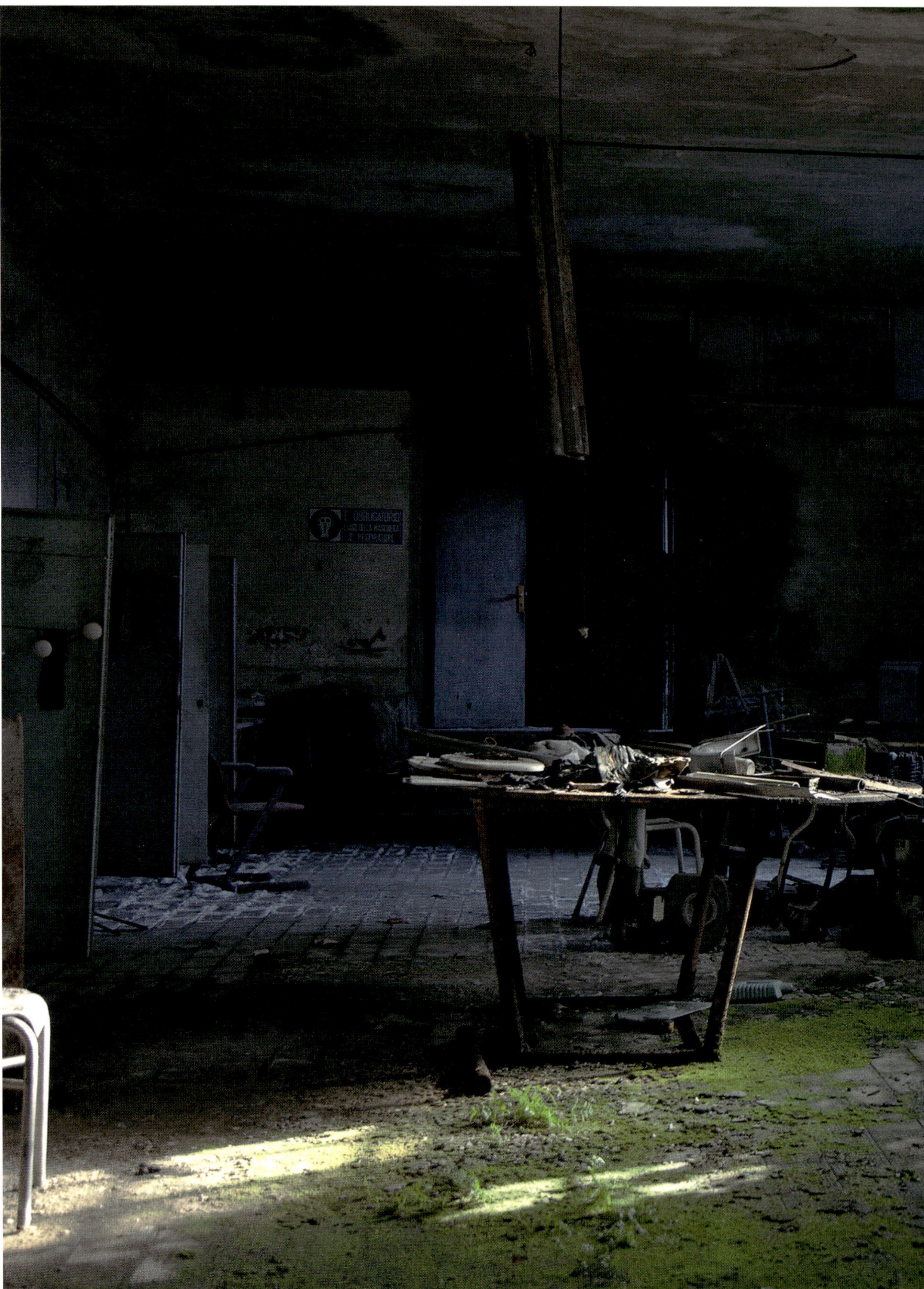

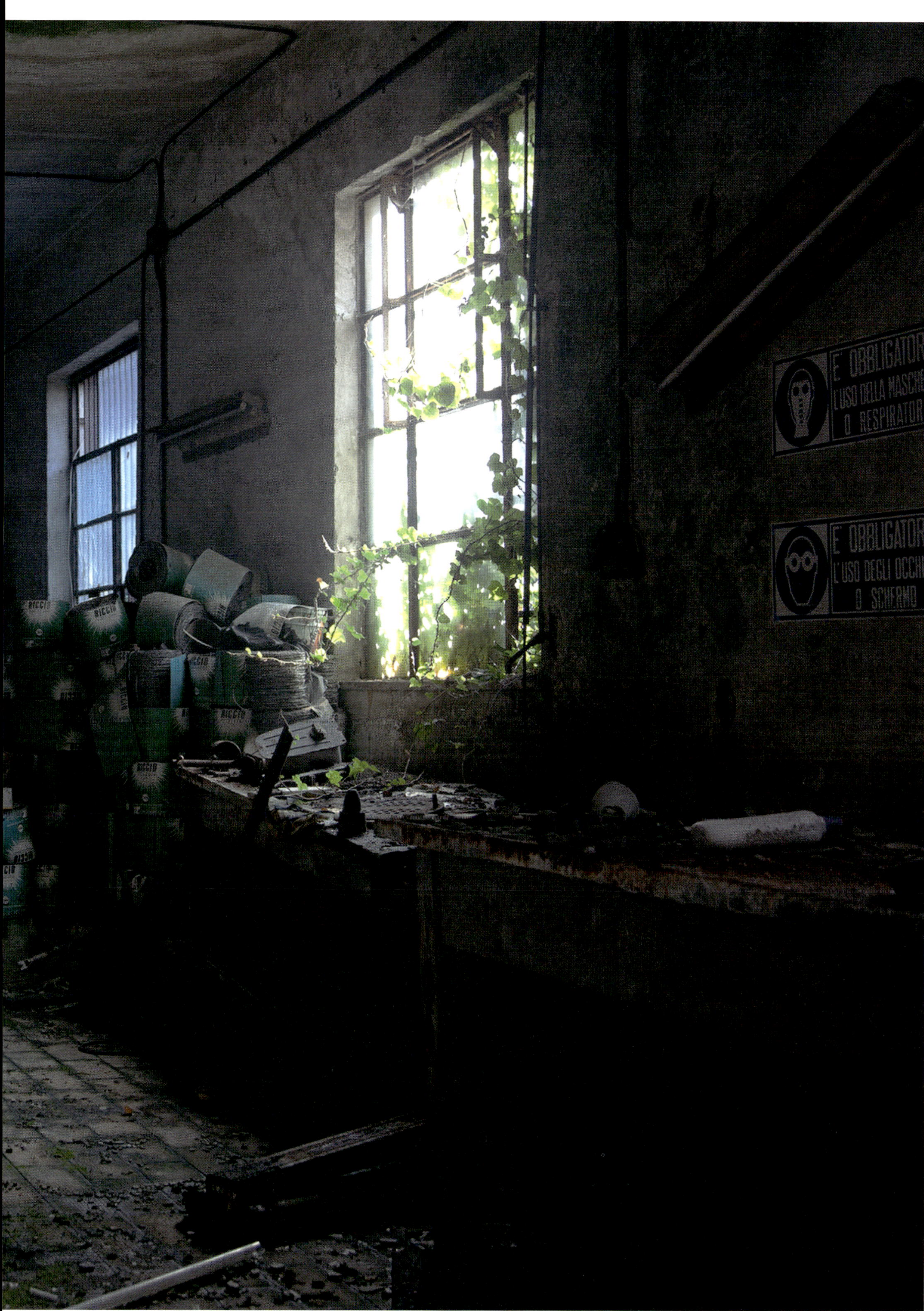
E' OBBLIGATORI
L'USO DELLA MASCHER
O RESPIRATORE
E' OBBLIGATORI
L'USO DEGLI OCCHIA
O SCHERMO
RICCIO

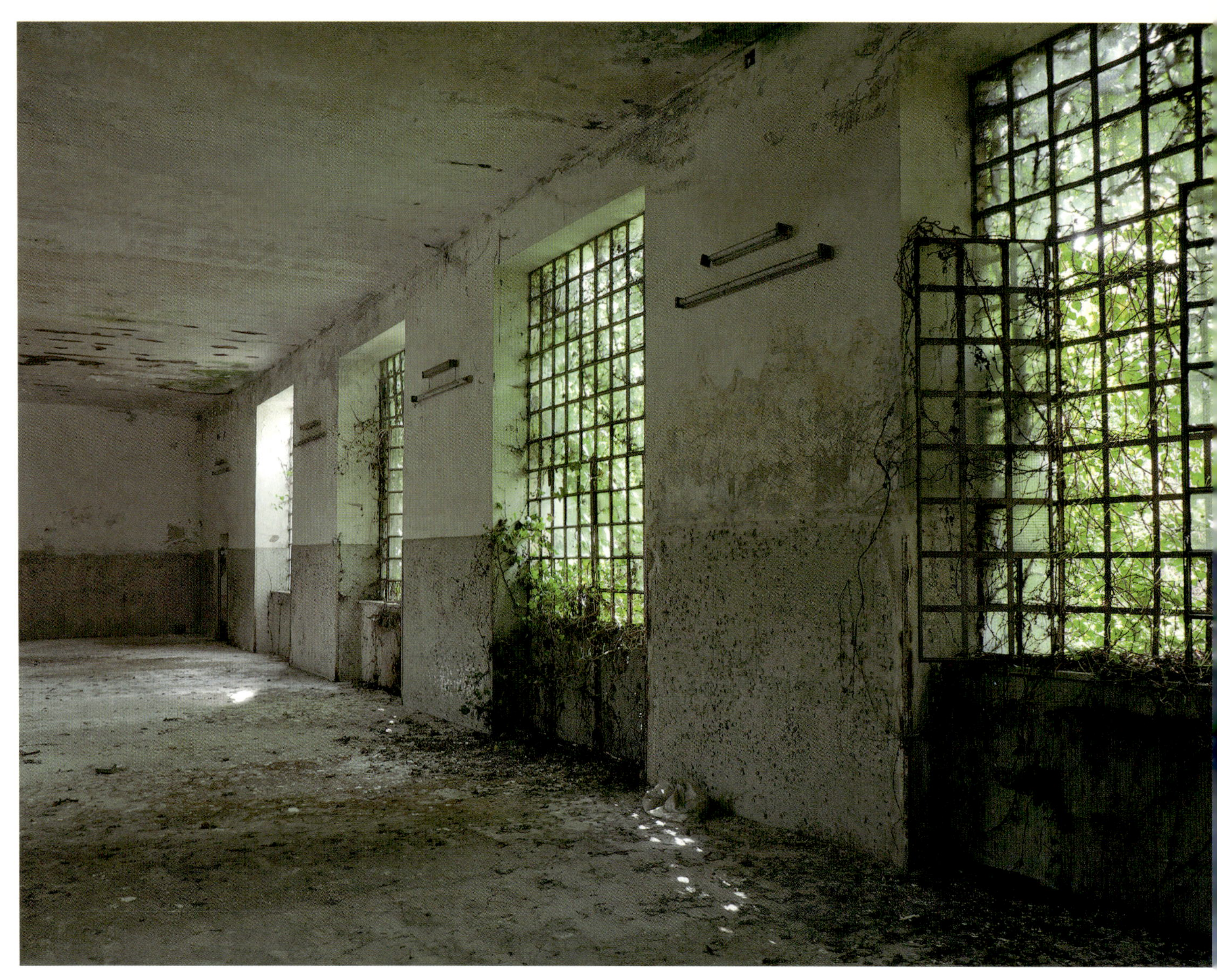

I. Abteilung Männer, Speisesaal
I. Sezione uomini, sala da pranzo
I. Men's wing, dining room

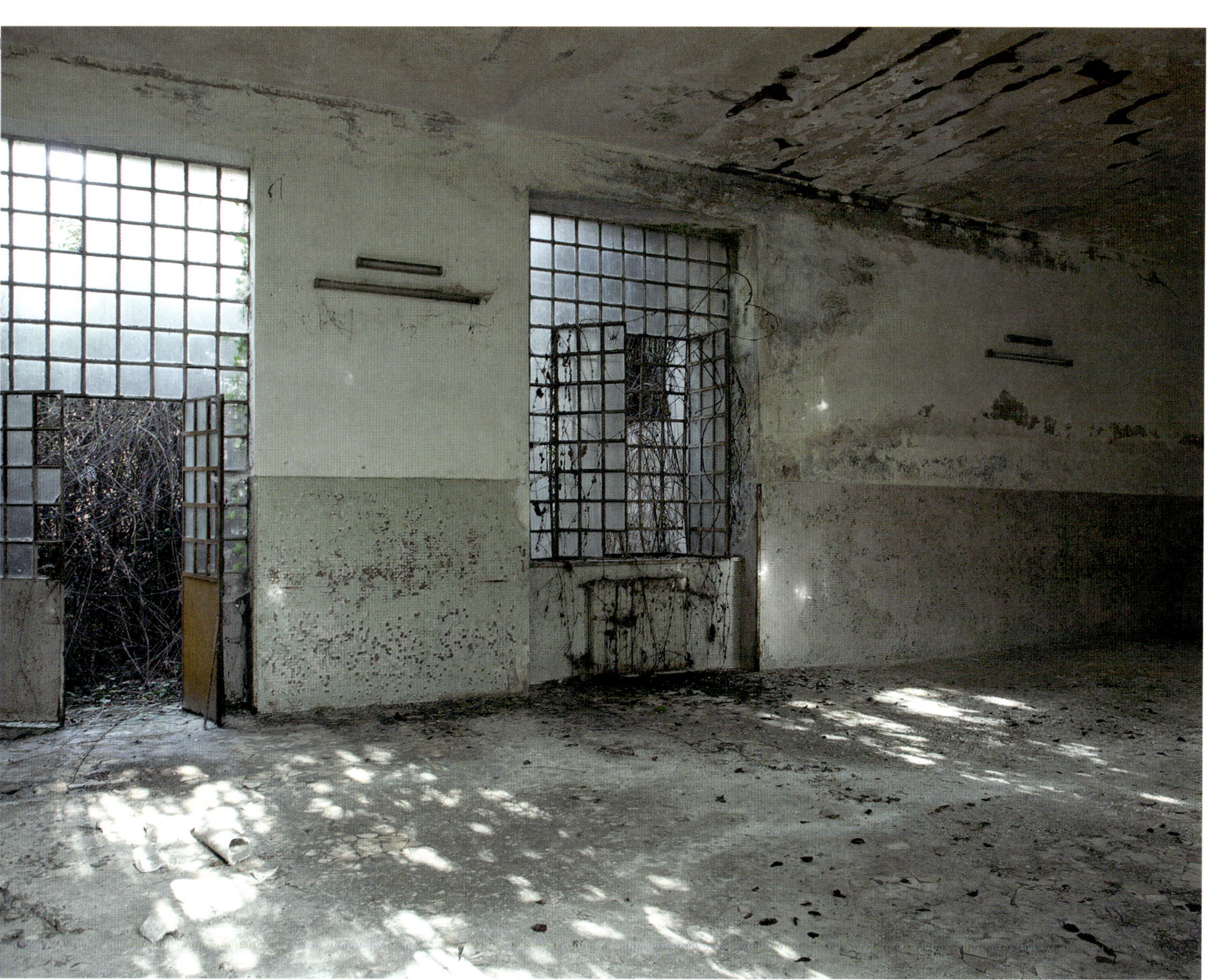

Chirurgie, Operationstisch
Chirurgia, tavolo operatorio
Operating theater, operating table

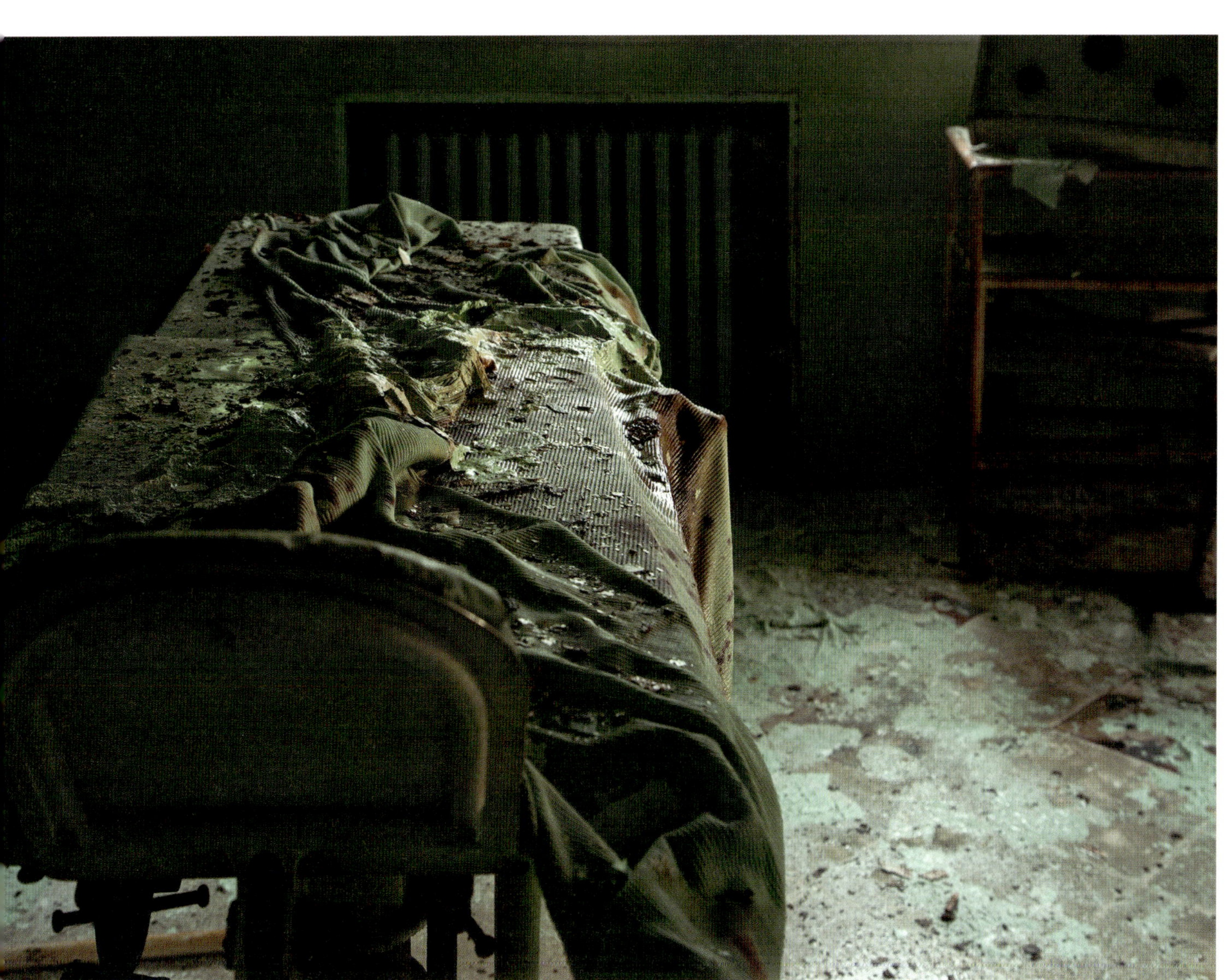

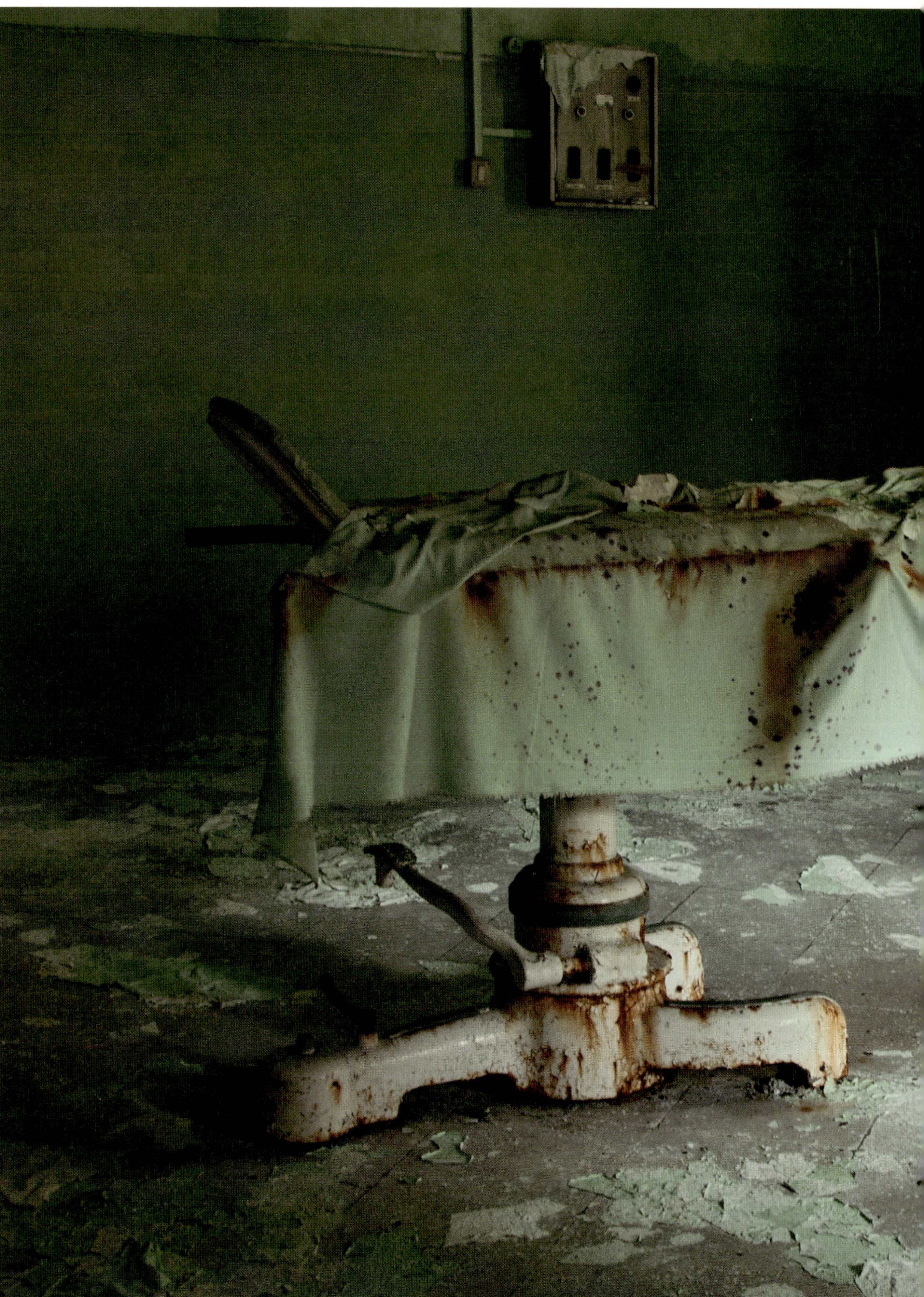

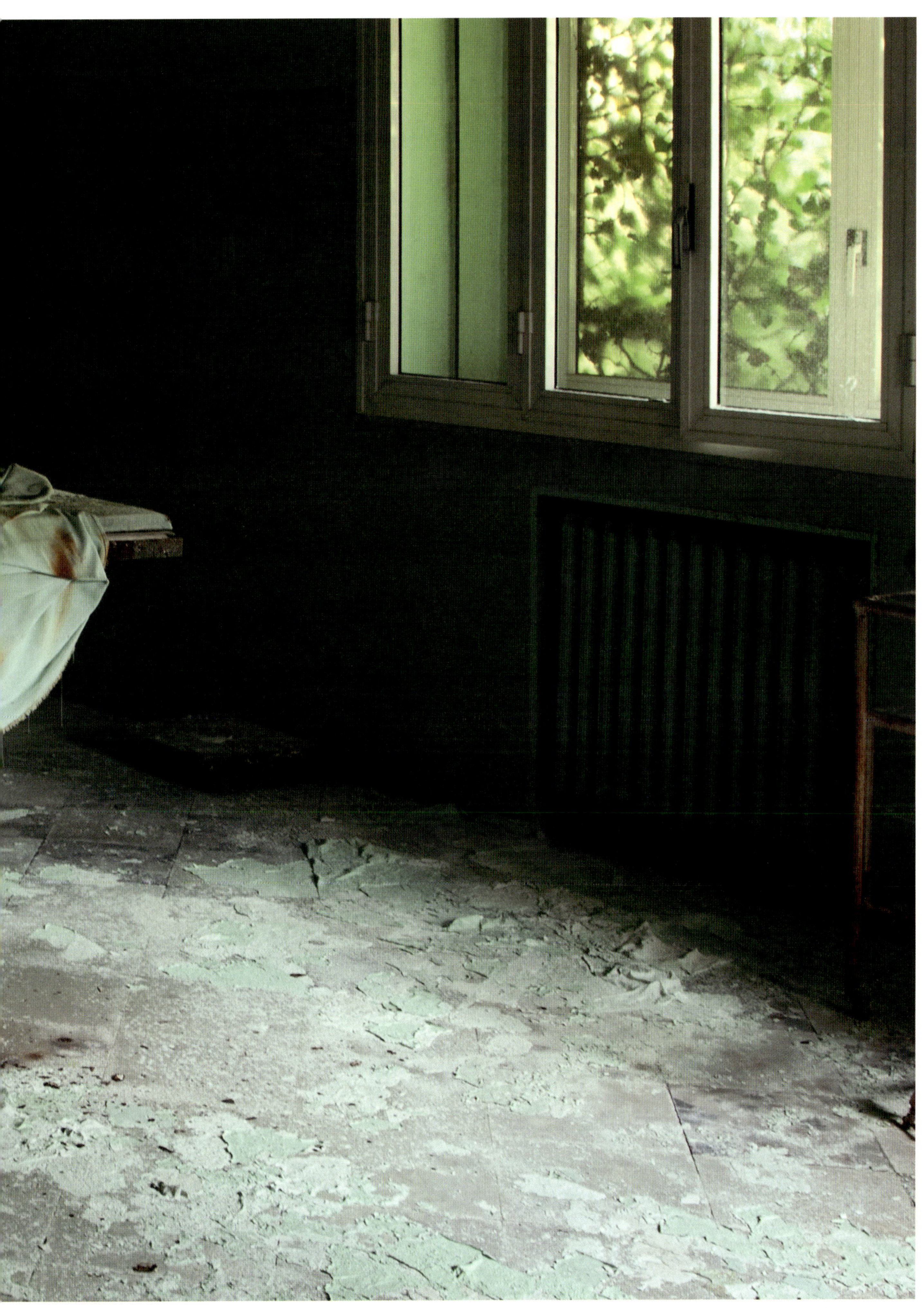

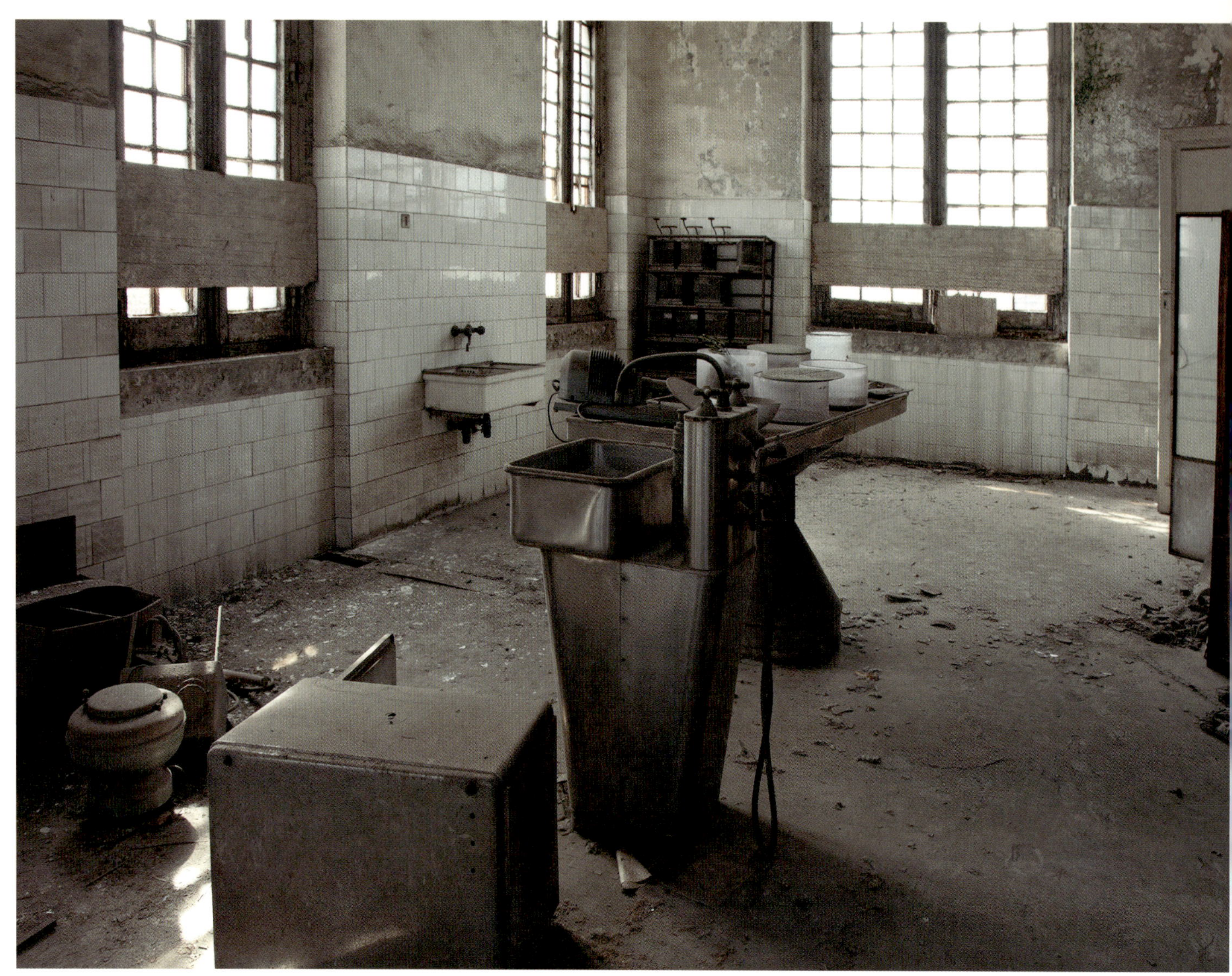

Nekroskopie
Necroscopia
Post-mortem room

Nächste Doppelseite pagina successiva
next double page

Bibliothek
Biblioteca
Library

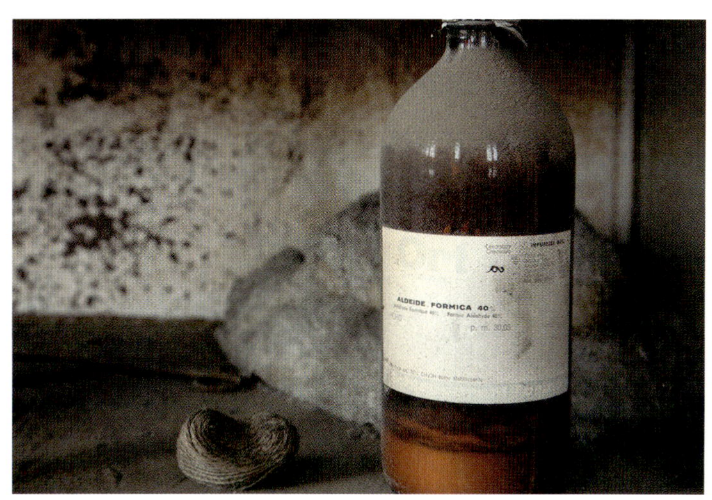
ALDEIDE FORMICA 40%
p. m. 30,03

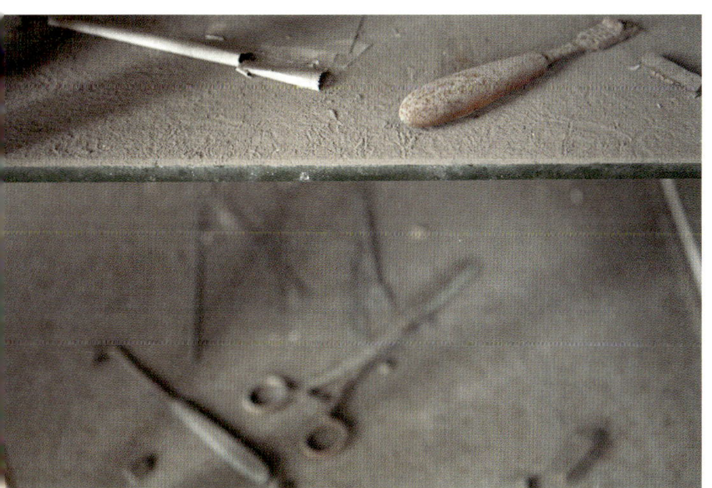

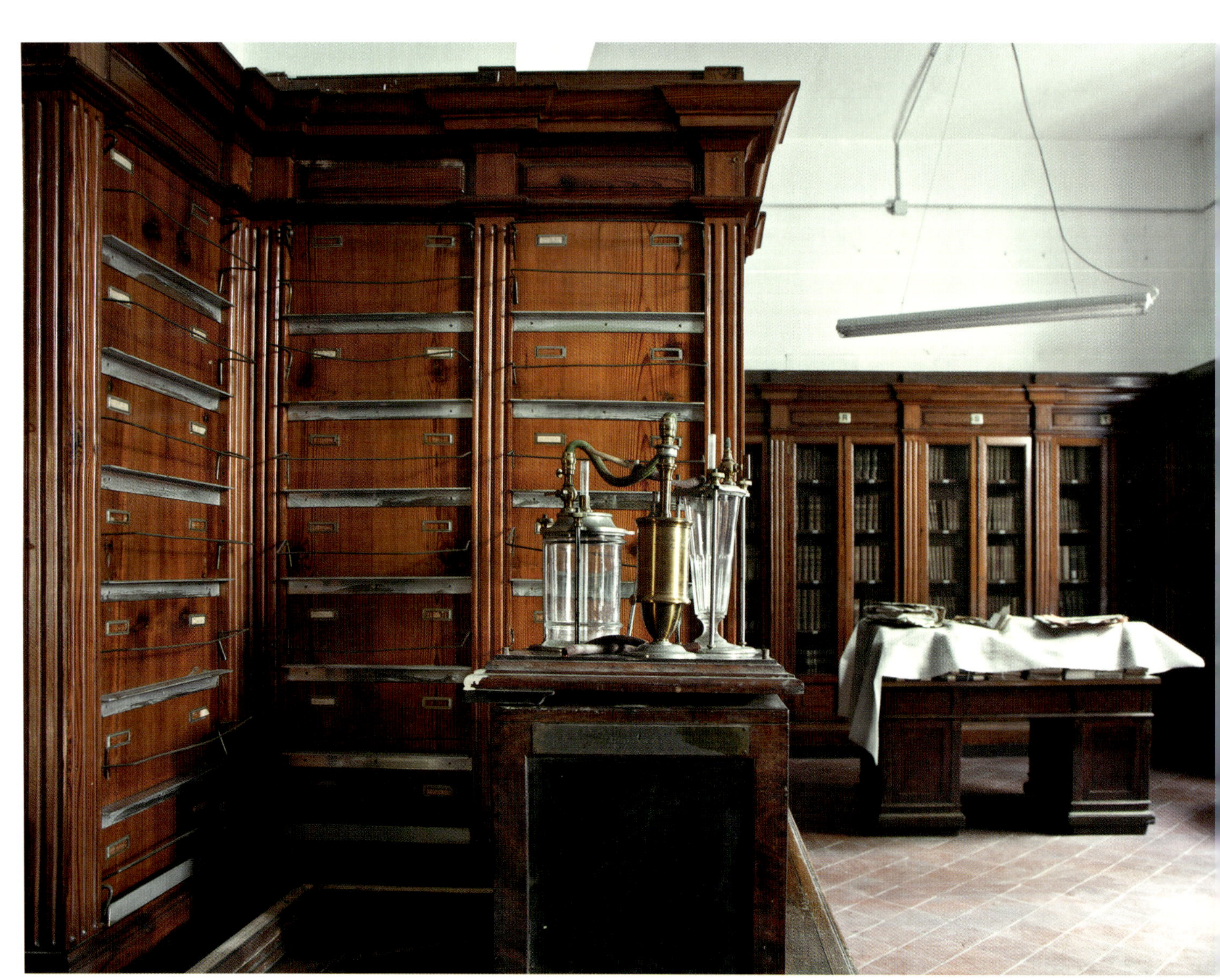

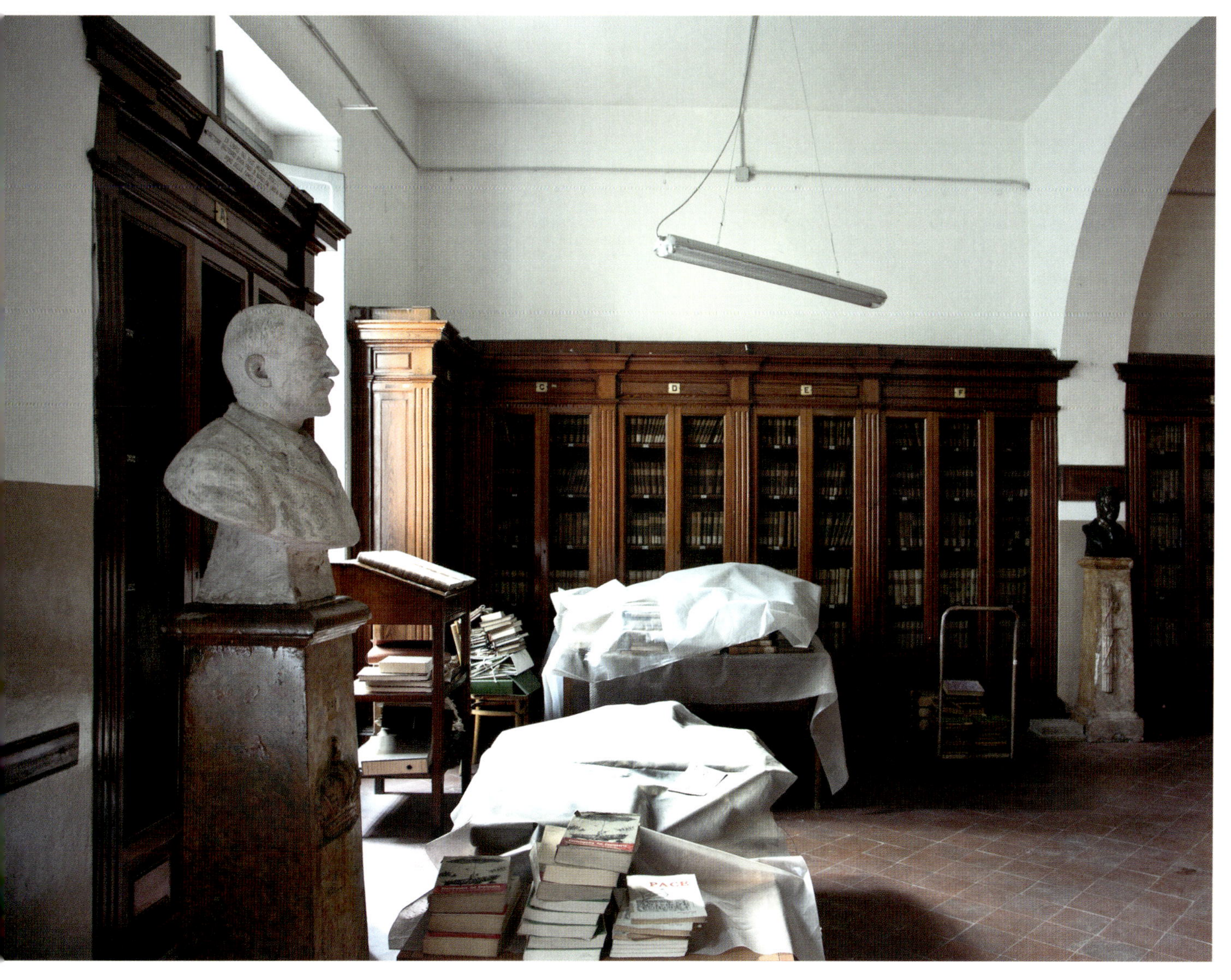
C
D
E
F
PACE

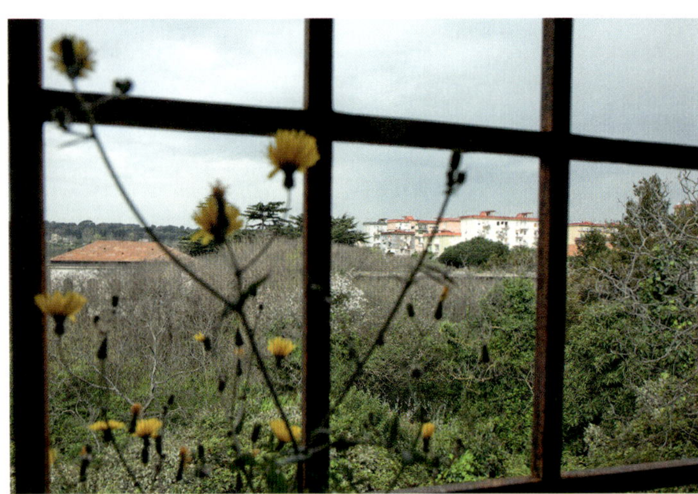

Fardellario (1921 — 1973) *

Register of Inmates' Belongings

* The registers with the names of the inmates of the asylum showing the list of personal belongings to be found in the bundle that each one of them deposited on admission, and which they either collected when they were sent home or which was returned to their family on their death. According to the regulations issued in 1889, if the bundle was not claimed within two months of death within the asylum, its contents were to be sold and the money raised would go to the institution (*art. 200*).

The following possessions and belongings were those that the inmates of the asylum had brought with them. These were all withdrawn by the Bursar on admission.

These were:

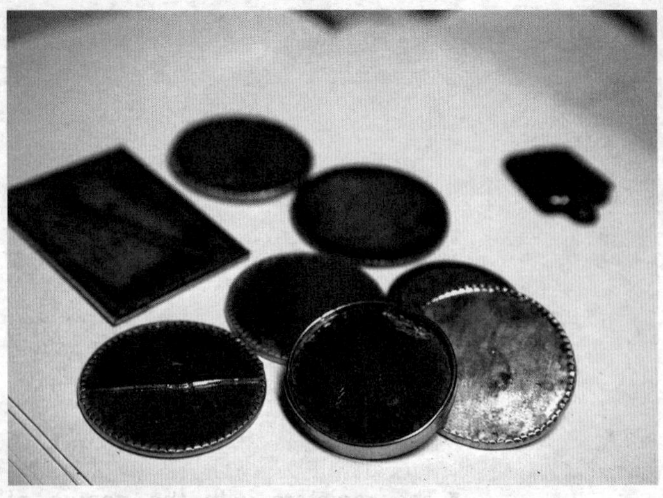

Beschlagnahmte Spiegel der Insassen
Specchietti sequestrati ai ricoverati
Small mirrors taken from the inmates

Men

A boy's suit.

Jacket, overcoat, shoes and hat.

Rags.

Jacket, waistcoat, trousers and rags.

Jacket, waistcoat, trousers, shirt, vest, collar, tie, socks, shoes, hat.

Overcoat, jacket, waistcoat, trousers, shirt, vest, underpants, collar, tie, braces, socks, shoes and hat, watch and chain (both made of fake metal), wallet with personal documents, coffee grounds.

Rags.

Jacket, trousers, overcoat, two vests, underpants, shoes, socks, leather strap, peaked cap.

Overcoat, jacket, trousers, waistcoat, shirt, underpants, vest, socks, shoes, collar, tie, hat, cuff-links made of fake metal.

Jacket, overcoat, shoes and hat.

Overcoat and trousers.

Overcoat, jacket, trousers, 2 pairs socks, shoes, tie, vest, waistcoat, hat, underpants, parcel with personal documents and gloves, two pairs of glasses, a small white metal chain, two Austrian securities, one for ten thousand crowns and one for a hundred crowns.

Rags.

Shirt, two vests, underpants, jacket, trousers, waistcoat, braces, shoes.

Overcoat, jacket, waistcoat, trousers, shirt, two vests, underpants, socks, shoes, braces, peaked cap, two cuff-links made of fake metal, yellow metal ring.

Hat, jacket, waistcoat, trousers, shirt, vest, underpants, socks, shoes, sock garters, shirt garters, strap, hat, suitcase with six shirts, two vests, two pairs of underpants, a hand towel, a jacket and trousers, three pairs of short socks, a pair of shoes, four collars, three handkerchiefs, two ties, a piece of soap, shaving brush, a box with a razor.

Rags.

Jacket, waistcoat, trousers, shirt, two vests, underpants, socks, shoes, hat.

Rags.

Overcoat, jacket, shirt, underpants, vest, socks, shoes, braces, shirt bib, hat, yellow metal ring.

Overcoat, jacket, waistcoat, trousers, shirt, underpants, braces, sock garters, socks, shoes, collar, tie, hat.

Jacket, waistcoat, trousers, shirt, two vests, underpants, socks, shoes, strap, scarf and hat.

Overcoat, jacket, waistcoat, trousers, shirt, underpants, vest, socks, shoes, hat, braces, collar, tie, two cuff-links of white and yellow metal, a pair of glasses with a white metal case.

Overcoat, jacket, waistcoat, trousers, three shirts, six pairs of underpants, two vests, two hand towels, two handkerchiefs, tie, hat, tattered scarf, suitcase with rags, the sum of nine Italian lire and 95 cents (lire 9.95), bill n. 27/n. 27 bills.

Rags.

Shirt, two vests, underpants, jacket, trousers, waistcoat, braces, socks, shoes.

Overcoat, jacket, waistcoat, vest, trousers, shirt, underpants, sweater, light shoes, socks, straps, hat, collar, wallet with identity card, metal cigarette case. All in a bundle.

Jacket/tunic and trousers of plain weave, shirt, underpants, socks and shoes.

Overcoat, jacket, waistcoat, trousers, shirt, underpants, vest, socks, shoes, shirt bib, hat.

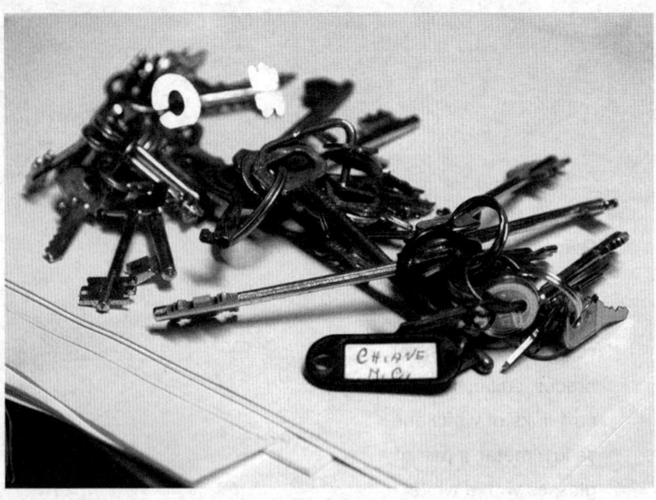

Women

Blouse, knickers, two underskirts, dress, coat, shoes and stockings.

Rags.

Three blouses, two vests, two pairs of drawers, two frocks, three pieces of underlinen, coat, shawl, scarf, three pairs of stockings and shoes.

Blouse, vest, drawers, petticoat, two frocks, small shawl, stockings and slippers.

Blouse, vest, drawers, frock, coat, stockings and shoes, small scarf.

Frock, light coat, blouse, vest, blousette, drawers, shoes, two pairs of stockings, a handkerchief and a leather bag.

Blouse, vest, drawers, petticoat, two frocks, small shawl, stockings and slippers.

Dress, blouse, drawers, clogs.

Jacket, dress, blouse, drawers, petticoat, shoes, handkerchief.

Coat, frock, petticoat, 3 blouses, drawers, clogs, 1 towel, 1 pair of stockings, one hundred and two Italian lire and 10 cents (102.10 Italian lire).

Frock, blouse, drawers, petticoat, clogs.

Blouse, jacket.

Frock, blouse, petticoat, drawers, clogs.

Skirt, blousette, jacket, bra, vest, stockings, shoes, a yellow metal wedding ring.

Skirt, vest, underskirt, T-shirt, bra, suspender belt, stockings, shoes, a bag, eight interest-bearing securities for a hundred thousand Italian lire and three for fifty thousand Italian lire, a bank book (Banco di Napoli) with a credit of 50,143.5 Italian lire, a small yellow metal chain, a pair of yellow metal earrings.

Dress, light jacket, underskirt, knickers, bra and shoes.

Dress, skirt, jacket, 3 blousettes, 2 vests, knickers, shoes.

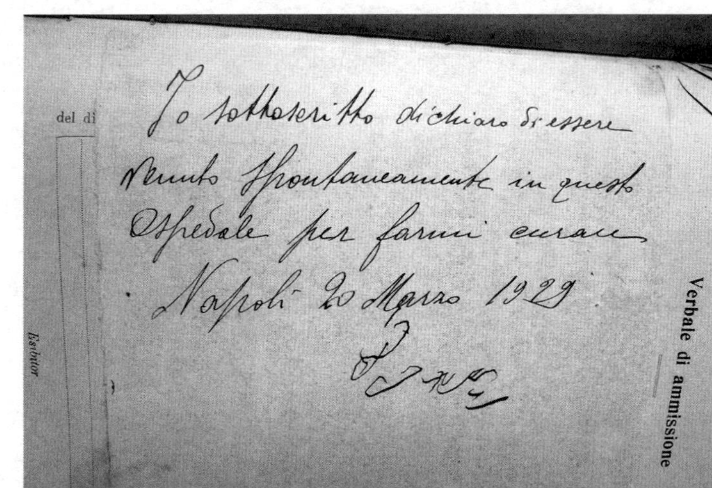
del dì

Io sottoscritto dichiaro di essere venuto spontaneamente in questo Ospedale per farmi curare

Napoli 20 Marzo 1929

Verbale di ammissione

Dress, jacket, blouse, skirt, underskirt, bra, T-shirt, knickers, handkerchiefs, 2 pairs of stockings, shoes.

A sweater.

Dress, light jacket, underskirt, sleeveless T-shirt, 3 handkerchiefs and shoes.

Two hats, six handkerchiefs, two silk handkerchiefs, corset, two underskirts, two blouses, three pairs of knickers, a vest, bra, eight sanitary towels, three dresses, three pairs of shoes, coat, stockings, belt and gloves, a basket of clothes for a newborn baby, a yellow metal ring, two small keys, two fake metal bracelets, a mother of pearl rose.

Blouse, vest, a dress, light coat, stockings and shoes, a pair of yellow metal earrings with white stones, a yellow metal ring.

Beschlagnahmte Schlüssel
Chiavi sequestrate
Keys taken from the inmates

Einverständniserklärung zur freiwilligen Einlieferung
Dichiarazione di ricovero volontario
Request for voluntary admittance

porter

post-mortem room

laundry

contagious women

chapel

contagious men

disturbed women

disturbed men

semi-disturbed women

semi-disturbed men

unwashed women

infirmary

bakery

infirmary

unwashed men

bathrooms

bathrooms

general utility room

calm women

calm men

calm women

calm men

observation area

offices

observation area

directors' quarters

porter

doctors' quarters

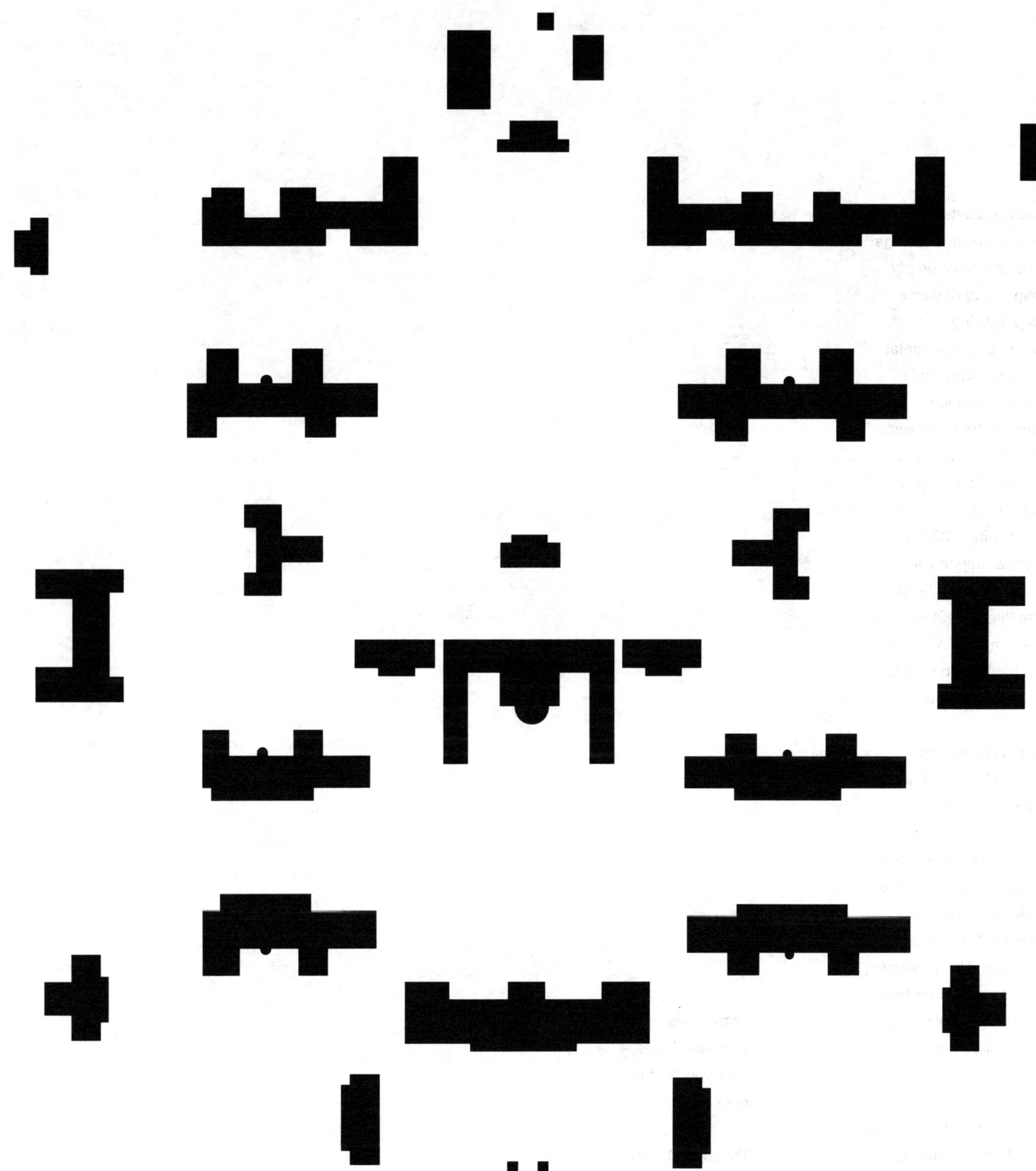

Grundriss des Hospitalareals
Pianta dell'areale ospedaliero
Hospital ground plan

Blouse, pants, pantie girdle, dress, stockings and shoes, an empty bag, a bag of waste paper, a ring and hat, a pair of yellow metal earrings with white stones, a yellow metal brooch, 28 small keys, two thousand, three hundred and eighty-four Italian lire and 65 cents (lire 2,384.65), coffee grounds, and two thousand Italian lire (lire 2,000) in a personal savings fund with related bill/N. 6/ with 6 related bills.

Two blouses, three pairs of pants, 4 under-skirts, 4 vests, 2 camisoles, coat, hat, eight dresses, fur coat, 4 towels, 2 hand towels, two sanitary towels, 1 sheet, scarf, raincoat, straw suitcase, two small leather bags, two pairs of glasses, two pairs of shoes, stockings.

Blouse, waist-skirt, vest, light blouse, apron, stockings and slippers, a pair of yellow metal earrings without stones.

Blouse, pair of knickers, waist-skirt, stockings, shoes, one hat.

Yellow metal earring with fake stones, a small watch of fake metal.

Blouse, vest, pants, dress, jacket, coat, hat, gloves, stockings, shoes, nine small keys.

Blouse, dress, coat, stockings, shoes, a yellow metal ring with no stones.

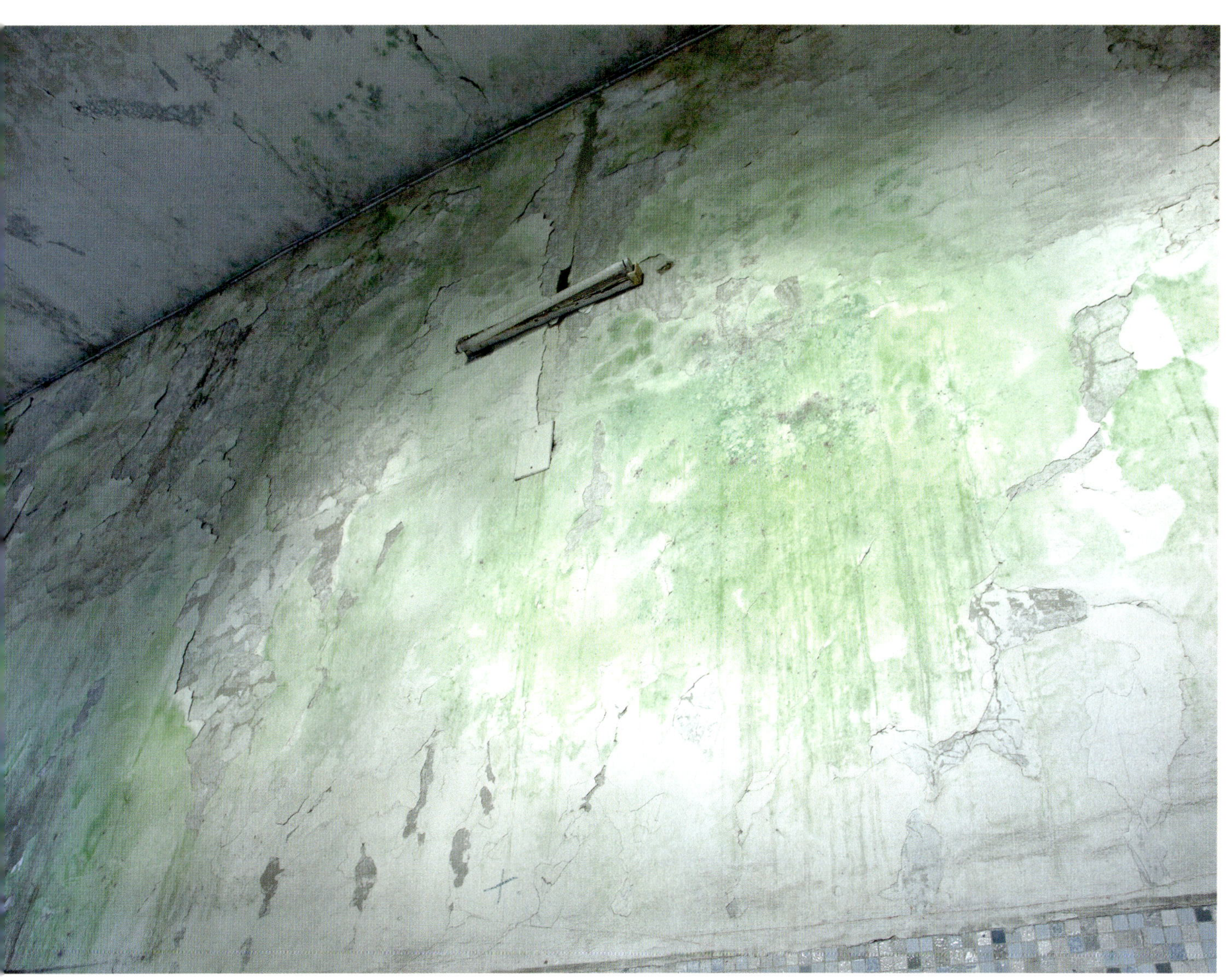

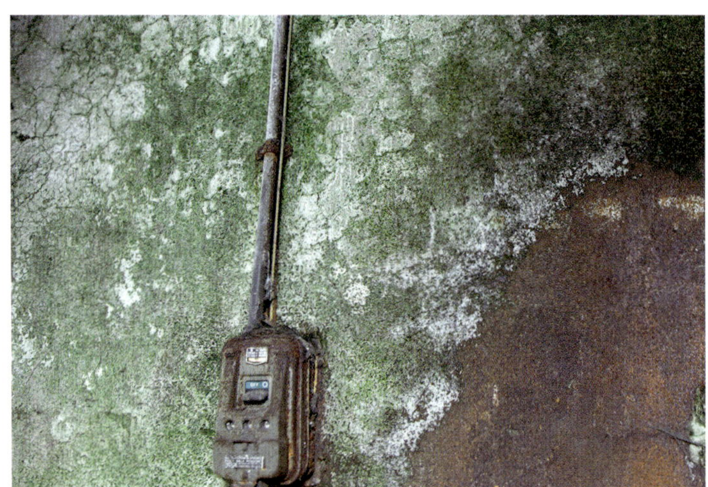

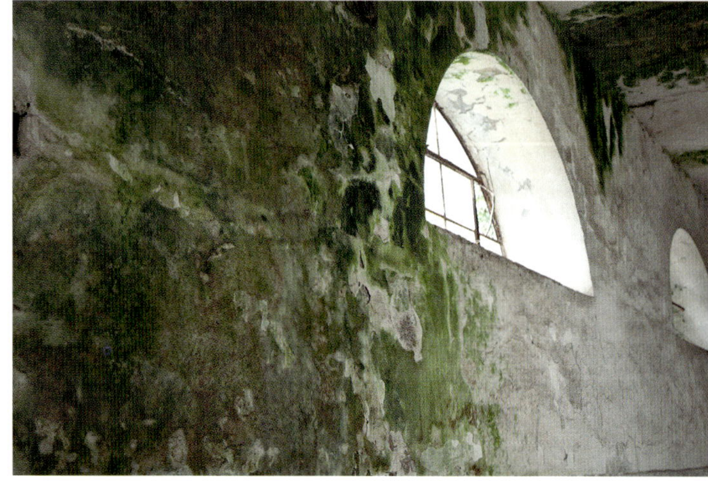

Topografie von Moos und Schimmel
Topografia di muschi e muffe
Topography of mosses and moulds

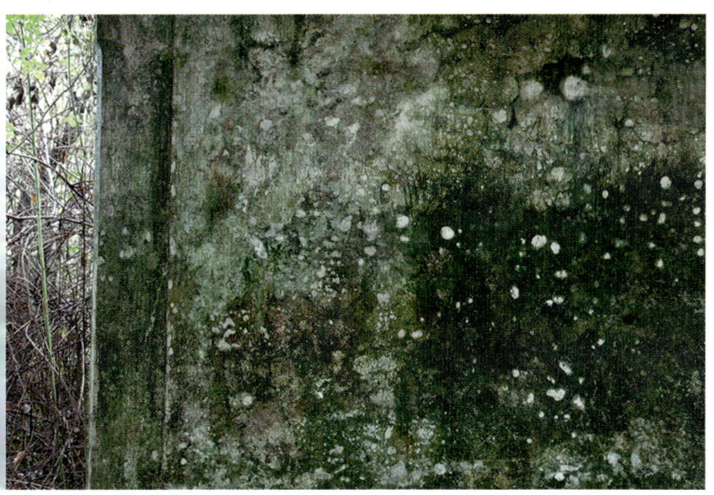

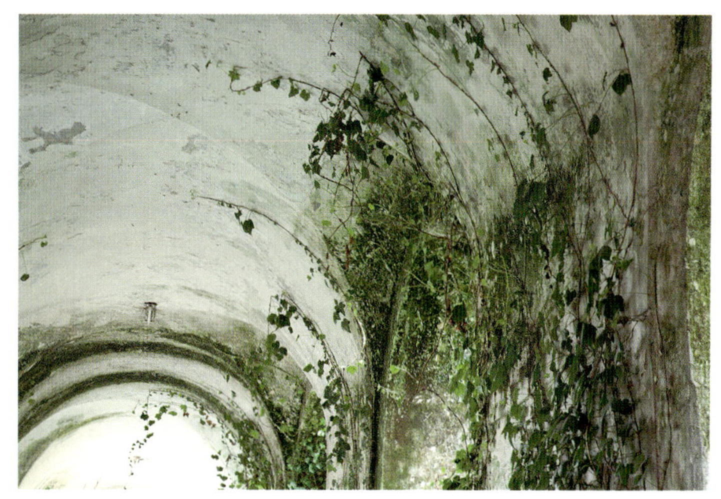

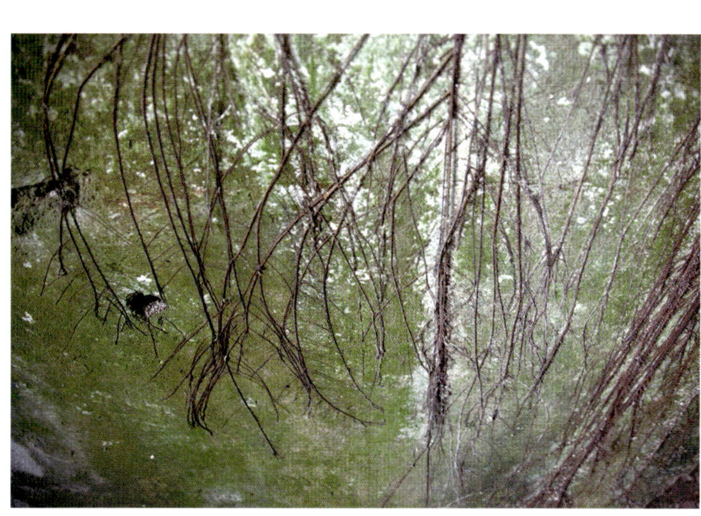

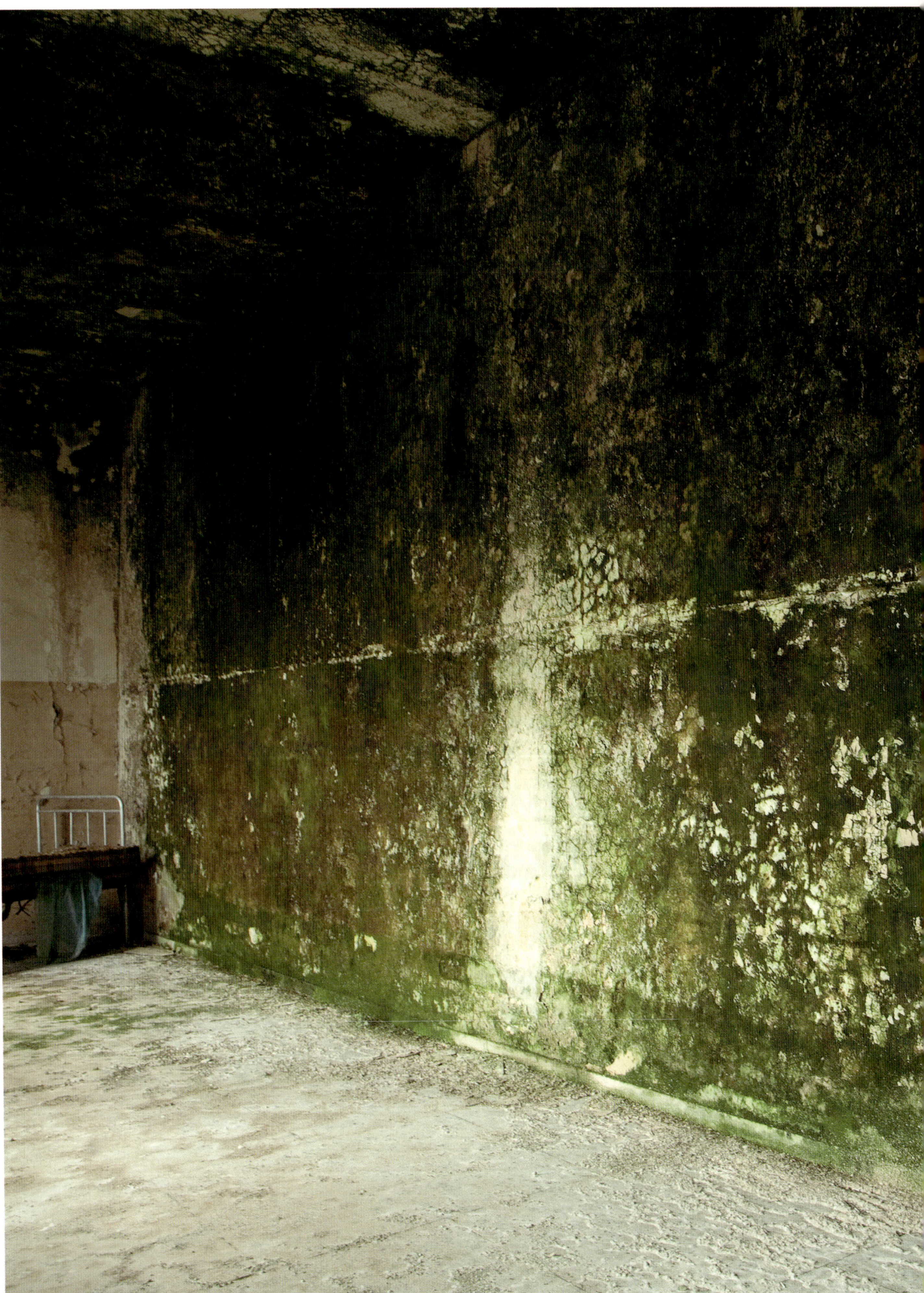

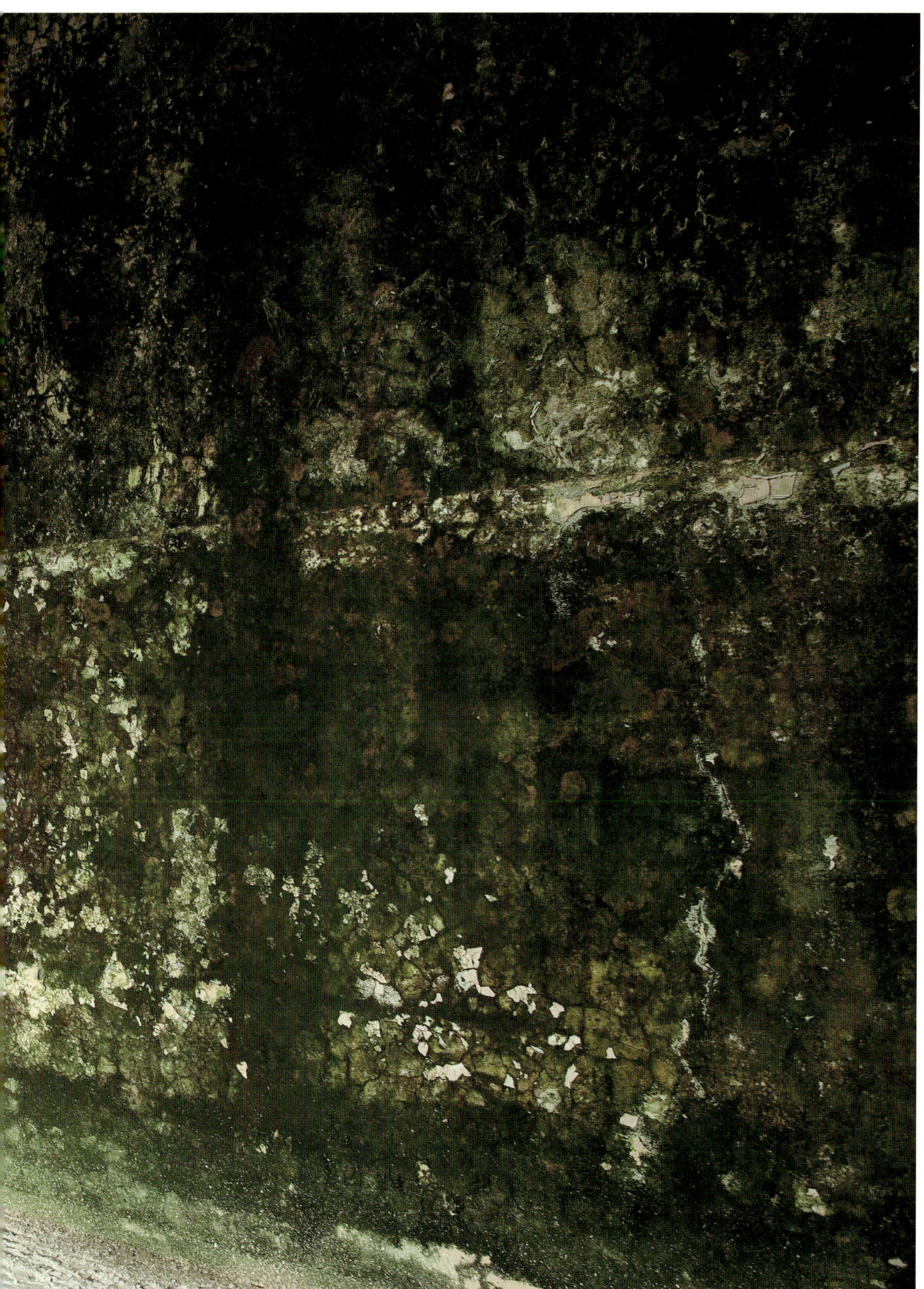

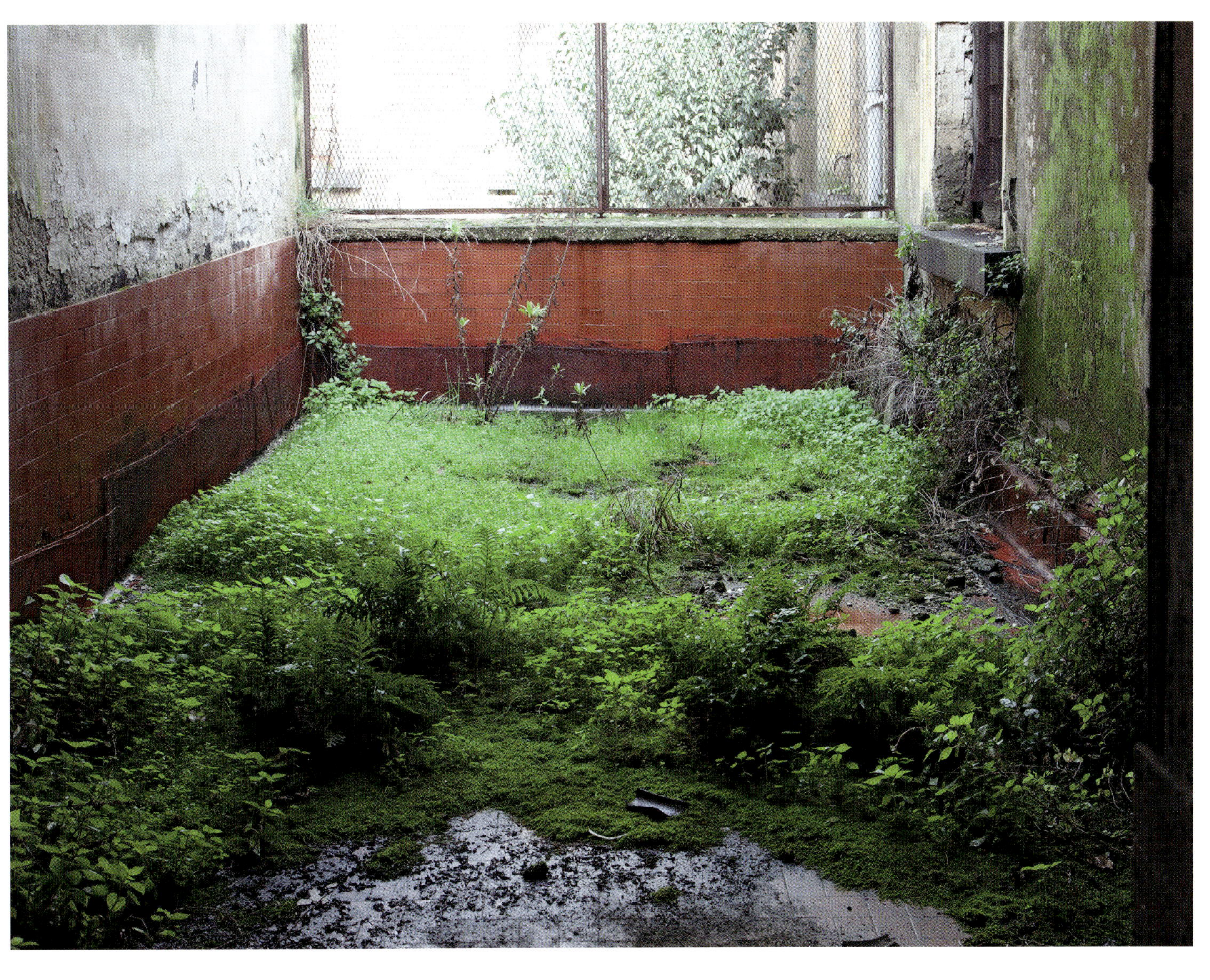

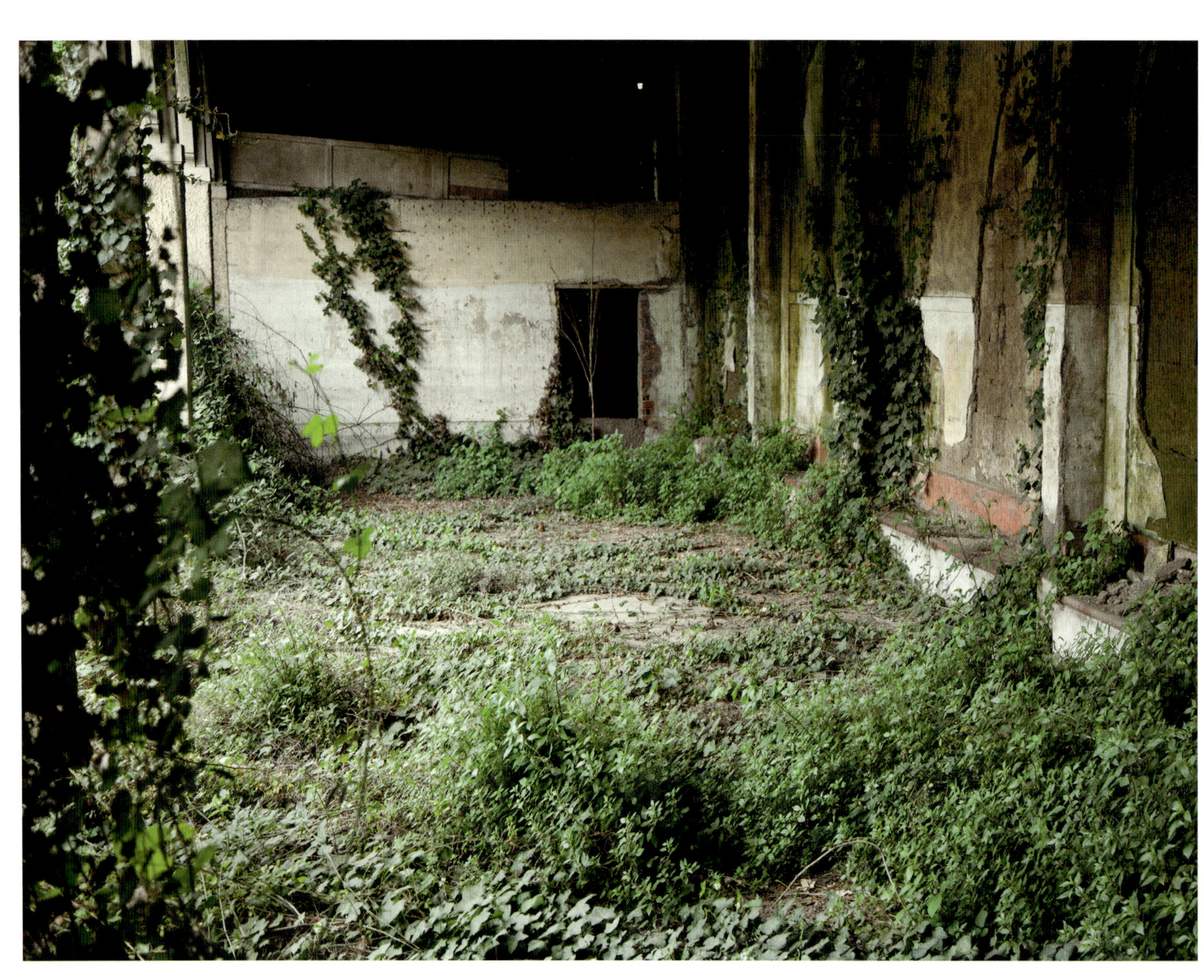

V. Abteilung Männer, Innenhof
V. Sezione uomini, cortile del piantone
V. Men's wing, courtyard

La casa dei matti
Anna Sicolo

La costruzione del nuovo Manicomio Provinciale di Napoli ha inizio ne l 1890 e termina, dopo varie vicissitudini, nel 1909. Prende il nome del suo primo direttore, Leonardo Bianchi, neuropsichiatra e parlamentare, sotto la cui guida divenne luogo di ricovero e cura tra i più moderni e spaziosi d'Europa, capace di accogliere fino a 3500 pazienti e circa 2000 unità di personale. Sin dall'inizio venne considerato centro di cultura e di ricerca internazionale.
La struttura architettonica è basata su un impianto simbolico coerente con la cultura del suo tempo. L'insieme, costituito da 54 edifici per una superficie coperta di circa nove ettari, è dislocato su un'area di venti ettari, ricca di verde. Questi enormi spazi, apparentemente aperti ma dove in realtà solo la luce non trova ostacoli, sono circondati lungo tutto il perimetro da un alto muro di tufo che li rende quasi invisibili. L'intero complesso è servito da una lunga rampa di accesso in pietra lavica che dà quasi l'idea di un ponte lavatoio e che conduce, attraverso un cancello, a un primo blocco di edifici; la palazzina di rappresentanza con direzione e biblioteca al primo piano, l'alloggio suore al secondo. I pazienti al loro ingresso venivano scortati al piano terra di questa palazzina dove c'era l'accettazione e poi alla cosiddetta "fardelleria": lì lasciavano tutto quello che avevano portato con sé, compresa la loro identità, per assumere il nome di "folle": cappotti, cappelli, orologi, gemelli, medaglie, sciarpe, mutande, maglie intime, occhiali, pettini, portamonete, specchietti da borsetta, monete, banconote, fotografie, lettere, agendine, calendari tascabili, ago e filo, ricette di cucina, tessere di partito, santini, chiavi, portasigarette, e ancora catenine, braccialetti, orecchini, spille e fedi nuziali, tutto in "metallo giallo", come veniva registrato l'oro in fardelleria. Due bracci laterali, perpendicolari alla palazzina e in continuità con essa, attraverso lunghi, risonanti corridoi, portano alla "degenza": a destra per gli uomini, a sinistra per le donne. Sarebbe da soffermarsi sul significato simbolico dell'endiade destra/uomo sinistra/donna.

Percorrendo i corridoi, si incontrano i padiglioni dei degenti, suddivisi per patologia, che si succedono progredendo in modo esponenziale, secondo il criterio di "gravità" assegnato: "folli tranquilli", "agitati", "contagiosi" e in ultimo i "folli furiosi". I due bracci, destro e sinistro, convergono in un punto centrale: la chiesa. Nella pianta architettonica, quindi, ponendo la chiesa all'estremo opposto all'ingresso, si realizzava l'idea secondo cui solo la fede cristiana poteva liberare l'anima dalle sue sofferenze terrene e garantirle la pace. Questo percorso, metafora della visione cristiano cattolica della propria epoca, veniva ulteriormente evidenziato dalla numerosa presenza di personale religioso, suore della Carità e preti, assunti in ruolo e ospitati negli alloggi che erano a loro riservati.

La finalità del presidio, capace di accogliere fino a 3500 pazienti e circa 2000 unità di personale, è quindi contenuta in tale concezione e ben riflessa anche nella tipologia architettonica dei suoi edifici. Il complesso ospedaliero era strutturato come una comunità chiusa ma autosufficiente, provvista di cucina, dispensa, lavanderia, sartoria, sala tessile, tipografia, con ambienti riscaldati, viali e giardini curati, e "fabbriche" per tenere occupati gli ammalati; un esempio per tutti, l'apprezzata produzione di mattonelle di graniglia. Ad un'attenta analisi si può affermare poi che la comunità interna era in piena sintonia con il mondo esterno, riproducendone tutti gli aspetti, positivi e negativi; sintonia che si interrompe alla fine degli anni '70, quando, sotto la spinta di un'opinione pubblica sempre più critica verso l'istituzione totale, venne approvata la legge 180 di riforma della psichiatria. La legge voluta e redatta dal Prof. Franco Basaglia, impose la chiusura dei manicomi, riconoscendo appieno i diritti e la necessità di una vita di qualità dei pazienti psichiatrici. Essa prevedeva tra il resto, anche il reinserimento degli ex degenti degli ospedali psichiatrici nel tessuto sociale, nei territori di origine, favorendone il rientro in famiglia o in case famiglia e la messa al bando definitiva di pratiche terapeutiche costrittive se non brutali (camicia di forza, elettroshock, lobotomia).

Sono questi gli anni in cui comincia la mia esperienza all'interno del Leonardo Bianchi. In quei primi giorni non mi colpì tanto il degrado, la puzza, lo sporco, le grida disumane, le figure informi, terrificanti, che vagavano chiedendo ossessivamente soldi, sigarette, caffè. Ma invece forte fu la percezione di ciò che mancava: nel manicomio non c'era lo specchio e non c'era il calendario. Questa "assenza" denunciava in modo eclatante come in quel luogo venissero negate alle persone la fisicità e il tempo.

Quando Carmela, sessant'anni circa, da quarantacinque in manicomio, si vide riflessa in uno specchio che avevo portato, timorosamente avvicinò le mani al volto, sfiorandolo e percorrendolo tutto lentamente, poi mi disse: "Quella sono io?!"; l'abbracciai, e nel farlo ero entrata anch'io nello specchio accanto a lei: un primo faticoso, piccolo passo verso il futuro. E c'erano anche Raffaele, panettiere, ricoverato perché impotente. Renato, figlio dell'avvocato antifascista combattente in Spagna, internato insieme alla famiglia in un campo di concentramento in Francia, cresciuto diffidando degli estranei, associava la vita al silenzio. Fu inviato in manicomio: non ha mai parlato ed è morto in silenzio. Marisa, messa in un orfanotrofio, dopo tre anni si accorsero che non parlava e non camminava, allora la tolsero dalla culla nella quale l'avevano dimenticata. Quando a tredici anni ebbe la sua prima mestruazione, ne rimase sconvolta, nessuno l'aveva preparata: fu ricoverata in manicomio per isteria. Modestina, figlia di un medico condotto, cresciuta senza mamma e senza guida, divenne adolescente con la voglia di piacere: fu internata come ninfomane. Elena, invece, era una ragazza povera, la sposarono a un vecchio che la violentava. Alla prima ribellione fu ricoverata: matta aggressiva. Il piccolo Antonio, rinchiuso in manicomio a tredici anni: "oligofrenico sudicio". Era ancora sudicio a cinquant'anni. Alessandro, depresso, scappava appena poteva per raggiungere la via dov'era la sua casa; nessuno gli aprì mai quella porta per trent'anni: è morto fuori quell'uscio. Liliana, prostituta veneta, finita in manicomio perché "disorientata", chiedeva solo un piccolo spazio tutto per sé e i suoi pensieri : non lo ebbe e non si orientò. Teresa, abbandonata alla nascita, più volte data in adozione, e sempre restituita: "sono certo posseduta dal diavolo se tanti mamma e papà non mi vogliono". Fu rinchiusa come "allucinata". "Tendenza a profumarsi, ad adottare voce e gesti femminili, instabilità del contegno, fatuo, manierato, puerile. Viene ricoverato per le continue proteste dei coinquilini..." – questo è scritto nella cartella clinica, e per questo Umberto, universitario, abusato dal padre, è entrato, ha vissuto ed è morto in manicomio. Di Adriana, parrucchiera, si legge: "sindrome delirante in soggetto che dice di vedere il Papa e di parlare con lui". Entrò in manicomio a trent'anni: "irriducibile". Con un chiodo o con il rossetto scriveva ovunque di libertà: sui tavoli, sui vetri, sui vestiti e sui muri. Un giorno trovò carta e penna e scrisse al Papa. Il Papa le rispose: fui proprio io a consegnarle la risposta. Lucia, paraplegica e basta, dolce, furba, curiosa, aveva un desiderio forte: vedere il mare. Glielo regalò a settant'anni Franco Basaglia...

Oggi sono l'unica responsabile dell'ex ospedale psichiatrico Leonardo Bianchi, custode della biblioteca, dell'archivio storico, delle cartelle cliniche e dei ricordi qui dentro racchiusi. Spesso qualche parente viene a cercare qualcosa. Ma questa è un'altra storia.

The Madhouse
Anna Sicolo

The building of the new provincial mental hospital in Naples was begun in 1890. After various delays, work was completed in 1909. It was named after its first director, Leonardo Bianchi, a neuropsychiatrist and a member of parliament. It was under his direction that the asylum became one of the most modern and spacious care centres of its kind in Europe, capable of housing 3,500 patients and around 2,000 members of staff. From the beginning, it was considered a centre of international culture and research. Its architecture is based on a symbolic plan that reflected the culture of the time. The 54 buildings that make up the complex cover around nine hectares of land in a park, rich in vegetation, of twenty hectares. These enormous spaces, apparently open but where really only light could enter freely, are completely surrounded by a high perimeter wall of volcanic rock which makes the buildings almost invisible. The whole complex has a long access ramp, also of volcanic rock, that almost gives the impression of a drawbridge. This leads through a gate and takes us to the first building, the office block, with that of the director and the library on the first floor, and the nuns' rooms on the second. It was to the ground floor of this building that the patients were escorted on their arrival. They were taken to the reception and then to the so-called "fardelleria" or luggage deposit. This is where they had to leave everything they had brought with them, including their identity, to take the name "mad": coats, hats, watches, cufflinks, medals, scarves, underpants, vests, glasses, combs, purses, make-up mirrors, coins, banknotes, photographs, letters, diaries, pocket calendars, needle and thread, recipes, party membership cards, pictures of saints, keys, cigarette cases, and still more, little chains, bracelets, earrings, brooches and wedding rings, all in "yellow metal", as any items made of gold were registered. Two side wings, perpendicular to the building and continuing from it, cross long, echoing corridors, and take us to the hospital itself: to the right for the men, to the left for the women. We should just stop and think about the symbolism of this twinning of words: right/man and left/woman.

Walking through the corridors, we come to the wards, each one following on from the other. These were divided according to pathology and to the "seriousness" of each case; the mad who are "calm", "agitated", "contagious" and in the last, "crazy". The right and left wings converge on a central point: the church. By placing the church at the opposite extreme from the entrance, the architect's plan incorporated the idea that only the Christian faith could free the soul from its earthly sufferance and guarantee it peace. This route to the church is a metaphor of the vision of the Catholic Church of the time, and this can also be seen by the presence of many members of religious orders, Sisters of Charity and priests who worked in the hospital and who lived in their own quarters.

The scope of this institution,which at any one time could house up to 3,500 patients and around 2,000 staff, can therefore be found in this concept, and this can also be seen from the architectural style of the buildings themselves.

The hospital block was organized like a closed but self-sufficient community with a kitchen, larder, laundry, a tailor's workshop, a linen room, a printing press. The rooms were heated, and the paths and gardens were well looked after. There were "factories" to keep the inmates occupied. Just one example was the lucrative production of bricks made of grit. After a careful analysis we can see that the community within the wall was in perfect harmony with the outside world, and that it reproduced all its characteristics, both positive and negative. This harmony was broken at the end of the 1970s when, in response to increasing public criticism, the Psychiatric Reform Bill 180 was passed by the Italian government. Prof. Franco Basaglia was the man who conceived and drafted the Bill that approved the closure of the mental hospitals, in full recognition of the rights of psychiatric patients and their need for quality of life. Among other things, the Bill also provided for the reintegration of the ex-inmates of the psychiatric hospitals into society, in their home towns, encouraging a return to their families or to residential homes,and the banning of brutal therapeutic practices of restraint, such as straightjackets, electric shock and lobotomy.

It was during this time that I started to work at the Leonardo Bianchi. In those first days, it was not so much the decay, the smell, the dirt, the inhuman cries, the terrifying formless figures who wandered around obsessively asking for money, cigarettes, coffee. It was rather the strong perception of what was missing: in the mental hospital there were no mirrors or calendars. This showed in the most striking-way how the people there were denied confirmation of their physical existence and a sense of time.

Carmela was around sixty years old when I met her, and had been in the hospital for forty-five years. When she saw herself in the mirror I had brought, she shyly put her hands to her face, stroking and exploring it slowly. Then she asked me: "Is that me?" I hugged her and in doing so I too was reflected alongside her in the mirror: a small, unsteady step towards the future. And there was also Raffaele, a baker, who had been admitted because he was impotent. Renato, son of an antifascist lawyer who had fought in Spain, a prisoner along with his family in a concentration camp in France, who had grown up distrustful of strangers, who associated life with silence. He had been sent to the hospital: he had never uttered a word and died in silence. Marisa, who had been put in an orphanage, after three years they realized that she didn't talk or walk. Only then did they take her out of the cradle in which they had left her, forgotten. When she had her first period at the age of thirteen, she was traumatized, nobody had explained to her what happens. She was sent to the asylum because she was hysterical. Modestina, daughter of a town doctor, who had grown up without a mother and without anyone alongside her as she grew up, entered adolescence with a desire to sample the pleasures of life, and was sent to the asylum as a nymphomaniac. Elena, however, came from a poor family who had married her off to a man much older than her, who abused her. At the first sign of rebellion she was labelled "mad and aggressive"... and was sent to the mental hospital. Little Antonio, locked up in a mental hospital at the age of thirteen as a "dirty little freak". He was still dirty when he was fifty. Alessandro, depressed, at the slightest opportunity he would run away to the road where he had lived. But in thirty years no-one ever opened the door to him. He died on the doorstep. Liliana, a prostitute from Veneto, ended up in a mental hospital because she was "disorientated". She only asked for some small private space for herself and her thoughts. But she didn't find it and couldn't settle down. Teresa had been abandoned at birth and had lived with various adoptive parents who had always given her back to the home. "I must be possessed by the devil if so many mums and dads don't want me". They told her she was hallucinating and locked her up. In one case history, we can read: "he tends to cover himself with perfume, uses a feminine voice and gestures, it's not always possible to control him, silly, affected, immature. He was admitted to the hospital after continuous protests from his neighbours". And this was the reason for which Umberto, a university student who had been abused by his father, entered, lived and died in a mental hospital. The case history of Adriana, a hairdresser, reads: "delirium in a subject who says she can see the Pope and talks to him". She entered the hospital when she was thirty: "unyielding". With a nail or a lipstick she wrote about freedom on anything she could find: on the tables, on the windows, on her clothes and on the walls. One day she found a pen and some paper and wrote a letter to the Pope. The Pope answered her saying "it was actually me who sent you there". Lucia was a paraplegic, and as if that wasn't enough, was also sweet, smart and curious. She wanted more than anything to see the sea. Her wish was granted at the age of seventy, thanks to Franco Basaglia ...

Today, I am the only person left here at the ex-psychiatric hospital Leonardo Bianchi. I'm in charge of the library, the archives, the case histories, and of the memories of those who were locked up here. Often some relative will come to search for something. But that's another story.

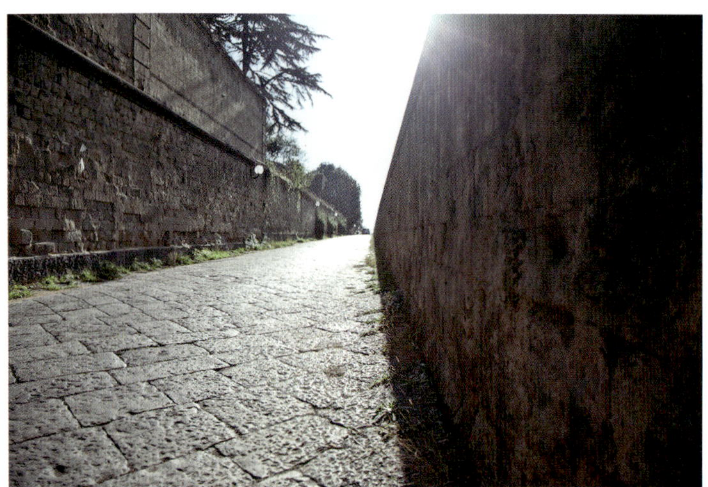

Eingangsbereich, Kirche
Rampa d'ingresso, chiesa
Access ramp, church

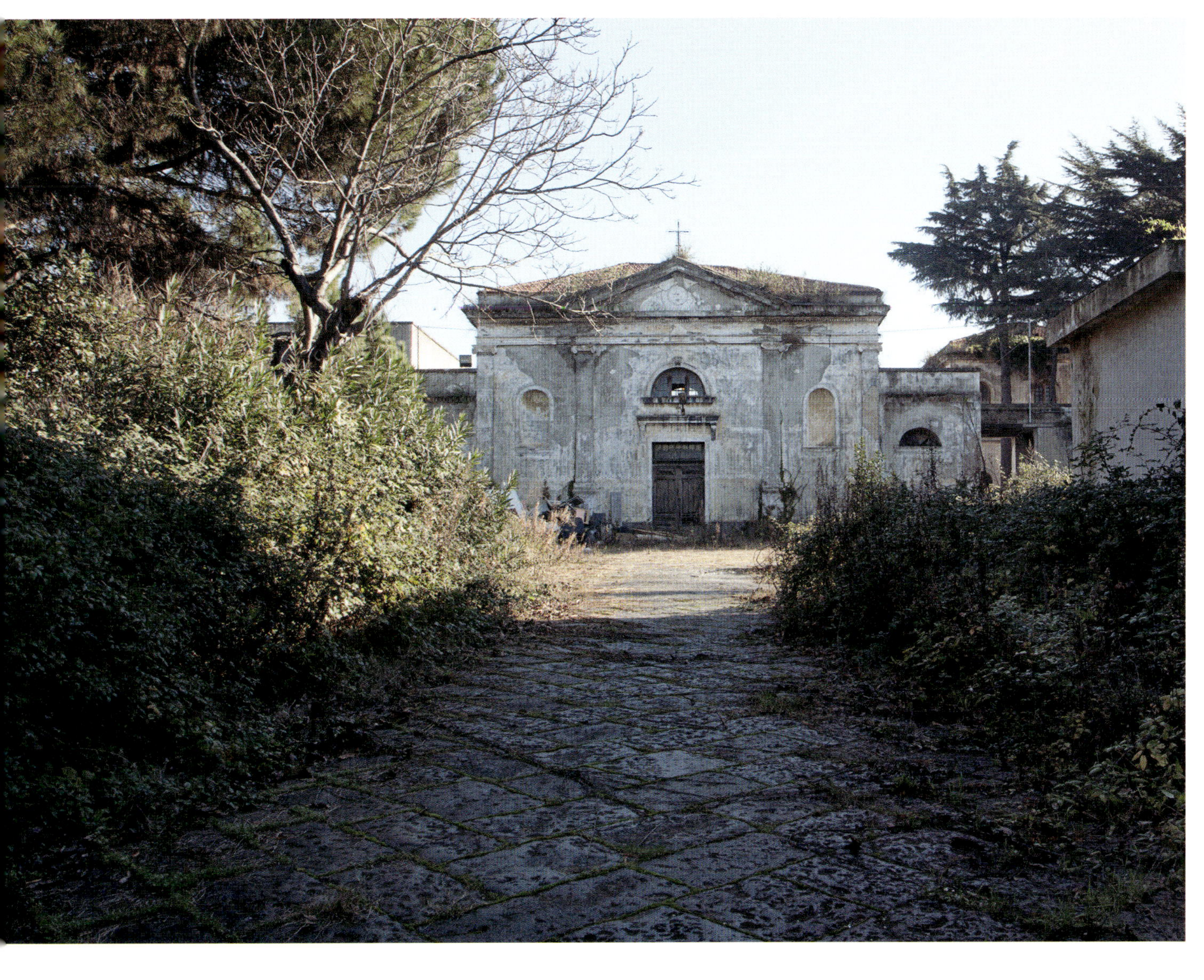

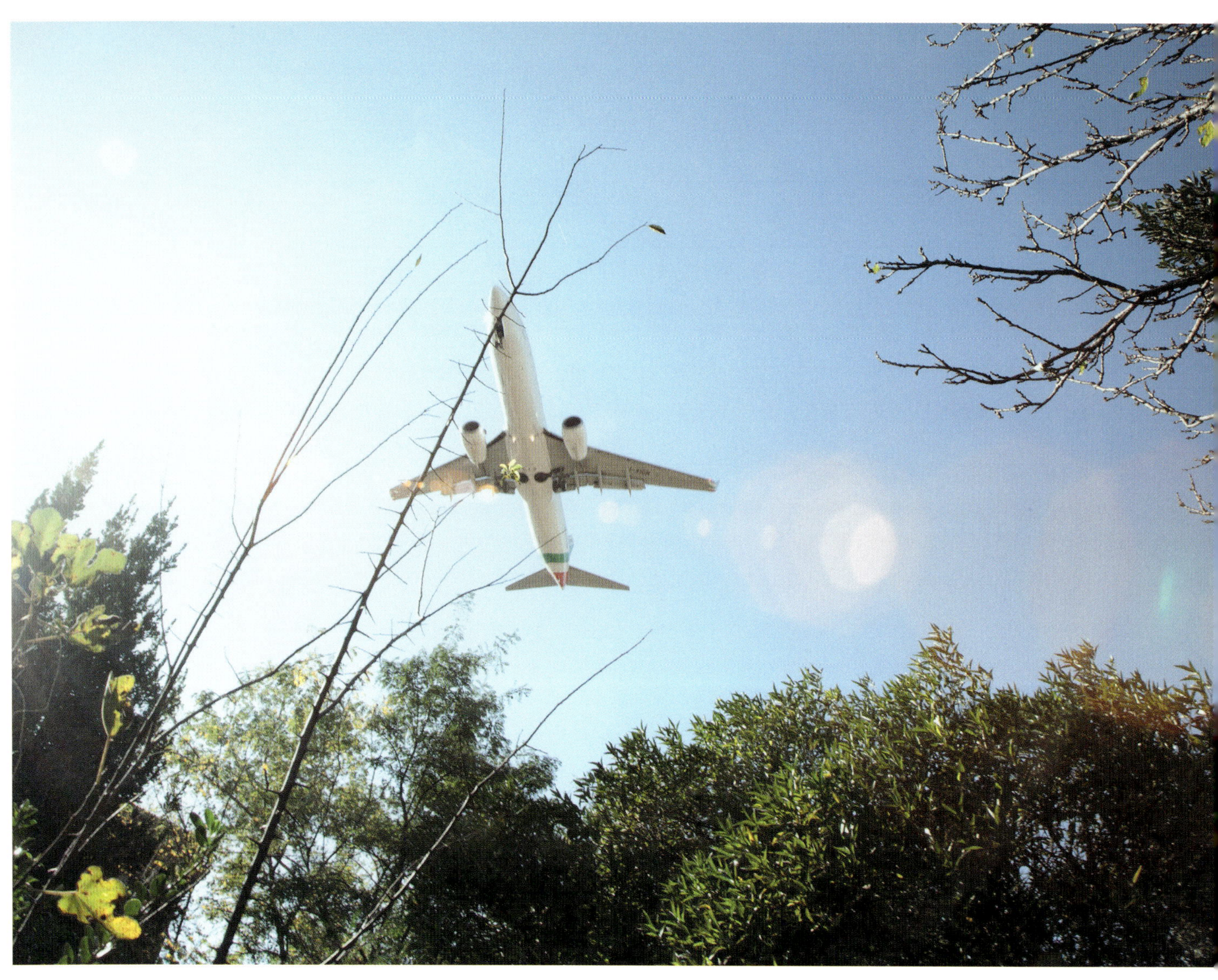

Der Fluglärm des anliegenden Flughafens Napoli Capodichino bricht immer wieder die Stille.
Il frastuono del traffico aereo dell'adiacente aeroporto di Napoli Capodichino scandisce ritmicamente il silenzio.
The silence is broken at regular intervals by the roar of the passing planes from the nearby Naples Capodichino airport.

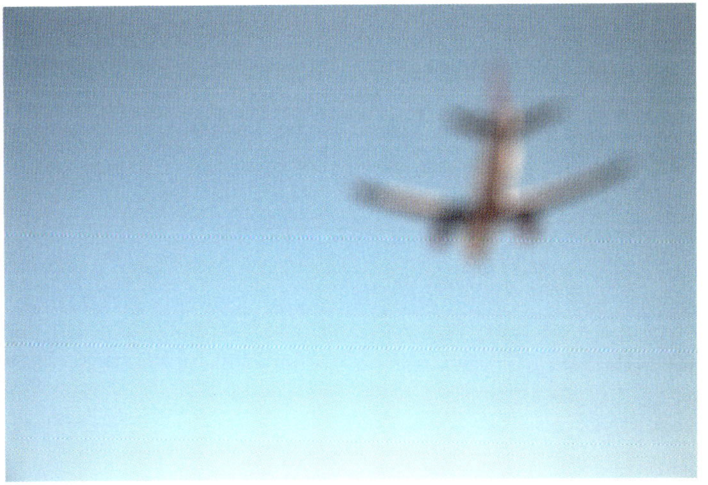

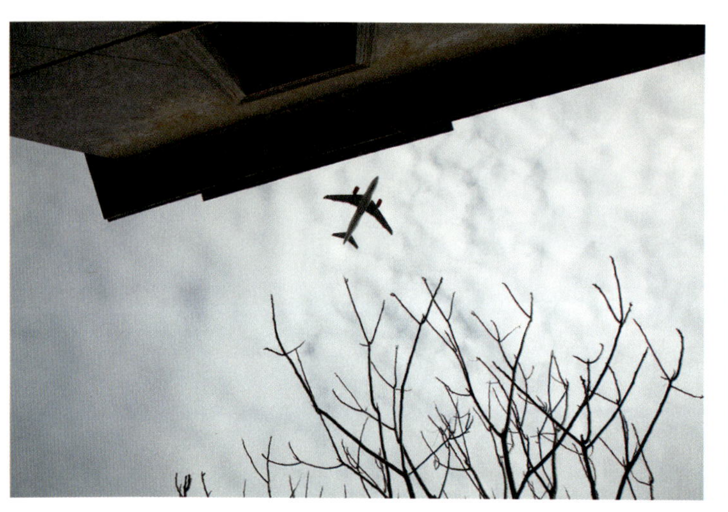

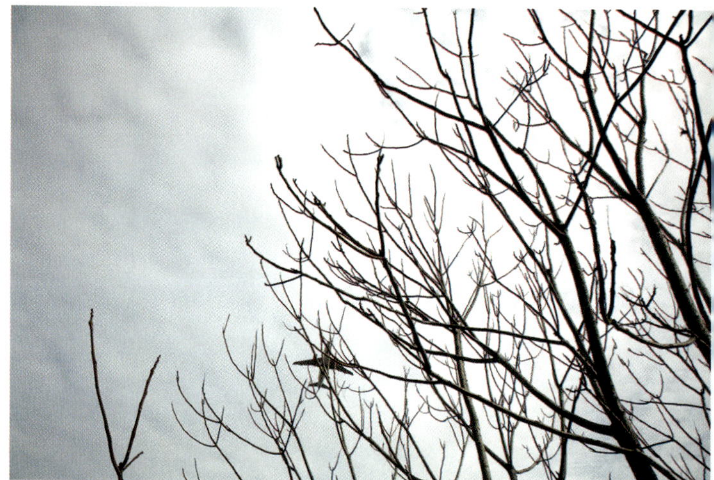

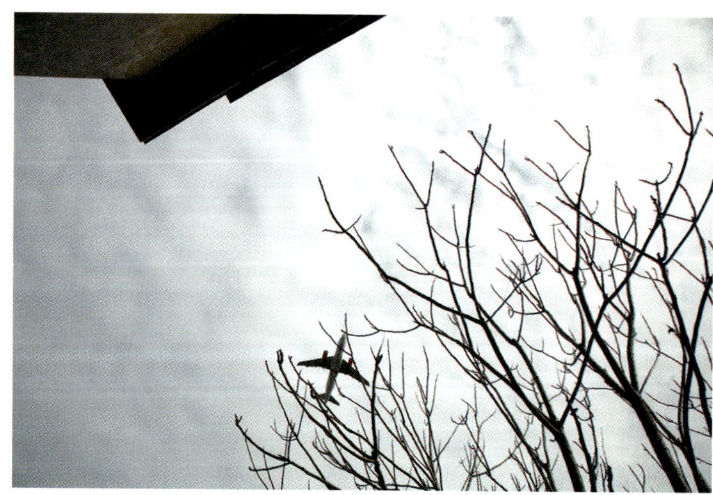

Silvie Aigner studierte Kunstgeschichte an der Universität Wien sowie Kulturelles Management an der Donauuniversität Krems und absolviert ein Ph.D. am Institut für Kulturwissenschaften an der Universität für angewandte Kunst Wien. 1991 bis 1994 Leitung des Wiener Büros von Artscope International. Arbeitet als Autorin, Herausgeberin und Kuratorin vorwiegend im Bereich der zeitgenössischen Kunst für internationale Museen und Institutionen. Seit 2011 Kuratorin der *bäckerstrasse4-plattform für junge kunst*, künstlerische und organisatorische Leitung der Ausstellungsprojekte, aktuell in der Passagegalerie im Künstlerhaus Wien oder im Österreichischen Kulturforum in Washington DC. Seit 2008 Verlagstätigkeit im Rahmen der edition dispositiv. (www.dispositiv.at)

Silvie Aigner studied art history at the University of Vienna and Cultural Management at Danube University Krems and is taking a Ph.D. at the Institute for Cultural Sciences at the University for Applied Arts Vienna. From 1991 to 1994 she was director of the Vienna office of Artscope International. She works as a writer, editor and curator mainly in the field of contemporary art for international museums and institutions. Since 2011 she has been curator of the *bäckerstrasse4-plattform für junge kunst*, artistic and organisational director of exhibition projects, currently in the Passagegalerie in the Vienna Künstlerhaus and in the Austrian Cultural Forum in Washington DC. Since 2008 has worked in publishing for the edition dispositiv. (www.dispositiv.at)

Emanuela De Cecco è critica d'arte e curatrice. Dal 1990 lavora nella redazione di *Flash Art*, dal 1996 al 1998 come capo redattore. È stata responsabile dei progetti di formazione presso la Fondazione Sandretto Re Rebaudengo di Torino (2002–2005). Ha insegnato Cultura Visuale (Università di Ferrara, 2001–2006); dal 2007 è professore associato presso la Libera Università di Bolzano. Pubblicazioni principali: *Contemporanee* (con G. Romano), Costa & Nolan, 2000; *Zingonia. Arte, integrazioni, multiculture,* A + M Bookstore (Milano 2002); *Non toccare la donna bianca. Conversazioni con le artiste,* Fondazione Sandretto (Torino 2004); *Tacita Dean,* Postmedia Books (Milano 2004), *Arte-Mondo. Storia dell'arte, storie dell'arte* (2010). Mostre principali: *Fuoriuso* (Pescara, 2000), *Transforms* (con R. Pinto, Trieste, 2001); *Arte all'arte 7 (2002), Maria Lai – come un gioco,* Museo d'Arte Moderna di Nuoro (2002); *Tacita Dean – Baobab,* Fondazione Sandretto (2004), *Passaggi a Sud Est. Storie, memorie, attraversamenti,* XII. ed. Biennale Donna (2006).

Emanuela De Cecco is an art critic and Associate Professor of Contemporary Art at the Faculty of Design and Arts at the Free University of Bolzano/ Bozen in Italy. She graduated from the Faculty of Modern Literature in Genoa with a thesis on the History of the Art Critic. From 1990 to 1998 she worked for *Flash Art,* the art magazine, becoming its managing editor in 1996. From 2002 to 2005 she was responsible for educational projects at the Fondazione Sandretto Re Rebaudengo in Turin. From 2001 to 2006 she taught Visual Culture at the University of Ferrara. Her most important publications include: *Contemporanee* (with Gianni Romano), Costa & Nolan, Milan, 2000; *Zingonia*, 2007; *Art, integration, multiculture*, A & M Bookstore, Milan; *Tacita Dean*, Postmedia Books, 2004; a collection of interviews with the artists invited by Francesco Bonami to participate in the exhibition *Don't touch the white woman* at the Fondazione Sandretto in Turin; *Arte-mondo. Storia dell'arte, storie dell'arte*, Postmedia Milano, 2010. Exhibitions (selection): *Fuoriuso* (Pescara, 2000), *Transforms* (with R. Pinto, Trieste, 2001); *Arte all'arte* 7 (2002), *Maria Lai – come un gioco,* Museo d'Arte Moderna di Nuoro (2002), *Tacita Dean – Baobab,* Fondazione Sandretto (2004), *Passaggi a Sud Est. Storie, memorie, attraversamenti,* XII. ed. Biennale Donna (2006).

Elisabeth Hölzl ist 1962 in Meran geboren. Studium der Bildhauerei an der Kunstakademie Bologna, Stipendium für New York 2003 und La Havanna 2004, seit den 1990er Jahren rege Ausstellungstätigkeit im In- und Ausland. In ihren fotografischen Arbeiten setzt sie sich vorwiegend mit dem Thema Raum und dessen vielschichtigen Veränderungen auseinander.

Ausstellungen (Auswahl): *three rooms*, Imperialart, Meran, 2010; *Vakuum*, Galleria il Vicolo, Genova, 2010; *Premio Agenore Fabbri, Giovane Arte Italiana,* Stadtgalerie Kiel, Palazzo Ziino, Palermo, 2010; *From&T(w)o*, Kunst Merano Arte, Meran, 2010; *New entries*, Museion, Bozen 2009; *Hotel Bristol*, Antonella Cattani Contemporary Art, Bozen; Emanuel Walderdorff Galerie Köln; Artambassy Berlin, 2008; *Die Kunst des Alterns*, ArgeKunst Galerie Museum, Bozen 2007; *Ti voglio bene, from Italy with love*, Raid projects, Los Angeles 2005; *Fuori tema/italian feeling*, XIV Quadriennale di Roma, Galleria Nazionale d'Arte Moderna, Roma 2007; *In faccia al mondo*, Museo d'Arte Contemporanea Villa Croce, Genova 2003; *Warm up*, Galleria Neon, Bologna 2002; *ne stè a vene tüa tera, tüa vita*, Außengestaltung, Museum Ladin, Ciastèl de Tor 2002; *escaping blue*, Villen am Lohbach, Parkplatzgestaltung, Innsbruck 2000; Publikationen: Fotoserie in *Roma und Sinti*, Studienverlag Innsbruck 2005; *Hotel Bristol*, Folioverlag Wien/Bozen 2008.

Elisabeth Hölzl was born in 1962 in Merano, where she still lives and works. She completed her studies at the Academy of Art in Bologna, and won scholarships to New York and Havana. Since the 1990s, the artist has intensified her activity with exhibitions both in Italy and abroad, gaining recognition and acclaim. In her current works, Hölzl concentrates on the concept of space. Throughout her numerous photographic series, she documents the material nature of space and the transformation it undergoes with the passage of time. Her most important exhibitions include: 2010 *Vakuum*, Galleria il Vicolo, Genoa; 2010 *Premio Agenore Fabbri, Giovane Arte Italiana*, Stadtgalerie Kiel, Palazzo Ziino, Palermo; 2010 *From&T(w)o*, Kunst Merano Arte, Meran; 2009 *New entries*, Museion, Bolzano/Bozen; 2008 *Hotel Bristol*, Antonella Cattani Contemporary Art, Bolzano/Bozen; Emanuel Walderdorff Galerie Cologne; Artambassy Berlin; 2007 *Die Kunst des Alterns*, ArgeKunst Galerie Museum, Bolzano/Bozen; 2005 *Ti voglio bene, from Italy with love*, Raid projects, Los Angeles; 2007 *Fuori tema/italian feeling*, XIV Quadriennale di Roma, Galleria Nazionale d'Arte Moderna, Rome; 2003 *In faccia al mondo*, Museo d'Arte Contemporanea Villa Croce, Genoa; 2002 *Warm up*, Galleria Neon, Bologna; Public Art: 2010 *three rooms*, Imperialart, Meran; 2002 *Ne stè a vene tüa tera, tüa vita*, Museum Ladin, Ciastèl de Tor; 2000 *Escaping blue*, Villen am Lohbach, Innsbruck. Her publications include the photographic series: *Roma und Sinti*, Studienverlag Innsbruck, 2005; *Hotel Bristol*, edizione Folio Wien/Bozen, 2008.

Anna Sicolo nasce a Napoli nel 1950. Si laurea in medicina e chirurgia a Napoli e si specializza a Bologna. Dal 1994 lavora nella struttura organizzativa della direzione sanitaria del L.Bianchi per la preparazione e l'attuazione del "Programma di dismissione degli ex ospedali psichiatrici dell'ASL Napoli". Dal 1997 si occupa della costituzione della rete di residenze territoriali. Nel 1998 ricopre l'incarico di responsabile della gestione organizzativa assistenziale residua. Nel 2002 la direzione del DSM le assegna il ruolo di responsabile della conservazione e gestione della biblioteca e dell'archivio storico del Bianchi. Dallo stesso anno dirigente del dipartimento di salute mentale dell'ASL Napoli e referente responsabile del "residuo manicomiale".

Anna Sicolo was born in Naples 1950. She graduated in medicine at the University of Naples and finished her specialist school in Bologna. She started working at the L. Bianchi in 1994. She was part of the organizational team that prepared and put into effect the *Local Health Authority* project in which inmates of the mental asylum where to be reintegrated into the community. Since 1997, she has been responsible for setting up the mental asylum support network. In 1998, she took charge of the final part of the project. In 2007, she was given responsibility for the conservation and management of the library and historical archives of the Bianchi. In the same year, she became director of the Department of Mental Health of the Local Health Authority in Naples and is in charge of what remains of the mental asylum institution.

Impressum / Colophon / About this publication

Herausgeber / a cura di / Editor
Elisabeth Hölzl

Gestaltung / Progetto grafico / Design and Layout
Studio Lupo & Burtscher, Elisabeth Hölzl
Cover
Studio Lupo & Burtscher

Übersetzungen / Traduzioni / Translations
Anne Freckleton, Steve Tomlin

Lektorat / Lettorato / Proofreading
Eugenia Fera, Silvia Jaklitsch,
Steve Tomlin

Printed in Italy, Lana Repro

Erschienen im / Editore / Published by
Verlag für moderne Kunst Nürnberg GmbH
Königstraße 73, D-90402 Nürnberg
www.vfmk.de

ISBN 978-3-86984-311-7

Mit großzügiger Unterstützung von / con il sostegno di / with support from

Kulturämter der Autonomen Provinz Bozen-Südtirol
Assessorati alla cultura della Provincia Autonoma di Bolzano-Alto Adige
Antonella Cattani Contemporary Art Bolzano
ES contemporary art gallery Merano
Gärtnerei Schullian Bolzano
Firma Niederstätter Bolzano
Firma Durst Brixen
Kulturkreis Algund

Besonderen Dank an / un particolare ringraziamento a / Thanks to

Herta Torggler
Dott. Vito Villani
Dott.ssa Anna Sicolo
Mimmo Armento
De Simone Raffaele
Marcello Fera
Marco Vitali
Leonardo di Costanzo
Linda Egger
Jutta Telser

Bibliografische Information der Deutschen Nationalbibliothek
Die Deutsche Nationalbibliothek verzeichnet diese Publikation in der Deutschen Nationalbibliografie; detaillierte bibliografische Daten sind im Internet über http://dnb.ddb.de abrufbar.

Segnalazione bibliografica della Deutsche Nationalbibliothek
La Deutsche Nationalbibliothek ha incluso questa pubblicazione nella bibliografia nazionale. Dati bibliografici dettagliati sono disponibili al seguente indirizzo internet http://dnb.ddb.de

Bibliographic information published by Die Deutsche Nationalbibliothek
Die Deutsche Nationalbibliothek lists this publication in the Deutsche Nationalbibliografie; detailed bibliographic data is available on the Internet at http://dnb.ddb.de.

Vertrieb für Großbritannien /
Distribuzione nel Regno unito /
Distributed in the United Kingdom
Cornerhouse Publications
70 Oxford Street,
Manchester M1 5 NH, UK
phone +44-161-200 15 03,
fax +44-161-200 15 04

Vertrieb außerhalb Europas /
Distribuzione fuori dall'Europa /
Distributed outside Europe
D.A.P. Distributed Art Publishers, Inc.
155 Sixth Avenue, 2nd Floor, New York,
NY 10013, USA
phone +1-212-627 19 99,
fax +1-212-627 94 84

AUTONOME PROVINZ BOZEN SÜDTIROL
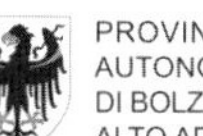
PROVINCIA AUTONOMA DI BOLZANO ALTO ADIGE

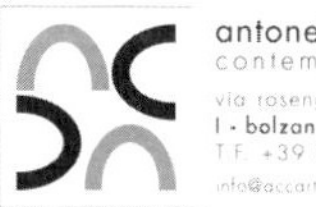

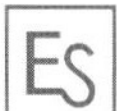

contemporary art gallery Meran/o
es-gallery.net

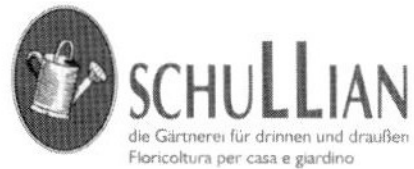

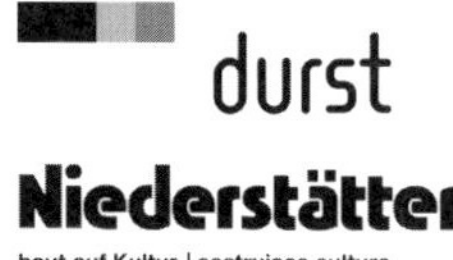

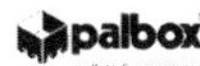